Grieving Still

Finding the *Other Side*

Pamuela Halliwell

105
PUBLISHING
EST. 2020

To my mother, Queen,
Thank you for always loving me and for never giving up on
me. Your love, strength, and devotion have made me the
strong Black woman that I am today. It's your love that has
helped me to become someone who can try to help others.

To anyone reading,
I hope this book provides you with mild entertainment,
distraction, and most of all comfort as you continue your
own journey through grief and loss. Mourning is this place
where we try our best to adapt to life without them, but in the
process, we can find ourselves again and we can find
something new as we still work to incorporate those we have
lost.
Hold on gently. Don't give up. There is a life after.

To two teachers that inspired me more than they know,

Ms. Darwin, thank you. I still remember fondly being selected for the front page of our high school English class newspaper. Mrs. Finegan, thank you. You were such an incredible source of support as I came into my own. Teachers are invaluable, you teach us all to reach for the stars and inspire us. Thank you both for allowing me to dream.

To two gentlemen that met me at different times in my life but nonetheless inspired me to grow,

Ross Ambers & Kurt Buis, though you're no longer here, your memories and the experiences we have shared live on in me. They've helped me to be a better therapist.

I want to thank security guards everywhere, mental health providers, teachers, healthcare workers, you're often times the underdog and I want to thank you all for trying to help many of us get through the darkest times in our lives. You are heroes.

I'd also like to thank our military members who often are fraught with challenges trying to survive through mental health trauma just for working their job.

Anyone and everyone that has done something positive to stand up against racism, discrimination, homophobia, transphobia, misogyny, and supported equality so we can all be seen and treated as equal, I sincerely thank you and my heart goes out to you.

And to anyone who needs to read this to know you matter, you do. No matter what we look like or where we came from, we deserve to be here. Never let anyone dim your light. Shine bright.

Contents

1

Rothing Gold Can Stay

He was on his knees, shrouded in a forest of faceless men and their thirst-seeking shadow selves, who were finally able to come out, even if only for a little while, as they were concealed by anonymity. The men were not merely here out of desperation and thirst, but they came to a place they knew they could find refuge, explore their curiosity, be and feel safe, even if only during the hours where they could be shielded by the cloak of the night sky and slivers of the moonlight.

The tall, over-arching, entwined eucalyptus, jacaranda, and weeping fig trees provided further luxurious shade that allowed their shadow selves to step out of the template they were expected to follow. Societal stereotypes, ideas of masculinity, ideas of heteronormativity, the expected script that they were doomed to follow from the start to the very end of their lives. Only the white from the moon peeking through the cover of the trees allowed everyone to find what they felt they needed. With the scent of testosterone in the humid air, the heat only enticed more to follow the trails, and everyone knew to follow the unspoken rules: speak not, let your body do the talking.

Doug couldn't use his light to find this man in the day, but under the cloak of the moonlight, without a cloud in the sky, on his knees in the park, he had found him. Standing tall, with broad shoulders, a plaid shirt, denim blue jeans, and Adidas, Doug made eye contact with the gentleman and used his charms to entice the man over to underneath the trees.

The man walked as if in a trance, buying into his urges and seeking the instantaneous relief he knew was awaiting him on the other side. Doug unzipped the man's denim blue jeans, and with excitement and exhilaration, pulled his raging manhood out. In the magic of the forest, people only see what they want to see, and that night, Doug could blur out any and everything he didn't want. All he wanted to see was right in front of him in this moment; a riveting, throbbing, hard black cock.

He took a moment to admire it, imperfectly perfect, but he couldn't last long. He knew where this belonged or else the others would snatch it away in no time. The exhilaration filled him up. Doug opened wide as he allowed the thick mushroom head to fill his mouth and enter the very back of his throat, taking his time to allow his own juices to surround the pulsating cock that was filling his throat.

Doug was initially sad that the man had arrived already in an erect position, it had robbed him of his opportunity to bring him there, but he was now too occupied in his thoughts to pay attention to anything else but serving this man, doing what Doug knew he was good for. He first started licking and playing with the tip of his head, licking it slowly, massaging him patiently with his lips and his seductive tongue.

Doug basked in the man's moans as he began to lose his balance and decided it was best to lean against the bark of the tree behind him. Doug paid it no mind; he couldn't go but two seconds without him in his throat at this point. Doug then moved slowly and seductively, with a grin, to the man's ball sack, gently licking and then sucking each testicle, enjoying the softness of his curly pubic hair and enjoying the scent of satisfaction.

Doug could only imagine what the man was feeling right now and if he could see. If it wasn't so dark, in a few moments, he would see the man's eyes rolling into the back of his head once Doug opened his mouth wide and took all of him deep in this throat, where mercy couldn't be found. He could tell the man needed him, the man needed this relief, so relief was what Doug would give him.

Standing tall, and crushing leaves underneath his feet, for the next fifteen minutes Doug did everything necessary to bring this man to ecstasy. On bended knee, Doug swallowed him as if he had been stranded in a desert for days. As the man began groaning, trying to stop Doug from continuing, Doug couldn't stop.

Doug fought the man's attempts to slow down the waves of orgasm quickly reaching its peak. He had come too far now; he was at the cliff, and it was time for him to jump off. With great passion and dedication, Doug continued sucking him, causing the man to forfeit and give in to what his body had wanted to do in the first thirty seconds of this encounter, cum. Doug sucked his sperm out as if he needed it to breathe. He sucked this faceless gentleman as if he was digging for gold, as if receiving his cum in his belly was thick, creamy, heavenly juice that could fill his stomach up for an entire week.

Men swarmed around as they always do when they detected motion, dropping their pants, and stroking their cocks. Doug longed to find a Black man to connect with; he had a yearning for the deep connection that he witnessed other non-Black people getting to have, but Black people like him rarely experience that with each other, which always left disappointment, envy, and resentment in the pits of his churning stomach. But outside of the park and the cloak of the night, this was the closest people like Doug could get to touching one, tasting one, serving one, but never being able to be loved by one, not as he really was. So, this was the only option, the next best thing, these fragile moments that last no more than a day, if only a few hours.

All thoughts escaped Doug as he felt the hand from the chosen one on the back of his head. He knew what he needed to do next. The moaning he was soon able to hear, the shivering he saw and could feel coming from the man's legs, and his throbbing penis in his mouth wasn't enough of a giveaway. Doug took him from the tip of his tongue to the very back of his throat so that he would not only remember Doug but remember Black people like him still found other Black men attractive. So that he didn't leave that night under the misconception pushed by social media that most Black people don't desire each other. Doug wanted him to know that tonight he wanted him, that probably tomorrow night he'd want him to if he could. And that he wanted more than just this moment, his aching heart crying out.

He stayed inside of Doug as they were now joined by several other faceless men who were stroking each other, one going down on another, taking the opportunity Doug provided to use for their own satisfaction and pleasure. Doug didn't care. He had found the one he desired, and he wasn't letting him go until his dick would not be able to rise again. So, he continued to suck. The arousal of satisfying this man led to something rising within Doug, but he had to hide it. He needed it to go away. He despised moments where he had to remember what he was.

One of the men inched closer, waving his uncut white cock near Doug's face. Doug wouldn't budge. His mouth stayed fixated on the man he was there to drain, not until every drop of his life essence was in his stomach would he leave. Doug continued to suck and slurp. The slurping was something Doug learned to do to make sure he was pleasuring every single angle and crevice of a man's penis. Doug admired the penis, and its beauty and felt it was a shame to allow any area of the penis to go untouched, unnoticed, neglected. He especially enjoyed going down lower and taking his balls in his mouth, feeling his curly, kinky pubic hair and sucking his tender balls, warming up the tea until it was ready to blow.

He felt the man's cock getting bigger and bigger, growing more and more sensitive and he loved it. This seemed to be all that he could do to get a man so this he had perfected. He could tell he was only seconds from exploding so this time he stopped, slowed down, teased him, then continued again, and he kept this pace until he was ready for him to fill his insides with his DNA. And then he did. Doug could hear the loud moaning of pleasure and relief and taste the explosion of warm juices inside his mouth, and then he swallowed it. Every drop, he swallowed. He had filled his insides with his DNA.

Doug proved to all the onlookers that he could please a Black man every bit as good as they could. But Doug didn't stop, he lingered, sucking until he made sure every drop was gone. The gentleman tapped out, motioning that he couldn't take anymore, pulling up and zipping his shorts. The show was over, folks. He left. Doug never got his name or saw him again, but it didn't matter. Under the shadows of the wide-branched cove of jacaranda and weeping fig trees, this was the norm. One never learns his name. One never speaks. You give each other a glance, hover, get closer, and show him that you want to serve him. If he is wearing a ring, you act like you don't see it. You make sure your cell phone ringer is off. And you make sure to leave by 10 pm before the patrol comes and finds you.

If you are found, you must run through the woods to reach your car and hightail it out of there before you receive a citation, or worse, before you get found out. And when they stop you, they know. They know what you were doing. They know something you don't want common people to know, and you hold your head down in shame. The moment you're caught, you must accept your fate. You cannot look away anymore. You must face it.

The crowd began to break up, but Doug still waited, searching for more. He knew his life was going to change in the next few hours and he would never be able to return here so he had to enjoy this for the last time. He walked around, stretching out of the isle of wide branched eucalyptus trees to the garden path, walking between more tall, bushy trees and thick shrubs, continuing to look around for a man in need. He may have just received two life essences, but this couldn't be the end.

There were steps leading from the path to a decline that gave way to a forest of additional trees and far-stretched greenery. This area was used for disc golf during the day, and you could surely find all the opened condom wrappers and empty lubrication bottles. But at night, all you could see were the faceless men and all you could hear were the whisperings and unspoken language that brings you closer to the men.

He looked beyond the two immediate men that were clearly wanting to be alone with each other and ventured outwards. A few minutes later, coursing through another patch of forest, he discovered three men who appeared to be circling one tall man in sweatpants, polo shirt, and a hat to cover his eyes. Much is left to the imagination but when his penis emerged, the men became like vultures, instantly circled, and zoned in for their prey. A few feet away, you could hear the casual fucking of a top mindlessly fucking a bottom who sounded like he couldn't fully handle the hardon that was tearing a part his ass. Doug glanced over but was never one to watch.

A little deeper into the forest, he finally found another man of mahogany complexion that was in need but instantly saw that a white man had gotten to him first. Doug walked over, tried to be inconspicuous, but the man of mahogany paid him little attention. Doug stepped closer and the man moved further away. The white man that was circling him seemed to understand that he wanted to go somewhere private. *Yes, you want to be private in a public park where anyone and everyone can see you at any time, makes perfect sense,* Doug thought to himself.

Doug was unwilling and too stubborn to give up. He followed them, easily overhearing them a few seconds later, and found the white man on his knees sucking his Black cock. Doug was hurt and furious. How dare this Black stranger not see what happened twenty minutes ago? Didn't he see how magical Doug had made the last two Black men feel? Didn't he see him standing there? Or did he see him standing there and decide to un-see him because they both had the same skin, because he too had melanin in his skin?

He walked around for a few seconds, trying to catch his breath, breathing deeply, feeling the energy pulsating through his veins. Doug struggled with the awareness that he should go home, but he was too aware of the prejudice that this Black man had just discriminated against him for being Black, as they both were. And making matters worse, this was the same kind of discrimination that has been done by white folks to Black folks since coming to this country. Doug couldn't take it anymore.

The spray was out of his pocket and in his hand before he knew it. His legs led him to them faster than he could have possibly imagined. He could smell the scent of mace in the air before he had even sprayed the Black man in the face, the man's pants down while the white man was sucking him. To re-iterate, he sprayed both of them in the face with long bursts of mace until the can was nearly emptied. He had been discriminated against by someone who should have understood the full impact of this more than anyone else and he was enraged.

The Black man went after him as if training for a decathlon…and Doug ran. The man was no longer going to have his erection. Well, since Doug wasn't going to get to suck it, what did he care? If he wasn't going to get to suck it, no white, Asian or Latino man here was going to get to suck it either.

What's more, no other Black person would be made to feel inferior to them because of it. Doug continued to run. He could hear him trying to carry after him but he couldn't. Doug had grown accustomed to the placements of the trees and the geography of this park for years, to the extent he could see it and know exactly where he was in pitch black with nothing but the sliver of the moon above guiding him.

Doug had lost him. And soon he discovered he had lost his own apartment key that had been safely secure in his pocket. What was he going to do? He went back and searched for it. Surprised that others weren't assembling to come after him yet, he frantically tried to spot his key under the dark veil of secrecy, but to no avail. He had to return home without his house key. He was panting.

Doug took on last look out over the park, at the men still hanging around, looking for the next best thing in this break from their real lives, hoping to never be seen, never be identified beyond the veil of secrecy known in this park. He prepared to say goodbye to the life he knew, knowing that he would never be able to come back here again. The same way that he was tonight, it would never be again. He could see the crescent moon shining between the slits of vision he had left as he prepared to start his journey.

*   *   *

Doug believed he had packed everything he needed for their trip. Anti-bacterial cream, enemas, Tylenol, crossword puzzles, filled prescriptions, and printed out directions for post-operative care. His mother was waiting in the living room in her favorite chair, probably worried about getting on her first ever airplane flight or worrying about the Airbnb they would be living in for the next four weeks in San Francisco. She tended to worry about everything, and when she couldn't find something, she would make something up to worry about.

In this case though, the reason for the flight was more than enough reason to worry. They had known about this for well over a year after receiving the required letters of recommendation for surgery, one year of hormones, and the dreaded one year of being this ugly duckling in-between being the you, you never were, and also being the you, you really are but no one can see yet. Waiting patiently while following protocols that make you feel like you have to prove to everyone else who you really are.

As he placed the last of the items he would need to start this four-week venture in the Bay Area in his suitcase, he was nervous, excited, terrified and aware that nothing would be the same again. Looking into his room for the last time, that eeriness of feeling like you are doing something different, changing the course of the way things were going to be until you made this decision, and making things anew. That feeling that something is happening, that if it weren't for this thing, you'd be doing something else, watching TV, drinking coffee, going for a walk, but instead you're headed on a flight, Doug's first ever flight, with his mother to San Francisco where his life would change, never to be what it was and never to be the same again.

*   *   *

How much longer before we lift off? Doug pondered to himself while seated in the aircraft in the window seat. Always hating planes, he anxiously awaited this part of the journey being over so the next part could start. Seat belts fastened, he noticed his mother had a quietness about her, one he had learned that over the years was a tell-tale sign that she was worrying, again. She was worrying about all the things that could go wrong. She hated being out of her home, even for a day, and was processing being gone for four weeks at a complete stranger's residence.

Everyone could hear the jets, the air conditioning fans kicking on blowing that warm air, the muttering from other passengers behind them. Movement was decreasing. Doug could hear the pilot's voice through the intercom, but he was too lost in thought to listen. *What if we crash? What if I don't survive what we are about to do? What, if after all this work, this waiting, this preparing, this getting myself mentally, physically, and emotionally ready, what if I'm still not ready for this? What if this isn't the right decision to make?*

The plane was moving. Rather slow-paced, getting in line to take off. There was still a plane or two in front of them. Doug could feel his heart beating faster. He could feel the anxiety pumping through his chest and reverberating down his arms and legs. He wanted to move. He wanted to stretch. He wanted to do what he always did, pace. He wanted to move his hands, but he couldn't. There was nowhere for them to go.

He was lost in the worst place he could be right now, his own thoughts. *Mindfulness they say. Breathing. Closing my eyes and visualizing good things. How about bombs detonating two inches from your face? I can't lose it now. We've come all this way; we have come so far. My mother is here and if I can't keep it together, she's shit out of luck. I'm made to be this man to make sure she is okay, even though that's not who I am. Prue, you can turn around right now, yell 'Fire!' on this bitch and get off. What's it going to be?*

He saw that the plane was at its mark. It was picking up speed, 30 mph…60 mph…90 mph…engines blaring, high speed, interior shaking. They had taken off. Clouds surrounding them. Soon they would be flying over the sun, gliding through the sky. The beautiful journey began.

2

Transcendence

Everything felt like it was in a fog. As her eyes opened, a distant light above became clearer and focused in position. She had become more alert. The sound of a ventilator machine beeping reminded her that she had made it, confirming that she was alive. Looking around the cold, sterile room composed of four bare white walls, and a large rectangular window on the farthest wall.

Medical equipment was scattered about throughout the room. A whiteboard with many words hung on the wall directly in front of her. She wasn't strong enough to make out all the words yet. There was a feeling inside of her that told her to move, to try to get up, to try to see if this was real. She wanted to move towards a mirror to see who would be looking back at her. She wanted to see if this was real.

There was a heaviness on her chest that she was unfamiliar with. A tightness, coolness, and numbness between her legs. Clouds quickly moved through her mind as if they were still walking over the sun. An image of herself floating while peering out into the clouds, wondering what the shapes meant. Seeing a bird, seeing a dove, and the shape of Martin Luther King Jr on the top of Mount Rushmore. Floating higher, she could feel her gown blowing in the wind, memories of her life before passing by and welcoming a new chapter that she had long been waiting for, she had waited for such a very long time.

In an instant, she was back in the hospital room, the beeping reminding her again that she was alive, that she had returned. It wasn't strong enough though to keep her. Within seconds, the bursting waves of the Atlantic Ocean were surrounding her, crashing into her legs, her feet. She rushed up to the top of the hospital bed, but she couldn't escape. They were all around her.

Suddenly, she was underwater. The lights above had faded to a single stream. Afraid and unable to swim, she tried to keep herself from sinking by trying to hold onto something but nothing would hold her. She reached for the IV pole but as soon as she touched it, it turned into sand. She stretched her arm to touch the hospital phone, but her hand fell off. Suddenly, her arm grew a new hand, and she tried again, but this time her hand ate itself and didn't regenerate.

The violent waves crashing caused the electrical outlets to spark with bursts of electricity, sending shockwaves to her arms and legs. Amidst feeling the volts of electricity running through her veins, she removed the equipment that was now acting as handcuffs and chains, holding her down. But it was becoming too late. She was losing strength and her spirit ever more so evaporating. She was trapped between the oxygen and monitoring tubes that had made her hospital bed become her personal prison, and now her place of execution. She was sinking, the light becoming dim in an abyss of blue.

"Doug- I mean Prudence, are you okay?" With a panicked voice, a familiar woman shook her arm and began slapping her face. "Nurse, my daughter isn't waking up. Prue, wake up!"

Something about this voice brought her back. Something was pulling her back to her body. A silver string, she barely noticed in the glimmer of her eye. It appeared attached to something.

"Doug! Prudence! Oh God, please!" As the woman who resembled an older image of herself wailed, her daughter opened her eyes. She had returned. "Oh my God. I was so worried about you. Are you okay? The nurse is here."

"That was a close one. Prue, how are you feeling?" She recognized this name as her own, but it also felt different and new at the same time.

"I feel like I died," Prue exclaimed.

"Well, you didn't, you're just on a lot of medications right now to manage your pain." The nurse turned to the other nurse. "Let's decrease his- I mean her dosage to help with his pain management so that she won't slip back into unconsciousness."

It felt like everything and nothing at once. She noticed the bandages on the top of her chest, the holster bra, the bags of ice on top as well as the large heavy bags of ice on top of her genitals. She could feel and not feel all at once. Though she couldn't feel it, she knew that it happened. What was once there was no longer. For the first time, she would be seen as the woman she has always known herself to be since she was three. She was becoming her. Feeling all of her emotions, sadness, fear, anxiety, fear, happiness, FEAR. The thoughts were too much. She had used up all her energy just to make these connections. The room began to swim, the waves were crashing again and she had no more energy to hang on.

*   *   *

She could hear a faint voice from a nearby room. It sounded like it was coming from someone's phone. No, from a television. No, voices from the hallway, gasping, crying, in shock. As if her soul was re-entering her body, the voices and her audio comprehension aligned as she made out the voices saying, "And in local news, Kaleb Jackson, an inspirational leader for our youth who worked at the local high school's afterschool program for over ten years was killed this morning. Freak accident in an airplane crash. No survivors." The words didn't make sense. The news continued, "Kaleb, along with his teenage son, local star seventeen-year-old Marco who aspired to enter the MLB franchise are dead. None of the one-hundred-sixty-four passengers made it out alive, their lives tragically cut short."

Prue was also in disbelief. She literally could not believe the words that were said. It was in that moment her heart stopped. It felt like she couldn't breathe anymore. Tears instantly rushed to her face before she knew what to do with them. This couldn't be true. There had to be a mistake. She thought she had heard Kaleb was signaling to the paramedics to find them, where the crash was, signaling so the other passengers could be helped. She swore she heard one of the newscasters say this. She thought that was what they said. So, it couldn't be true that he or anyone else had passed away that morning.

Prue tried to get down on her knees, but she couldn't move. She couldn't feel her body anymore, but she knew she was there. All she could feel was the coldness between her legs and she knew soon the waves would begin crashing again. Staying in her hospital bed, she prayed. She felt guilty, but she prayed it was anyone else. She prayed that maybe the others had passed away, but not him and not his son, as she knew that would have killed him.

Somehow, she was able to stumble out of bed and make it onto her knees, the bed alarm going off. She didn't care. He couldn't be dead. She didn't know why this impacted her so much. She wasn't related to him, hadn't known him in any real meaningful way. But she felt like she could die at this moment.

As the news continued pouring in for hours, it became more real. It became real that they had lost someone significant who had made a positive difference. And he had been lost while innocently traveling with his son to visit a potential college offering him a scholarship to play baseball.

Nothing made sense. While thieves and robbers and cheaters and liars and rapists and child molesters and drug dealers and wife beaters get to live, Kaleb, his teenage son and almost two hundred other people all met their untimely death in a tragedy that no one could see coming or ever understand. The world didn't know what it had just lost.

3

Guilty Before Proven Innocent

The two men briskly walked through the doors of the corner store, a quarter to closing. It was the moment between the sky shifting from dusk to twilight, their shadows collided into an emerging realm they never expected to experience. The clerk hurried around, frantically cleaning the aisles, impatiently looking at the time, clearly ready to go home. The two men with mahogany skin, full lips and auburn eyes scrolled the aisles, looking for snacks to devour. They could be overheard chanting, "Go Aztecs!"

The cashier was at the front of the store, counting and putting away the cash from the drawer. The men appeared jovial, laughing and gallivanting to the counter near the double glass entrance doors. The only thing on their mind was preparing for the final half of the Monday night Aztec basketball game at the local state university. They were so consumed in their own excitement that they missed the obvious signs because everything within this store knew that it was closing time. Placing their items on the counter, Derek fumbled around for a few bucks in his pocket and managed to find three one-dollar bills and a nickel. Dwayne looked at his friend, shook his head, reached into his backpack for his credit card and handed it to the cashier.

"You guys must be big Aztec fans," the cashier motioned to the Aztec gear, most prominently the Aztec logo on Dwayne's shirt.

"Are you kidding? This is like the only reason I enrolled in this school." Derek laughed along with Dwayne.

Dwayne noticed out of the corner of his eye the impatient clerk near the doors. Dwayne turned towards the cashier, "Sorry man, I see you're about ready to close. Just wanted to get a few things before heading back to the dorm. We've got to study later anyways."

"No worries, man. What are you guys studying?" the cashier asked.

"I'm a business major, and my friend Derek here is in computer engineering."

"Wow, that's cool guys."

"What about you? Do you go to state too?" Dwayne couldn't help but notice the cashier looked about their age, a little shorter than them, thin frame, his face hidden by his thick brim oak brown glasses, but they couldn't take away his youthfulness.

"Actually, no. I don't think I'm the right fit for college life."

Dwayne appeared shocked. "What do you mean? College is the land of opportunity for us all. There's no one way to be."

Derek patted Dwayne's shoulder. "You shouldn't have said that to Dwayne. He's our resident gospel advisor. Inspiration to us all, day end day night."

"I think it may be easier for you guys. I didn't exactly come from anything."

"Neither did we," Dwayne interjected. "You make the most of what you got. We don't have to let our past and how we got here define us and dictate where we go the rest of our lives."

The cashier looked down, as if he was trying to find a way to hold on to this moment for when he was ready to use it. He handed them the receipt. Dwayne took the receipt and out of his pocket pulled out and gave the cashier a card. "Give them a call sometime if you change your mind and you're ready to get over that fear and give yourself a chance."

The cashier took the card, it read the name of an enrollment counselor at the local university in the Outreach and Engagement Department. As they headed out of the store, Dwayne looked back, "They really have helped a lot of people like us. Give yourself a chance."

As they walked to their car from the store, footsteps rushed behind them. "Put your hands up!" said a man's voice from directly behind them. Derek and Dwayne were used to that authoritative voice. It was a tone familiar to men with mahogany skin, full lips and brown or auburn eyes, the voice of a man who believed he could own another man, the ancestral voice that was used to incite fear in generations of other men and women of mahogany skin. Instinctively, they put their hands up and slowly turned around. To their surprise, the police officer was holding a gun less than ten feet away, aimed at both of them.

"Officer, why are you pointing that at us? What did we do?" Dwayne tried to remain calm and in full control of his voice and mannerisms knowing full well what the consequences were if he didn't. He had been taught to be this way since he was old enough to tell the difference between people with mahogany skin and people with pale skin. As he aged, he even learned that there were other shades of mahogany that he never knew of, sepia, caramel, mocha, peanut, coffee, carob.

"Just keep your hands up!" the officer demanded, in his full police officer regalia, his full head of black hair, bulging brown eyes, and sleek black shoes. His gold-plated name badge read Lt. Hunter and his shiny gold badge appearing as a flash of light in the darkness of the night underneath the faint warm glow of the streetlights on the sidewalks and the corner store's neon sign flicking on and off.

If Derek and Dwayne weren't focused on trying to save their lives, they would notice the three additional black and white squad cars approaching and pulling up just 50 feet from them. The red and blue lights, and the sirens sounded, alerting everyone nearby to come to their windows, peek out of their doors, stop what they were doing and watch. Derek and Dwayne would have noticed that they were the main event that night, that all eyes were on them, they would have heard the sounds and seen the lights. But it was impossible to see and hear anything but one's own beating heart in one's throat, hoping to stay alive just one moment longer.

"I know my rights. Tell me what we did. Why are you pointing a gun at us?" Derek shouted, the fear fiercely fighting through him causing him to move around and not remain still.

"Stay where you are! Calm down!" yelled another voice from behind them.

At this point, Derek and Dwayne were facing the store windows. Dwayne motioned to Derek to try to remain calm, sensing his fraternity brother's anxiety rising. They were the same age but Dwayne knew what could happen if he didn't stay calm, he knew how quickly things could escalate and he didn't want to see his brother hurt. Nothing he could do seemed to relax Derek though, and Dwayne couldn't blame him. If you had a gun pointed at your face and the officer pointing it yelled at you to calm down, how likely would you be to calm down? After all, we are in a country where officers have killed unarmed Black men before for less. It was a good thing that they hadn't turned around to see the choir of guns pointed at them from behind.

"Don't tell me to calm down. You calm down. You're pointing the gun at me, motherfucker. Why are you targeting us? What the fuck did we do?" Derek was inconsolable. He couldn't stand there any longer. Without thinking, he started moving forward, away from the gun. Dwayne tried to whisper to Derek to stop moving. Derek couldn't help it. He felt fear running, leaping throughout his entire body. In this moment in this time, where his feet stood and the crescent moon rose in a foggy sky, this could be his last moment.

The phone rang. Derek reached into his pocket to pick it up.

Thirteen, fourteen shots rang out and instantly penetrated his body, the body that once held his soul for 26 years. Twelve more shots that appeared to emerge from a menagerie of face-less officers hitting his lifeless body, three shots entering the adjacent brick stone building, two cracking the corner store windows where the cashier stood using his privilege to take a stand. When in the beginning it was one, now they were surrounded by officers in their black and blues. He couldn't look back. He knew what would happen if he did. He'd realize he was standing there alone and that his friend, his fraternity brother, his brotha, had already departed, as a bird falling in a broken sky.

There were bursts of screams but also pin-drop silence. He couldn't tell where the screams were coming from. It was as if he was so shaken that he had lost complete control of his limbs. As the police approached, the main officer in charge, Lt. Hunter, yelled to his fellow officers, "Shit! We've got the wrong guys. The bank robbers are still out there. Report to dispatch."

"What? Wrong guys?" the voice came out.

Lt. Hunter kept his eyes to the ground, surveying the murder scene, ignoring his question.

"What the fuck do we look like? You just saw us walk out of that store. How the fuck could we have robbed a bank?"

Lt. Hunter tried to keep his gaze low so that he wouldn't have to make eye contact. Perhaps he was thinking not making eye contact would make this easier, as if he wouldn't have to face himself, he wouldn't have to see what he did. Lt. Hunter turned away and motioned to the other officers to come forward, saying, "We should get him to EMT before the bleeding from his shoulder and leg get worse." The man of mahogany skin looked down and noticed the bleeding from the bullet wounds that had grazed him, his body fully intact before coming into contact with the police, but he was unable to feel anything.

Anger filled his voice instantly. "Hold up. We just walked out of the fucking store. You come up to us pointing a gun because we fit a fucking description. You shoot us and…" he stopped himself, acknowledging his voice breaking up. He couldn't bring himself to say the next few words.

Lt. Hunter refused to make eye contact. "Guys, let's go." Lt. Hunter turned briefly towards him. "You can file a report at the police station if you have more questions."

He was beside himself, and now, without any moaning or uttering from his wise friend, he knew he was alone. He turned around. There laid his brother Dwayne, dead in a pool of his own blood, bleeding out on the concrete. The same concrete they had walked on moments earlier to enter the store to get snacks to watch the Aztec game. The same concrete where moments before they were supposed to return to their dorm to study for their exam. He wouldn't have his business exam tomorrow; he was gone because of an impatient clerk who wanted to go home and a police encounter that ended with his friend Dwayne dead.

This moment would become the metamorphosis of something greater than anyone could have imagined. Someone using his privilege took a stand to memorialize what happened that night so the world could see, hoping it would make a difference and hoping it would catapult society to a much-needed change in an imperfect world.

*   *   *

Devon woke up in a disarray as he often did. Opening his eyes, he could hardly recall whose bed he was in and which lover he was with. Attending his last year at the local state university, he was motivated and determined to complete his studies in finances and become the first college graduate in his family.

Originally from Jamaica, he and his family immigrated to the United States when he was a small child. He used his military experience as an opportunity to see more of the world than he was used to, that included spending time overseas, returning to his home country and seeing distant relatives who had not been able to legally move to the states.

He did not escape his naval career without injury. Years spent being in the field caused him carpel tunnel, arthritis, back pain, body aches and experiences he could have gone without. Lord knows he tried to distract his mind as much as possible with beer, hard liquor, women, and sex, typically in that order. There were times that when he couldn't achieve that formula, he would mix it up: beer, hard liquor, men, and sex, but his formula was very restrictive, he always had to be the MAN.

He would receive oral pleasure; he would dominate, but he would never give. He was a taker. Although enjoyable, not a preference he was extremely comfortable with and not one he shared with others.

There was a time where Devon was a man that he himself was proud of. Three years ago, he was on track to marry the love of his life, the woman whose children he took in as his own and loved and cherished more than he could have ever thought possible. But, due to certain indiscretions on his part, his fiancé found out and decided to end it all.

A shattered, broken man who had done all he could to hide the things he had done from his love, and then groveled and apologized to try not to lose the love he had been accustomed to; he grew to accept that she would not change her mind.

Then Devon changed his, by embracing another part of his soul that most people keep hidden deep inside until they decide they have nothing left to lose. The shadow within him had come to feast and what Devon would never do with a man, he chose to do with his heart and compassion, and that was to submit.

He resigned the parts of his soul that made him human and embraced the shadow of himself that everyone else projected, a big, tall, strong, masculine, emotionless Black man who was dominant, assertive, smart when it suited him and blessed and highly favored due to what swung between his legs. So, Devon decided to open a lot of legs and that morning woke up in an unfamiliar bed where he had done just that.

"Good morning, Daddy." He turned to find a petite pale faced flat-chested, blonde hair blue-eyed girl cuddling next to him, wearing panties that said *Cum Slut*. He felt like he needed to immediately leave. The moment was over, he knew he gave her his seed last night but this morning he was ready to go and explore. Intimacy was overrated.

"Morning. How late is it? I'm running late for class."

"There isn't class today. They cancelled all classes today because of what happened last night," she responded.

He looked puzzled. "What happened last night?"

She cuddled up closer to him, playing with his curly black hair and kissing on his earlobe. "A man was shot and killed last night by police." He reached throughout the crisp white sheets and ivy comforter for his cell phone. "It happened around 10:00 last night. The video is all over the news."

He had not been successful finding his phone but had found his boxers and socks loose between the sheets. "Who was he?"

"I don't know. They haven't released his identity yet." She paused and then pressed her index finger to her lips. "So that means you can stay over. I can make you breakfast." She leaned over to give him a kiss and reached down to hold him in her right hand. He could feel himself in her hand, but he wasn't alive as he was last night. "Oh, I know what to do."

Finally finding his cell phone, he noticed eight missed calls, and twelve unanswered text messages. Feeling himself rising between her lips, he was jolted back to reality when he read a text saying, *They killed him, bro. The racists pigs killed Dwayne.*

Suddenly, the bliss that he was about to fall into for the next ten minutes wasn't going to happen. The blood that was pulsating below immediately stopped and was diverted to the pits of his stomach. His friend Dwayne was dead. They had studied all four years at State together. Spending extra hours in the library studying late at night into all hours, navigating the campus as the only three Black men studying Business and Finance in a sea of white faces, grappling with maintaining their culture while knowing they had to lose parts of themselves in order to find success in their fields.

Dwayne felt like a brother to him, they were part of the same fraternity, Alpha Omega Psi. They had been through so much. The pain of this was too much and in a Black man, pain quickly is seen and projected as anger and being feared. Immediately he became aware of his Blackness when just a few moments ago he was allowing a white woman to send him to a paradise with her backstroke. He felt uncomfortable and angry and knew he had to leave. "Where are my clothes?"

4

Lost in a Memory

The deepest of blues, he felt as though he was swimming beneath the ocean, experiencing the parallels of fragility and infinity, relishing the ocean's gift of liberation and freedom. He sat immersed in steamy soothing pools of lavender-scented heated water flowing and gently crashing into his body. Cloud puffs of lemongrass and clary sage filled the air.

Taking his stand on the pool deck, he was aware of the people all around him, every echo, extra towel, and the faint smell of chlorine. He became even more aware of his goal and his ambition to climb to the top of the diving platform and out score his competitors. Especially Johnson, Jacob and Jones, the triple threat, putting them to shame and making the score to get Coach Scottie's recommendation for the U.S. Swimming Olympic Trials swim meet coming up in a few short months.

His sights were on making that team, no matter what, and he wanted nothing more than to show everyone who didn't believe in him that he was worthy, that he was enough, and that he was a winner. And as aware as he previously was of the totality of voices, chatter, gossip and dozens of discussions all around him, in an instant the volume was turned down, treble dissipating, and only the bass present, but subdued in the background.

The deepest of blue ocean water with its ripples, moving swiftly without effort. Suddenly, a small duck appeared on the water. The duck was covered in khaki plumage, with its dark brown head and greenish-colored bill. The scene didn't make any sense. A look of shock remained on Gus's face. The duck moved about, flapping its wings as if it could fly, and although wild ducks can, this one didn't seem to. Out of the corner of his eye, he recognized the glimmers. The oh so familiar scent that he had grown to loathe while in high school but over the past several years had made him fight back tears.

"Are you just going to keep standing there like a chump?" He recognized his voice. And right away, all of it made sense. "Gus, let's go. There's no way you're going to beat my record for the dive."

He was afraid to turn around. He could tell the voice was coming from behind him, but he knew what would happen if he did. He knew he would get lost in a memory that had long since passed. Even at this time, the area of the Sapphire Elite Athletic and Swim Club that was bold and bright, sat overcast in shadows. The see-through 80 foot tall, oval shaped, glass panel ceiling that moments ago shown beams of sunlight now only illustrated overcast skies. The clock he was able to see so well before on the wall, with its big numbers, was fading away. He was remembering less and less of this memory, that all he could really hold on to was this part. But still he turned around.

His brother, David, was standing there dripping wet, holding his favorite towel that had his initials DB inscribed on the bottom, the same towel that got him kicked out of Mr. Cooper's class for throwing it at Casius. Grinning, only that big, sneaky grin that big brothers do, he threw the towel at Gus and dared him to jump higher than he did, to finally reach and touch the glass panel ceiling. They never could when they were younger and because of them, they had to build the Notarium even higher than before to accommodate their high jump dives.

Gus was always smaller than his brother. He never allowed himself to grasp his full potential as long as his big brother was there. He always felt he stood in his big brother's shadow. Even after. He worked to make a name for himself, and did, but never alone, never without his big brother pushing him somewhere within. But even the spirit within was starting to fade as now his brother was the only part of the memory that was light. His brother's body was shrouded in grey.

Gus allowed himself to get carried away. He ran up to the diving board, paced himself, visualized himself carrying out the dive to its completion and the crowd going wild. Wait, there was a crowd. He could hear voices again. The bass turned back to full volume. The treble returned. It was as though all of his human senses were amplified, but the sense he needed for his brother was now muted. He was overwhelmed with sense, he could feel everything now, he was aware of everything now. This probably would have all been fine if this wasn't happening while Gus was diving off the dive platform heading towards the pool beneath.

Losing his concentration would cost him. As he heard the laughter, he knew that would answer any questions about whether or not he would impress Coach Scottie below and get him to choose him for the Olympic Swim Meet. He met the water belly up, as graceless as a meteor hitting planet Earth. The humiliation made his cheeks feel they were on fire and his head ache beyond repair. He knew that he was losing the last part of him that he could hold onto and that he had disappointed himself. Gus wanted to fly away right now, so desperately.

*   *   *

Dive after dive, no dive was good enough. He had waited until the gymnasium was empty again and had snuck back to continue his diving practice, after all, if he was going to be an Olympic swimmer, he had to learn to never give up. After that performance this morning, he couldn't stand to see

his face in the mirror. He knew he had to do better. He knew
he had to be better. So, he ran endless laps in the pool until
he was a mile past exhausted. He worked on his breaststroke,
his backstroke, butterfly laps and crawl. He swam deeper and
deeper underwater in the 50-meter-long bottom-less pool,
developing his breath control and core endurance. He took
dives off the diving platform at 10 feet, 15 feet, 20 feet, and
25 until his body couldn't take it anymore. And when he felt
he was leaving his body, he tried harder, remembering the
feeling of failure and the laughter of the crowd that seemed
to find the holy spirit from his utter defeat.

In the deepest of the ocean, he was searching but he
knew he couldn't find him again. He tried to conjure up the
image of David, but all he was left with was the Khaki
Campbell duck. He needed to do better. He needed to try
harder. The water strokes turned to hours and the darkness
that he became started to witness hints of amber dawn, and
faint light shining through the glass walls. He knew in a
matter of moments, the pool staff would open the
gymnasium and his fiercest competitors would rush in, ready
to practice, hoping to be legendary and win.

Gus knew he had to get out of there, he had to show no
sign that he had the potential to beat the triple threat.
Suddenly, he heard something stirring. He looked around,
immediately jolted with his own image, leaving him with a
confused expression on his face. He took off his goggles and
ferociously rubbed his eyes, unable to believe what he saw,
but when he opened them, he found nothing and no one. It
must have been time for him to go.

His exit was delayed as he couldn't open his locker and
eventually realized that he was trying to unlock the wrong
one. It took him a few moments to realize his locker was the
one right next to this one but it was so peculiar since the lock
was so much like his and he was the only one there. He then
proceeded to lose more time by changing his clothes and
then having difficulty finding his car keys where he thought
they were in his duffle bag. He was, however, able to find his

secret stash. During one of his bathroom breaks, he had drank most of what he could and had found a temporary relief from his thoughts when he injected a mysterious fluid into his arm an hour ago. He found his speed improved by the feeling and appreciated the extra energy it gave him. Finally getting himself together, he shoved the half dozen empty cans into his duffle bag, made his way to the parking lot and though his hair was still wet, he was ready to drive off.

Finding his keys became a "Where's Waldo?" exercise. He had them in his pocket but as if little magical gnomes had moved them, he couldn't locate them. No sooner had he found them, did he lose them again, along with his sunglasses that were hiding in plain sight over his bloodshot eyes. The keys, he eventually found in the ignition. He knew it was time to go and although his mind seemed to know this, his body seemed to bounce to a different drum. When he tried to move his left foot, amazingly his right foot would respond. He had gone everywhere and nowhere at the same time, exerting so much energy to drive the car, but starting and stopping to the extent that he was certain someone was coming to haul him away to the psych ward. Alas, he seemed able to summon the power in his right foot to step on the pedal and he was finally moving.

He tried to remind his brain where he was, because it seemed it was on vacation. He was tired and faint, so he rolled the windows down, but now that they were all rolled down, he felt as though the wind was suffocating his larynx. He couldn't decide, more or less, couldn't remember where he was even going. He knew it, held onto it for a second, but then watched it fade away, knowing it was there while watching it disappear.

While driving, he started witnessing the blurry numbers on his dashboard. 35. 45. 67. 93. And the numbers he was able to see outside in his neighborhood, although these numbers were much lower. 30. 30. 25. Shapes that he could see. Triangles. Hexagons. Yellow hexagons. And colors.

Yellow. Red. Red. Red. He could feel something was happening. He could tell. He could see the truck. He could hear the sound. He could feel the shock.

5

Grieving Begins

Prue had arrived home only a short time ago and had already found herself slumped into the sofa. On days when she wasn't becoming one with the couch, she was spending evenings and afternoons walking aimlessly up and down the hallway and kitchen of her mother's apartment. She had managed to earn some of her strength back, but it showed most in fleeting moments. She couldn't conceive of this new feeling within her, these thoughts that were surrounding her, this dark grey cloud that had abruptly taken over her life without sign or warning and had completely swallowed her whole.

Up and down, she was up and down, tearing up, crying, trying to not cry, giving up, trying to not give up, trying to understand, trying to remember the moments before, trying to remember everything before as if this was a dream, a nightmarish dream. She believed that if she could remember all the details from immediately before it happened, all the memories, his voice, and his personal items that grounded him, that proved that he had lived and that he couldn't possibly have died, that this would bring him back. She just knew that if she kept thinking about this, that if she kept looking for a way, she could figure out how to change this.

It couldn't be true, it couldn't be. He couldn't be gone. It was Kaleb. Everyone in town knew Kaleb. He had single-handedly brought the high school basketball team back from their years of defeat to each and every championship trophy. He created a space for hundreds of at-risk youth who had nowhere to go after school, no parent at home to look after them, no father in their life to be a role model. Well over a decade, he was the friendly face in the basketball gym, the smiling coach on the track field pushing each student to be their very best and to never let anything or anyone get in their way.

He was the friendly tutor who taught you that you were smart, that you could be anything you wanted to be if you put your mind to it. Even after his own personal challenges, his back injury that night on the court leading him to early retirement, the divorce that followed, the strained relationship he was rebuilding with his son, he practiced what he preached. Kaleb was loved.

He allowed nothing to stop him. He allowed nothing to get in his way. While the rest of us were learning how to shovel, he had already created a luxurious town of colonial 19th-century sandcastles surrounding us with a ten-inch-deep moat and mermaids resting against the wooden drawbridge parting the seas. Giving him more time, he surely would have figured out how to carve the dragons with actual fire roaring out of their mouths.

Kaleb made you believe you were better than you are, that you could do anything, that anything was possible, that with him on your side, nothing was impossible, and everything was possible. He was the bass voice in the locker room. He was the smile that you felt instantaneously cover your face the moment something made you feel light and happy. He was the quiet guy that was the role model, that helped you reach your full potential but knew how to give you your ass back single-handedly.

In his time, there were countless people, teenagers, families, community members who were better because they knew him or knew of him. The wings of his impact spread widely, very few could escape the effect of his mentality and his utter determination to help you be the best, even now he is leaving the lesson of the importance of appreciating the time you have because you never know when it's gone. He couldn't be gone. He was a good man. It would make no sense.

Prue remained paralyzed in a state of confusion. She couldn't understand how one particular day, how one moment could lead to the end of almost two hundred lives, people that had been alive for decades, even before her, suddenly ceasing to exist, ceasing to live and breathe again. It felt as if it couldn't make sense, as if thinking about it longer and harder would cause her to figure out how to fix it. If something had just happened to have delayed when they left the tarmac, or something had caused them to land early, or if something that caused them to have not flown in the first place, any of these things, any one change could have prevented this from happening. His son was going to become an MLB legend for sure.

So how is it possible that people today are living and breathing, going about their day, but people that had been alive for decades before suddenly weren't now? All because of one avoidable moment. One moment where if one thing had changed, there wouldn't be anything to grieve. Prue could instead be complaining about some other nominal thing in her life, which is a guarantee she'd find.

Somewhere out there, there is a gaping hole in the matrix and fabric of time now that the universe has taken him away, and while he was doing no harm, nothing wrong. It was impossible. Something, somehow, must be wrong. Someone must have messed this up and Kaleb would be so angry when he learned that everyone thought he and his son, Marco, were dead. He was going to come out and tell everyone that this was a mistake, but that he was happy folks were leaving him beautiful notes and posting their prayers and condolences and now honoring his life as they should have while he was living.

He would be happy to see that the afterschool program is receiving more financial support than ever and his students finally listening to him. Maybe that's what he was doing. He was waiting until this ridiculous story raised over a million dollars in support to the afterschool program, lord knows it was well needed, and once he was satisfied, he would come out and announce to everyone that it was just a mistake. Not before making sure the checks cleared though. That made more sense. He was always the mastermind; he could turn pennies to millions. There is no way that this would be how God chose to end his life. It would make no sense for God to choose this moment to take them away. They didn't deserve that.

She allowed herself to get lost in this narrative, bringing it up each time her mind needed her to, but it came with its share of consequences. To believe this, she would need to turn off the television, not check social media, not talk to her friends, and she'd have to be very careful where she went. No one would understand. Many times, this ritual worked, but the longer it took for him to come out and reveal this was a hoax, the more she found herself overcome with emotion where she couldn't do anything else but cry.

She would go to her room at her mother's house, pull the curtains down, turn the old-fashioned radio on with the volume turned all the way up to deafen her cries, and she would give in. Prue succumbed to the feelings inside of her. At this point, nothing mattered. Time flew by, minutes, hours, all the same. Nothing mattered. Time was just a construct, and she felt she didn't want, nor deserve, to live in this world anymore. She had no right to be here and didn't want to if he wasn't going to be here. He deserved to be here. He was a great person. He is a great person. She couldn't conceive him in past tense.

The knocking on her door did very little to startle Prue. On the other side, she heard her mother calling her, "Honey, are you okay?"

She knew her mother would be worried. She loved her mother but nothing inside of Prue worked anymore. The cloud that was around her had darkened and thickened. She couldn't see a way out. This made no sense. God should have protected them. They didn't do anything wrong.

She couldn't stop the explosion of tears that dimmed her light and made her want to give up hope. All she wanted at this point was to die. She was beyond feeling like a zombie. Her soul was crushed. The same images of the airplane crash, and pieces of the aircraft stretched out all along that mountain kept intrusively entering her mind on repeat. When her eyes were open, she saw it. When her eyes were closed, she saw it. When she tried to sleep, she saw it, and she could see it so vividly as if she was there with them.

She could make out the inside of the cockpit. It was easy, they had shown so many pictures on social media before she shut that shit down, it was ridiculous. She could see the inside of the airplane. She could see the pilots, one with his shades on and both of them wearing their headsets. She was amazed by all the buttons and switches all around the pilot's cabin. Peering beyond to the first class seating, she noted vanilla leather interior seating, and fancy technology including mounted high-def flat screen TVs.

And then she saw him. Kaleb was several feet back from the pilot's cabin with his shades on wearing his hoodie and sweats. He was looking down, texting on his phone. Marco was to his right, headphones on, orange soda in the console, looking out the window. It was so cloudy outside. You couldn't see anything outside the windows. It felt like they were engulfed in the eye of a swirling tornado.

At once, Prue was parallel with her own thoughts; she was in the airplane while also aware she couldn't really be there. Feeling fear and panic, sadness and impending doom, she was frozen in her emotions and felt completely powerless. Her body was there but she couldn't move, much less think. She could see from the aisle that Kaleb couldn't have seen what was going to happen. She had worried so much, *What if he saw what was about to happen? What if the reports that they held each other until the end were true?*

She couldn't live knowing that they felt a moment of pain. She had hoped that the final moments were brief, that something happened that caused them to immediately become unconscious and that they couldn't have possibly ever seen or felt anything after that.

She looked at Kaleb and Marco, she couldn't understand why this was going to happen. She saw the others behind them in their seats. She just wanted to hold him. She wanted Kaleb to know that everything was going to be okay, but she didn't know that to be true. She wanted to make everything okay for him. She wanted to protect him no matter the cost. She would give anything to be able to stop this moment from happening.

She had acknowledged her truth, that she didn't want to live in a world without him. Something within her began to move. Initially frozen in peril, this newfound energy ran through her and she felt the urgency to move, to go to him, so that's what she would do. She picked herself up off the floor, dusted her shoulders, and made her way towards him…and then everything went dark. No sound. No movement. No sense of feeling. Only her continual loop of thoughts; *This couldn't be right. He couldn't be dead. Why, God, did you abandon them like that? Why didn't you protect him? He was doing so much good; he was just getting his life back. He didn't deserve that.*

She could feel herself returning to her bedroom, the soft sheets beneath her skin, the music still blaring, jolting her back. But she would do what she had learned how to get through, shift it all out of her mind and pretend. Nothing else at this point mattered. All she wanted was to die now. Hearing the sounds disappearing in a world behind her, she wondered to herself, *Where is he now? Where are they?*

* * *

At this point, her mother was beyond concerned for her. Prue had taken the habit of leaving in the dark of night, aimlessly walking around the neighborhood, just looking up at the night sky. Passing strangers in the night, immersing herself in the buildings she had become familiar with, being re-awakened by new buildings and places she hadn't experienced that were on the path of the less traveled.

There was something mysterious about the night air and the outside that made her feel the winds of freedom, and strangely made her feel more connected to Kaleb. She didn't know why, it didn't make sense, and she didn't know if it was the pains of her grief talking, but every night, she became more and more aware of two stars that seemed to follow her wherever she went. One star shown brighter than all the others and seemed to stay in that spot. Not far from it, she saw a much smaller star, not as bright but making its presence known.

When she would return to her mother's home, she would rush past the old garage below her room, the one she used to rent so many years ago, and quietly sneak into the apartment. But still, she would find herself peering out of her bedroom window and reflecting, going over and over how she wished he was here, wondering to herself how she would get through another day.

Her mother didn't understand what was going on and why she was feeling this way. She thought the surgery had done something wrong, causing her now-daughter to act bizarre and distraught. She couldn't see that her daughter's soul was dying, that she wasn't able to hang on anymore. Prue couldn't find the words. If Prue had found the words, her mother could see, her mother's eyes would open, but Prue couldn't find the words. She held out her hand and could see the words, but she couldn't reach them.

It took all her energy just to get out of bed that day. Every minute that she didn't just crawl back under the covers and cry was a miraculous moment at this point. All she wanted to do was stop suffering, stop feeling, but every moment she was awake, she was reminded that he was gone, and she had no choice but to remember why. All she wanted to do was to stop feeling.

*   *   *

It was 2:24 am and she couldn't return to sleep. She had just experienced another dream where she was in the airplane again, doomed to watch it plummet to the earth. There was no feeling anymore. Nothing made sense anymore. She avoided the burial, the funeral, the celebration of life. She didn't want any part in any of it. It all just made the loss more real. The sad songs that were designed to make you cry, the beautiful eulogies that shouldn't be said because he shouldn't be dead. She compartmentalized all of it to the point that nearly every day had to exist in its own locked compartment just so she could make it through the next 24 hours. But not today. It was 2:25 am, and she could feel the tears rushing to her eyes, the desire to just throw something, to tear apart everything in the four walls of her room. She was so angry, she was seething. *God, how could he be dead like this? How could you take him this way?*

She headed out of her bedroom towards the hallway bathroom with a glass in her hand. She had already decided. It was 2:26 am. Sleep is what she craved; it was her only nominal relief from the pain. Watching the same TV shows, the same movies the day before the tragedy, these lies didn't last long enough to tranquilize her pain. Enough was enough. Tears ran down her face, she opened the medicine cabinet. She had run out of reasons not to do this. Her own thoughts had now become her worst enemy. *What a freak you are. No one will miss you. Your mother will get over it and be fine. You're just an embarrassment. Do it.*

Standing there, in front of the opened medicine cabinet, she saw exactly what she was looking for. Standing perfectly still, she stepped outside of herself, conversing internally if this was what she really wanted to do. The grief wrestling with her former self that was being suffocated by spirals of rampant, thickened, charcoal smoke for which she couldn't escape. Standing in front of the mirror, she could barely recognize herself and at 2:27am, she wondered who would win.

6

No Justice, No Peace

On a cold night, candle after candle lined the city street corner, their temper blue base and flicking sun hues, reflecting tints of sadness and fury. A light mist fell to the ground, the pavement unsure how to respond to this rare experience. A crowd of no more than 50 BIPOC community members stood together in front of the store where days prior Dwayne Harris had lost his life.

Posters of Dwayne and picket signs were furiously raised into the air by the crowd of people in mourning over yet another reckless and unnecessary murder of an unarmed Black man. Dwayne was just one of many Black men who had done nothing wrong but be at the wrong place at the wrong time, losing their lives over it. The police were both the judge and the jury, the officers managing to walk away without justice, without penalty, without much more than an apology.

Lt. Hunter and the other officers involved were being investigated and Dwayne's family had begun talking to a lawyer, but everyone knew where this would lead. Lt. Hunter already had a firm reputation. He had been on the force for a decade. He was coveted by the blue shield that would keep all of his actions hidden from the light, with deals and closed door conversations that would make sure they stayed that way. There wouldn't have been any evidence at all if that store cashier hadn't recorded the killing of Dwayne and posted it on social media. The police claimed to not have their body cameras on and surely would have supported each other's statements, viewing Dwayne's life as just another expendable soul.

The police officers responsible for the murder of Dwayne Harris were on administrative leave. Oh, the irony. While they were still being paid and were doing no work, many Black Americans were willing to work but unable to find it. This was something Devon knew too much about which only inspired him to do more and be better.

Between all the chaos and clamor of voices shouting in unison, arose a lonesome, rustic, wooden podium. Families and friends held each other, speaking at once both in dismay and disarray of the epidemic that caused them to have to gather once more. Police, both on and off duty, and citizens taking the laws in their own hands leading to the death of unarmed Black men was the epidemic. Killing unarmed Black men is an epidemic. Killing unarmed Black women is an epidemic. Killing unarmed Black transgender women is an epidemic. These epidemics need to stop. Black Lives Matter. Black Trans Lives Matter.

The same individuals had gathered not too long ago over the reckless murder of an unarmed Black man named George Floyd. They had previously gathered for the unjust unapologetic killing of Breonna Taylor. They had gathered still for the vigilante killing of a young Black man named Ahmaud Arbery, who was out for a run. And they stood together still as they heard the verdict of the killers finally receiving justice. The same group had to endure tragic killing after killing, over and over again, never having enough time to breathe, never having enough time to get air, never having time to stop, never having time to heal before being retraumatized again by the senseless acts of one man who felt he could take someone else's life into his own hands because of the simple fact that he could, because of the color of his skin.

Devon wore his thick leather coat and his favorite black durag. Inside, he could feel this tidal wave of animosity, frustration, and sorrow trying to pull him under. Every now and then the low tides would sweep in, trying to take hold and cover him up, but he could hide them better. He knew how to conduct himself in front of people. He wouldn't dare cry in mixed company, much less any company at all. He knew the danger of showing emotion as a Black man. Being with his own community may have helped, but if you're Black, there is never a place you can go where it's just your people, people who get you and share in your Blackness, your experience, your story because everywhere you go, you are Black, every day of the week.

Devon noticed others were starting to sit, and a tall Black man was headed towards the podium. Devon wondered where his friend had last stood. He wondered if he had been walking literally in his steps that night. He wondered where he was now. Devon looked amongst the crowd, now mostly seated facing the podium. He sought out his comrades and sat on the folded chairs amongst them.

"We are here, in this very spot, where we lost another brother, an amazing, man of Black excellence, Dwayne William Harris, who tragically was killed in front of this store a few days ago. He was doing nothing more but entering a store to make a purchase and return home to watch the local college game and to study for his business exam the next day." The man's voice had a vibrato that made him sound similar to the late Rev. Dr. King Jr. "This is murder. This is a heinous crime impacting our people. It should not have happened, and it needs to stop."

The crowd applauded as a call-and-response succession. "We as Black men should be able to go to a store and buy a stick of gum without getting shot at and never coming home again." Several men stood up, shoving their protest signs in the air. "We should not have to face this time and time again. We have a right to live like any other man. Police, if you hear me, you have to stop shooting at us first and asking questions later. You must. You must stop shooting at us first and asking questions later. We have a right to live. The constitution says freedom, liberty, and justice for all." The crowd rose in faithful accordance.

Another man wearing a hoodie approached the podium, and addressed the audience, "You cannot keep your mouth shut for Black rights and Black Lives if you open it for Black dick." The crowd was quieter in applause but held on to its devotion.

Yet another person approached the podium. Devon recognized her instantly. As she stood over the podium, her face said it all, and the crowd became so quiet, each and every word she spoke lingered. She gathered herself together and took a breath in and released it.

"This was my son," she spoke through her tears. "My son deserved to live." She looked down towards the crowd. "He shouldn't have died right here. He was a wonderful son. He was a graduate student. He was making something of himself. He was making us all proud. He had so many wonderful things that were waiting for him." She paused, trying to remain strong. "This has to stop. The police and vigilantes cannot continue killing unarmed Black sons, claiming their lives were in jeopardy when the officers always return home, but my son, our sons, do not. We have to fix this."

The crowd couldn't conceive how to console her, so they allowed their clapping to show her she was not alone and was supported. Several people who had been standing came over to gently pat her back and shoulder. Devon kept his head down. He did not want Mrs. Harris to see him in this crowd or he would lose it. He wouldn't be able to hold back the floodgates anymore. He averted his attention elsewhere, aware this tactic always made him seem aloof and unemotional, but this was how he learned to survive. Looking around, he became more aware of the police presence around the audience, squad cars, and uniformed officers standing on the outskirts. *What were they there for? Why the hell were they here now?*

Their presence didn't go unnoticed by Mrs. Harris. With a firm, deathly scowl, she looked at each one of them, moving her glance so that each officer could see and feel the words she was about to say over the microphone. "You had no right to kill my son. You had no right to kill my son! MY SON! How dare you?!" The crowd's clapping intensified, cheering her on. "This has to stop. I don't want another Black mother to ever be in this position where I'm standing right now, mourning the loss of their son. This has to stop. Stop killing our Black sons. Stop doing it. You haven't stopped since Emmett Till and you're still following the KKK, they just wear business suits now. I still see you, KKK. Stop killing our Black sons! NOW! Black Sons Lives Matters. Black Men Matter. Black Lives Matter. Stop killing us NOW!"

The crowd lost itself, breaking out in concert, chanting *Black Lives Matter*, chanting *Justice for Dwayne Harris,* screaming, *No Justice, No Peace.* Not giving up. Not standing down. Devon watched how the police would respond, several community members looking at them directly, anticipating if their lives would be lost next. Unsurprisingly, most of the uniformed officers were white.

Devon felt the urge to do something. He knew what had happened here was wrong, that his friend should be alive. He again felt his internal conflict to do or to not do what his instincts told him to. Truth was, he still feared that he would be next. Living in this country as a Black man, it often feels like it's only a matter of time.

Devon remembered thinking, maybe if he surrounded himself with white people, maybe if he fit in better with them, he would be less likely to make the 10pm news. But he knew that wasn't true. No matter what, he would still be Black, and the police don't know your personality when they pull you over or stop you the moment you have let your guard down. So the answer, never let your guard down, an impossible, traumatic task negatively impacting the mental health of millions of Black men in this country.

The crowd marched down the street, holstering up their picket signs continuing to shout *Black Lives Matter, Justice for Dwayne Harris, No Justice, No Peace*. The police in their special uniforms and masks and gear followed them, several staying in front of them. The community marched, staring the police straight in the eyes with each step they took, and Devon, for a moment, unafraid to die.

There would be a time for him to feel his grief but he knew the time wasn't now. Tonight, his grief would have to take a backseat as he stood with his community to make it clear that we were unafraid of the police and would not succumb to fear. We are not second-class citizens. We have a right to live freely and to live happily and it is not okay to kill members of our community. We helped build this country and we have a right to be here like anyone else. If the police want a fight, that's exactly what the people will give them.

7

When One Door Closes...

"Welcome to the grief and loss support group. My name is Alex Thomas, I use they/them pronouns and I am your group facilitator for the start of our healing journey together. I want to welcome you all to this group. I know that everyone here is dealing with a loss of some kind and I believe that with each other, we can help find a way through it. Who would like to introduce themselves first?"

The small number of group members exchanged looks, waiting to see who would break the ice and begin. The room looked bare, pieces of abstract and post-impressionism art hung on pearl white walls with carpet to match, leaving everything to mystery. Wheatfield with Crows and Sunflowers hung closest to the windowpane adorning ivory Mercuri, semi-sheer double curtain panels.

Plants were placed about the room in all the usual places you'd expect in a counseling office, plants that Gus couldn't easily distinguish if artificial or live. Great, more questions leading to deep, tantalizing reflections. To his far right sat a large rectangular LED aquarium with clearly plastic seaweed, bubbles floating to the top, and a rainbow-colored goldfish that he thought for sure was dead but he didn't know for how long. Gus thought to himself, *Maybe if this is a grief and loss support group, they should make sure the fish are living before we all come in here.* Everyone sat in a quaint circle, looking from face to face as if they had all forgotten the question.

After a long stretch of awkward silence, someone finally spoke. "I'll start. My name is Melissa. I've been coming to the group for the past four months after I lost my boyfriend. It's been helpful to be here but I still miss Marcus a lot."

"Thanks for sharing, Melissa. Grief takes time and I'm so glad you're here with us," responded Mx. Thomas.

Gus retorted to himself, *Basic support group shit*. He swore to himself that he would never drink and drive again, as long as it meant he wouldn't be stuck participating in another pointless piece of shit group like this. He didn't want to be caught within 50 miles of this dumpster fire.

As he sat there silently plotting to murder Coach Scottie for forcing him to come here, he began to worry when the chatter of the group stopped. He looked to his left, he looked to his right and then he knew, it was his turn to introduce himself. Taking a deep breath in and trying fiercely not to roll his eyes to the back of his head where he knew they would rest permanently, he exclaimed, "I'm Gus and I'm here because my coach made me come after I crashed my car. He said I couldn't compete for the Olympic trials unless I showed up for the next six weeks."

"Whoa, Olympics huh. Mister big shot," he heard from one of the members.

"Yeah, right," protested another group member with a scorn on his face.

"Nice to meet you, Gus," jumped in Mx. Thomas. "I know this probably was not your first choice and it sounds like you're hesitant, but that's normal and I'm glad that you're here. Do you mind sharing with us what caused you to crash your car, or why your coach thought it best for you to come here?"

"Actually, I do mind," the words escaped him effortlessly, faster than he could have restrained them.

"Okay, well, we are glad to see you nonetheless, and I hope you recover from those injuries you have. It looks like that was quite an accident." Mx. Thomas gestured to Gus's leg and eye patch over his left eye. "Thanks for being here."

Mx. Thomas seemed unfazed by Gus's response, and the introductions continued down the line through several other people Jamie (Caucasian), Peter (Caucasian), Elizabeth (Caucasian), Mariah (some kind of Caucasian.) But Gus paid special attention to the folks that looked the most like him. Although he didn't want to be here and wouldn't have if it weren't for his coach, he was open to hearing from other people that resembled him most, that he thought he could connect to more. He knew all too well how it felt always being the token minority in the room, or in his case, the Olympic training swim team, but he craved a sense of community, being with other people who he could connect with.

There was one person though who he had found a potential connection with, and they were speaking next. They had a slender body with long, black, curly hair. Their voice was soft and low but also sounded light and shrouded in mystery. Their figure resembled a plank; flat, but their face didn't seem to completely match the rest of them. Gus couldn't easily tell if this was a boy or a girl. The person appeared to have a female body but for some reason, their face looked more masculine, bigger features. Gus wasn't sure what to make of them but they were speaking next.

"My name is Prue. I'm new to this group." She had a heavy pause as she looked down towards her feet. "I'm not exactly sure why I'm here but I lost someone recently and felt that I needed to come here before it was too late."

"Welcome, Prue," said Mx. Thomas. "We are glad that you decided to come. When you are lost and at the end of your rope, that is usually the best time to reach out for support. Your own thoughts can start to really run wild and cause you to do things that you never would, taking you to a place that you can't return from. Thank you for your bravery

48

in showing up for you and everyone else that cares about you right now."

Gus played with a scab on his hand, thinking through what the facilitator had just said, our own thoughts can run wild causing us to do some crazy things that we wouldn't usually. His intrigue with Prue continued. Meanwhile, another Black person was next, the last person to introduce himself. He seemed to sit farther away from Prue, even though there were closer empty chairs. He sat in all denim and black, wearing a BLM shirt and a fresh pair of Jordans.

"Guess I'm next. My name's Devon. I lost someone that was like a brother to me. He was killed by the police for no fucking reason. I'm not sure why I'm here either. Thinking this may have been a bad idea now."

"What's giving you that impression, Devon? We are all here because we are grieving the loss of someone," Mx. Thomas responded.

"Yeah, but my grief isn't sadness. I'm not sad. I'm angry. I'm angry that because I'm Black, police think it's okay to kill me and people that look like me." The white people in the room looked down, clearly physically and emotionally uncomfortable. The minorities in the room became even more aware that they were minorities. "How is this group going to help me with that?"

"It's not uncommon that when someone has lost someone, especially abruptly like you lost your brother, the first feelings you have are anger. It's a part of grieving and usually is easier to feel than the sadness underneath."

"I don't feel sadness underneath, doc. I feel rage. How dare they kill someone like family to me just because he was Black?"

"Maybe they didn't kill him because he was Black..." said a group member wearing a red hat. Silence befell the room, fearful stares were exchanged, tension one could cut with a butter knife.

"What the fuck do you know? Of course, you would say some shit like that, whitey. Of course, they killed him because he was Black. He wasn't doing anything but going to the corner store and coming back." He stared at the group member dead in his eyes, "You think that's okay?"

Mx. Thomas appeared shocked by the energy that was now present in the room and was unprepared to discuss racial inequities and white privilege in group this evening.

"Why are you getting so upset at them?" asked Prue. "They don't know what happened, they weren't part of it, they're just trying to help."

"Fucking tranny, did I ask you anything?"

"Who the fuck are you calling a tranny?" Prue shouted.

"Who the fuck you think, *BRO*?" Devon shouted back, sneering at her and narrowing his eyes.

"You're directing your energy at the wrong person." Gus was surprised that this thought had actually become words that left his lips. Devon slowly turned to look at him.

"What the fuck are you talking about, pirate boy?"

"I can understand what you're talking about, but these other people here can't. The rage that you're feeling will consume you if you let it. You have to do something positive with it, something that allows it a way out so you can start healing," Gus advised.

"Yeah, right. I should listen to the alcoholic Olympic wanna-be who crashed daddy's car, walking around here with fucking crutches and a pirate-ass eye patch."

Gus maintained his cool. "You don't have to believe me. You can do what you want, but the rage will only consume you and you'll become the thing that everyone fears. Look around. Everyone in this room is starting to fear you. You have to control yourself."

"What the fuck do you know? I'm out of here." Devon grabbed his denim jacket and headed towards the exit.

"Running away doesn't solve anything either. You'll always just keep running back from where you started." Devon looked back and then stormed off. The group members looked around at each other, still in shock at what transpired.

At the slam of the door, the electricity in the room began to cause the lights to flicker on and off. "Nothing to worry about here. Just an old building," Mx. Thomas said with a quiver in their voice. Suddenly, the room filled with a deep buzzing sound starting from the ceiling lights at a slow pace and then moving around faster and growing in intensity before the room faded to black. The room filled with fearful shrieks. "Okay, everyone, let's meet outside in the downstairs parking lot for everyone's safety."

Group members began rushing to the doors. Gus was moving slower than everyone else, as he was still healing from his car accident, but the group members were too much in a panic to help him or even notice. Two group members ran past him so fast that they knocked him down. He tried to get up but he was having a hard time finding anything to hold onto between the darkness and now random flicking lights.

As Prue was exiting, she looked back and noticed Gus's predicament. She could tell the ceiling was not long from caving in but she felt she had no choice. She hurried back, helping Gus get to his feet and the two rushed swiftly out of the room, hearing the electricity racing faster and faster above them. Within seconds, the ceiling lights and tiles fell with a loud crash to the floor, live wires seething in fury.

Prue and Gus managed to exit the room just in the nick of time, but as everyone was exiting via the stairs, they had nowhere to go. Suddenly, Prue and Gus noticed a shadowy figure in an opened elevator directly in front of them. This was their only chance to escape. Without hesitation, they both headed inside moments before the elevator doors closed. As the doors shut, the shadowy figure turned towards them, and it was Devon, hot as fire, still seething from Gus's remarks. The elevator began moving.

"Fuck, what is the tranny and Olympic wanna-be doing here?" exclaimed Devon.

"Love the level of insight you demonstrate, Devon. Gee, why would two people enter an elevator?" Gus sarcastically retorted.

"Shut the fuck up, bitch. Don't think you're getting away with that either. Soon as we get downstairs, it's on!" Devon yelled.

"I'm a woman. Do not call me a tranny again," Prue demanded.

Before Devon could blast out his next line of insults, the lights in the elevator suddenly flickered off. The elevator instantly stopped. For several seconds, silence dissolved their ability to speak.

"Ummm--- this can't be good." Gus tried to shrug it off with humor. Devon began pushing on random elevator buttons, but nothing happened. Prue reached into her purse and took out her phone, deciding to use it as a flashlight to help guide their way in the dark. Instinctively, Gus followed the light from the phone to find the emergency button. Devon now stood in a daze. Gus pushed the emergency button but nothing appeared to happen. "Nothing's happening. What are we gonna do?"

"Does your phone work?" Prue asked, signaling to Gus to take out his phone. "Maybe we can call 911." She looked over at Devon, "Are you just gonna stand there staring out at space or are you going to do something, asshole?"

This was the retort he needed to spring back to life. With a grimace on his face and with light from Prue's phone, he was now able to see the buttons on the electric panel and decided to press the emergency button again, hoping his magical touch would make it work this time. Again, nothing happened. The doors wouldn't open and the elevator refused to start up again but as they continued moving around, they could feel the elevator beginning to swing below their feet.

"What was that?" Prue asked.

"I'm not sure, I…" Gus could hear wires above them and underneath the elevator tearing apart, the same deep buzzing sounds of electricity they had heard in the counseling room that caused the ceiling lights to fall. By the movement of the elevator, the group could also tell they seemed higher than they were upon initially entering the elevator. Gus tried to play it off though as if he didn't know what was going on, but the others already knew their lives were in jeopardy.

"Why was the elevator going up?" Prue looked towards Devon.

"I don't fucking know. It was supposed to go down."

"And now we are higher than we had imagined. This would be a great story if we live through this," Gus joked.

"If?" Prue gasped.

"The fuck, Gus," Devon balled up his fist.

Gus picked up his phone from his pocket and dialed 911 but there wasn't any cell phone reception. "No signal. That's okay. I'll look up ways to escape a death trap elevator box."

In sync, Prue and Devon rolled their eyes and said, "You have no signal!"

"Oh, yeah."

Prue wanted to scream but she was afraid her voice would cause her to feel dysphoria. She knew she was in a life-or-death situation, but the dysphoria would have debilitated her and felt so much worse.

"Why don't we see if we can remove one of the panels at the top and see if we can crawl out?" suggested Gus.

"That's not a bad idea. She can hold the light and we can try to remove the panel." Prue was surprised that Devon had addressed her correctly, but wanted to keep her happiness to herself until they were out of this situation.

Gus, being a little smaller than Devon, got on Devon's shoulders and pressed up at the top to see if one of the panels was loose and would lead to the emergency hatch, their way out. Any movement led to the elevator shifting its weight, moving at times swiftly and other times abruptly.

Holding Gus up, he was able to stretch out his arms but couldn't see where he was reaching.

"Prue, can you move the light up here?" Gus pleaded. Prue followed Gus's path, but the light seemed to startle Gus, causing him to quiver, leading to he and Devon falling to the floor.

Prue could hear something underneath them starting to break apart. She grew afraid. Gus and Devon tried again. "Guys, please be careful." It was too late. The elevator quickly began moving again, causing Gus to fall from Devon's shoulders to the floor once more. Moving at an expeditious pace, they had no chance to get back on their feet.

The three of them huddled together, holding on to each other's hands as the elevator continued to descend, faster and faster. Their hands began to feel warm. The space was black. They could hear nothing else as they awaited death. Warm distinctive lights suddenly began flickering around them. They appeared to be fireflies that had emerged out of nothingness.

Prue looked around at Gus and Devon, unsure if she was already dead, wondering if these fireflies were something she alone was seeing or were signals that her time had come to an end. Gus appeared to see the same fireflies that were now growing in number, shining brighter and brighter. Devon held Prue and Gus's hands, noticing the fireflies moving mysteriously unfettered by space and time. They knew their doom was approaching. Suddenly, the three were surrounded in light.

8

The Day Time Stood Still

Everything was dark. The light that had surrounded her was gone. There was nothing for her to see, it was as if there wasn't a Prue to interpret anything to see in the first place. And as swiftly as there was darkness, she felt this overwhelming presence, this need, this desire, something in her telling her it was time for her to finally open her eyes and see again.

So, she opened her eyes and to her surprise, the rays of light that were beaming in, that warmth, that presence she felt, was the sun peeking out of her window, trying to shine through her black-out curtains and covered blinds.

She was surprised to find herself in her bedroom, drooling on her pillow, pressed against her life-sized corduroy teddy bear that made her feel she was finally not having to sleep every night alone. This was the closest she had ever come to having a man in her bed the morning after.

All of what she had felt the moments before opening her eyes, the terror, the fear, the confusion, felt like a daze, felt as though she was in a fog and must have dreamed the whole thing up. She rationalized to herself that this had to have been a dream. Last she remembered, she was headed face-first to the metal floor of a man-made inescapable deathtrap, plunging to her end. The irony of surviving her difficult, life-altering surgery, only to then meet her maker trapped in a death box with strangers.

She made several attempts to lift herself up out of bed, still getting used to the heaviness on her chest. She turned on her television to hear the relaxing voice of Alex Wallace forecasting the next east coast storm in Philadelphia. She walked over to her bathroom mirror and took a long look at herself, finally seeing herself now. Standing, unclothed, she saw her body, the shape of her breasts, her medium waistline, her long, curly black hair that she bought from Malaysia, the scars on her chest. The shape of her virgin vagina. Her vulva, her clitoris. The smoothness, the softness of her vagina.

She could even sense wetness as she placed her finger inside to feel herself open. She was amazed to stand nude in front of this mirror and seeing herself like this, for the first time seeing more of her, not complete, but closer than she had ever seen herself before, closer than anyone had.

It still felt odd and shocking, knowing a penis had once been there. Knowing testicles that had been attached to her like a tumor all those decades was gone. That now she was free. She was free of that weight. She was free of those items that would grow and pulsate on their own accord with little effort from her. She was free of those genitals that defined who she could love, who she could be with, who she could sleep with, what kind of life she would have, who she was supposed to be, what jail cell she would be placed in, what restroom she could use, what someone else could classify her as for eternity. She was free of the thing that was most often used to deadname and dehumanize transgender women since the beginning of time because now her genitals matched who she truly was. She could look down and see what should have been there the entire time. The softness. The delicateness.

Everything about it that felt like it was her, that it had always been her, that it was worth the sacrifices and the risk of dying. She was a woman. She always had been and would always be no matter what anyone said. And still she felt this phantom sensation of what was once there each time she thought a tantalizing, arousing thought and she would look down, preparing to hide it. But it wasn't there anymore. There was nothing to hide. She was free.

She could still feel the stiffness, the pulsating, the feeling of something getting bigger and coming to life and the fear that embarrassed her and made her want to hide. But it wasn't there anymore. The stiffening, pulsating feeling was now her vagina pulsating, expanding, wanting someone to enter her, wanting someone inside of her. And Prue enjoyed this feeling. She was closer and closer to her own freedom and liberation. She was free.

She wasn't well enough to return to work yet. Helping others was her job but she was still needing to take care of herself. Growing tired however from recovering, sitting at home all day with nothing to do, her boredom was increasing. She knew she was supposed to rest and that she wasn't ready to have any company over, but the intimate parts of her body wanted much more than *company* and she knew she couldn't take the risk.

While the morning was still young, she put on some loose-fitting clothing, grabbed her special pillow for her to sit on, and went downstairs to enter her car. Wearing her shades, she figured she could reduce eye contact in case anyone saw her. Though she was closer to freedom, she could prominently see shadows of her male self and was unsure if anyone else could see this too. She didn't want to be seen as someone playing dress-up. She didn't want to be seen as a tranny, a word that she incessantly detested. She wanted to be seen as the woman she always was inside, even though her body had betrayed her.

While her classmates in high school were falling in love and meeting their happily-ever-afters, she couldn't even make deep, lasting friendships because she couldn't be who she really was. While her peers were able to go to prom and homecoming and explore their romantic interests, she was unable to.

She was forced to play with the boys and never be seen as someone attractive or ever an option for a romantic relationship. She was the sissy boy. She was the one no one wanted on their team. She was the dark one that didn't show up in class photos and always came out looking like an alien from ET but was told that she sounded white on the phone.

She was the one who would have to go to a prom in a tux, dancing with a girl that she didn't want to dance with, while the guy she liked humped blond-hair Heather in the backseat of her father's convertible. She was the one who was not allowed to be her true self so no one could develop that interest with her, nor understand her because she wasn't allowed to simply be.

She was forced to be someone else and she had no control of it because no one could understand. Her mother didn't understand. Doctors didn't understand. Teachers didn't understand. Principal after principal didn't understand. No one did, so for years, she would go home, and cry under her bedsheets watching the same old black-and-white movie over and over again until it was time to go to bed and start the same day again. Prue started the car and tried to experience her past as mere landscape passing by.

Out on her drive, it was a clear day. Hardly a cloud in the sky, the beautiful sun was stretching out it's warmth and light across the baby blue skies. A gentle breeze was felt as she rolled her passenger side window down, driving on a quiet road arriving at a four-way intersection.

There were beautiful trees all along the two-mile drive, luscious greenery and clean, well-paved streets, several cars passing by. 'Walking on a Dream' was playing through the stereo and not a care in the world entered her mind, just enjoying the moment and appreciating the landscape that brought her to this moment, free at last.

Without warning, a four-door grey sedan veered from the opposite direction and headed straight towards Prue's car.

Prue couldn't seem to register what was happening. She had momentarily left herself to enjoy this drive, this song, this breeze, and now suddenly her life was back in danger, a car was coming towards her but she wasn't reacting to it. She couldn't. She couldn't get her thoughts together to understand this car was coming towards her, NOW. The car was two seconds from crashing into her, killing her instantly. In shock, she released her hands from the wheel and covered her face, closing her eyes.

Moments passed in complete silence. Prue slowly opened her eyes. The car was inches from her. The music had stopped. The car had stopped. Her car had stopped. She was confused. She looked around. Everything had stopped. Nothing was moving. A bird in a distance was in the air, it's left-wing flap open, appearing frozen. Everything was still.

What was happening? Trying to control her breath, she started the car and after the surprise of the engine starting, she miraculously drove a few feet away to the corner where she could park. As soon as she parked, time restarted. The song jolted Prue, playing as if she had merely paused it.

The car that had almost hit and potentially killed her skidded behind her, trying to break and instead hitting a parked car. Airbags deployed. Prue got out of her car. The driver of the car jumped out, looking dazed and bewildered, but appeared okay. He looked confused, and so was Prue. Why was she still alive right now? How could time just stop on its own like that? How was this possible?

9

Before His Very Eyes

Sitting in the middle of class, Devon had his eyes
down, glossing over his Financial Accounting manual for the
fourth consecutive time. His teacher, Mr. Handshoe stood in
front of the class discussing business management and
accounting practices. Devon had learned to focus his
attention and concentrate, even on the most boring of
subjects. This was his final year before graduation and he
needed to prepare for the Uniform CPA Exam at all costs.

Devon's desire for finances evolved from having a
family that couldn't balance a checkbook and deciding that
he wanted to help others learn how to invest and not find
themselves in the same predicament, including himself. He
had to teach himself what he was never taught and he was
fraught with challenges from the beginning that still were
present every time he entered a classroom. He had learned
not to look around the room as he would always, without a
doubt, find that he was the only brown face there.

Mr. Handshoe was exceedingly animated,
gesticulating wildly with excitement as he always did.
Numbers and statistics seemed to really get him off. You'd
expect him to pull a rabbit out of a hat, he spoke with such
amazement and wonder over financial wizardry and
accounting software.

Nevertheless, his wizardry was not sustaining Devon as he found his mind trying to take him outside the four corners of the classroom. He could feel it. He could hear it and he knew for some reason that he didn't want to go. Devon would rather soak up every inch of this tedious and monotonous book, and his magician professor's lecture, than to allow himself to hear the words and voices in his own head.

Images of Dwayne crept into his head. The last time he saw him, Dwayne was talking to him about his goals and ambitions, being the beacon of light for something greater. Dwayne's passion and commitment to evolving and being the best he could be was contagious, it motivated Devon to do his very best, especially during moments he didn't think he had it in him.

Image after image played on repeat as if he was seeing him again right before his very eyes. Devon could see his friend smiling, hear his friend's voice, and remember both sad moments and happy ones as if they were on the very pages he was flipping in his textbook. Each page flipped to a different memory. Between page number 219 and the section header, Devon could see their last discussion taking place. The pages appeared to effortlessly move on their own, as if someone else was turning them.

As Devon tried to find comprehension, he postulated he must be drifting off to sleep or having a dream. To end this madness, he sharply closed his Accounting textbook, awaiting more magical financial renderings from Mr. Handshoe's jovial lecture.

When Devon looked up, he was no longer in Mr. Handshoe's classroom. He was still sitting at his desk, but the walls had disappeared. He was somewhere else now. He could see the store buildings, the typically busy sidewalks, the palm trees with their outstretched leaves blowing in the wind. When he saw the 30th and University sign, something felt familiar to him. He had been here before but how was this possible? *Where am I? Wasn't I just in Mr. Handshoe's Pepper Canyon Lecture Hall?*

The school had faded away and in its place were two white police officers pulling over a younger Black man with a Black fist bumper sticker on his car. Devon's shoulders and chest tightened up, he could feel the terror that the young man was feeling. The young man looked no older than twenty-one. He was wearing an HBCU shirt and Devon could see a bookbag in his passenger seat.

Devon couldn't hear what was going on but he could tell the young man was afraid, the way any other Black person would be when the police approaches. Their motto is to protect and serve, but that doesn't apply to everyone. The two officers appeared to be telling him to do something that the young man couldn't understand. Devon could see the young man pick up his cell phone from his book bag then holding it in front of him, possibly using the phone to record the encounter.

Things escalated quickly. One officer reached to grab the phone out of the young man's hand, the other with a shiny illegible badge reached to his holster for his gun. Both officers appeared to be yelling at him. The young man was sweating profusely, on the verge of tears, frantically moving his hands, as if he couldn't understand what was transpiring.

Once more, he reached into his bookbag and before he could pull out whatever he had, four shots rang out. Devon felt the sudden impulse to cover his ears and look away. From their shared Black experience, Devon could truly feel the remnants of the bullets penetrating through his body as if he had been the target.

A few moments later, Devon had to turn around and see what happened. The squad car was gone. The police had disappeared. *Where did they go?* Devon ran over to the young man and found him slumped over the steering wheel, bleeding from his ears, his face horrifically disfigured from the gunshots that robbed him of the life he had ahead. Devon noticed the young man's hand was still in his bookbag appearing to hold something.

Carefully, Devon took the man's hand into his to find what he had been trying to pull out. It was a cue card with a picture of a boy with an adult saying that he has autism. Devon was horrified, full of instantaneous rage. He held the young man in his arms, looking around for anyone that could help. Prior to this, the streets were filled with people and cars, but now it seemed they were all alone. He held the man, consoling him. *You'll be okay. Just a few bruises. We'll get you to the hospital and you'll be just fine.* But he knew it was too late.

Devon searched for his own phone to call the paramedics but noticed he didn't have it on him. He looked for the young man's phone, but after searching the front and back seat surmised the police must have confiscated it. There were no other cars on the street. No one was coming. Devon would have to leave him to find help. *I'll go back to where I was sitting. My phone's in my bag. I'll call 911. He'll be fine.* Conflicted, Devon moved away from the car, noticing the license plate that started with P01 and ended with Z before darting off to the bench to find his phone.

He attempted to run to where he believed he had been hiding when this scene unfolded, but as he ran, he couldn't seem to ever reach the wooden desk. He knew he had to have passed it. He had ran over to the young man within a few seconds, but it was taking minutes to find where he was sitting previously.

Outside his awareness, the air was engulfed in a growing fog that was starting to obstruct his vision. Tired and frustrated, Devon decided to run back to the car, but he wasn't able to see through the heavy, opaque haze that was now surrounding him. The tidal wave inside of himself was about to take him under.

Suddenly he was sitting back at his wooden desk, all eyes on him. "Devon are you okay?" Mr. Handshoe asked.

Devon looked around the room. He was back in the Pepper Canyon Lecture Hall. He didn't know what had just happened. One moment he was running through this haze to save a slain young man, and the next he was sitting at his desk again in class. It must have all been a dream, clear delusion from Mr. Handshoe's provocative lecture on statistics. But it felt so real.

Devon focused his attention back on his Accounting textbook, but as he flipped the page, he stopped. There it was, right in front of him, the shiny badge of the police officer who had killed the young man, *Lt. Hunter*.

10

Gus vs. Gus

Bouncing around on the pool deck, Gus had hoped he'd finally fit in with the others. After his calamity with car vs. pole, he knew it was by sheer luck and the grace of God that he was still able to walk through the doors of the Sapphire Elite Athletic and Swim Club, much less still be able to compete for the Olympic trials.

He remembered his deal though: he had to attend a rehabilitation outpatient program, attend weekly AA/NA meetings, and continue attending the mental health support group for the next six months or he could kiss any chance he had of making the U.S. Olympic Swim Team and winning gold this year to infinity. Gus knew he would have to go back to that depressing group but at the moment, that group was the furthest thing from his mind. He still couldn't shake that weird dream that he had of falling in the elevator, his death so close that he could almost touch it. He had known that feeling before, the day he lost his big brother, David. He didn't want to ever feel like that again.

Trying to look to the ground, he passed the maintenance worker, a man whose name he should have known as he had seen him many times before. Johnson, Jacob, and Jones were already up on the high dive platform, perfecting their dives the way the privileged always do, with great superiority. They were all gunning for the trials and to secure their position on the U.S. Olympic Swim Team except, unlike Gus, each of them came from money which pretty much was their ticket guaranteeing them an easier path in. Gus had family that could help, but it always required having to ignore half of himself to be accepted.

Adolescents were running around the pool deck, demonstrating their privilege by leaving a mess and expecting the workers to take care of it. Gus pretended not to notice, it frustrated him knowing that all of this was only a role-play for when the youngsters would get older and then use their white privilege to take over the world. In mostly a sea of white faces, Gus's was the only odd one out, the one that always stood out. He had been swimming for nearly ten years, swam against many competitors and in many heats, yet his skin tone was always the minority.

Towels were laid about all over the pool deck. The older swimmers wore their headgear and practiced their deep diving in the 50-meter pool below the high dive platform, taking each stroke seriously as if their lives depended on it, as if they were afraid one bad lap would cost them their parent's trust funds.

Gus' nerves were awakened. He knew he needed to head out of the pool and begin his high dive, facing his strongest competition. He knew Johnson, Jacob, and Jones would do the white boy thing and block him from practice. Gus would have to not care. He needed to practice to score high enough for Coach's team and he would have to work through his injury to do it.

The sounds of the stadium intensified as he neared the top ledge of the 20-meter platform. This was his favorite dive. From this perspective, he felt like he was on top of the world as if nothing and no one could touch him. So much of the world spends time trying to bring people with his skin tone down. But not up here. Up here, he was on top, at least before he took the next few steps, made a quick, calculated leap up into the air and then glided as light as a feather down below.

The sounds of the athletic club disappeared, the water overtaking his senses. He was still underwater. He shouldn't still be underwater. He tried to swim out to the surface but all he could see was only more of the ocean blue. In the very faint distance, he could barely make out an image but he couldn't hold onto it. Something seemed wrong. Try after try, he couldn't seem to get himself out of the water. He wasn't able to swim to the surface. His mind was working but his body had betrayed him. He was trying to feel where his body was adjacent to the pool. He was trying to sense where his hands were, where his right leg was, what direction he was going in. But he couldn't.

He didn't feel like he was moving at all. That was impossible. He had to have been moving one way or the other, either floating up or sinking down and he couldn't possibly be sinking. He had been diving for nearly ten years. That had to have been an impossibility. He tried to move his body, but the more he struggled, the more he became sure he was sinking, and with that realization, that his life was hanging in the balance. He didn't have time to think, he just needed a way out of this.

Surely, someone would notice that he wasn't getting out of the pool. The athletic swim club was full of kids running around. Someone had to have noticed him taking his leap and diving into the pool, struggling to find his way out. No, he hadn't been the best to make friends, was a little detached, a little socially awkward, but surely someone had noticed. He was Black but he wasn't invisible. Soon someone would be here to rescue him.

Suddenly, the sensation of heaviness and sinking dissipated. The weight he had been carrying turned to a feeling of lightness and calmness. The fear and panic he felt in every fiber of his being melted away. All signs of concern and worry vanished. He found himself suddenly without a care in the world. He felt like he was seeing things from a whole new perspective. The seeing didn't seem like it was coming from his eyes. He felt he was seeing somehow through something else, another sense, another line of vision.

He found himself standing in the athletic swim club again, his hair and body dripping wet; he could tell from the puddles of water around him. He didn't feel cold and he couldn't feel the typically cold pool deck underneath his feet. He didn't know where he was and he didn't recognize the man moving equipment around him, but the man seemed to know him as he quickly approached.

Gus realized it was the maintenance man he usually passed when he entered the facility. He appeared POC but Gus couldn't classify any further. His skin was fair, but he had hints of a dark complexion at the same time. His hair looked somewhat like Gus's, but his skin tone looked lighter. And his eyes looked lighter with a hint of olive.

The maintenance man approached him. "Gus, what's wrong with you? Are you okay?"

Gus was startled the maintenance man knew his name. He himself didn't know his and this was actually the first time he had heard him speak. Gus felt like he wanted to answer him but couldn't. He knew he hadn't by the expression on the man's face and the continued questions. From behind him, Gus could hear a few kids screaming in panic. The man turned away to see where the voices were coming from.

Gus felt overcome with the feeling he was floating so high above, simultaneously everywhere and nowhere with little desire for direction. Before he completely faded away, he found his attention directed towards a small shiny silver string. It looked like it was hanging from something, and his natural curiosity made him want to find out what. It was so hard to focus on getting to the string with how light he had felt, and how it seemed like nothing mattered anymore. But his will allowed him to get closer to the string.

On all fours, he was close enough to the string to finally pull it. All of a sudden, he felt himself gasping for air. The pain in his body made him feel real again. He felt cold.

He felt alive. He felt his dripping wet hair and his soaking wet body on the cold pool deck. He felt himself laying down, surrounded by faces he couldn't completely make out yet.

The lights above built into the high vaulted ceiling created a halo effect that seemed to blur everything. There were people's hands on him still, pumping his chest until he groaned for them to stop. "You're lucky, son. You shouldn't have been anywhere near that meter jump until your leg heals," he heard one of the men say.

Gus sat up. He didn't quite understand what was going on, but he was glad to be alive. He didn't understand how he became sucked up into the pool when he was an elite swimmer and had swam this same pool for a decade. *How could this have happened? What's wrong with my leg?* Gus didn't have any of these answers, but he did know that he needed to go. All of these blue eyes were looking at him and he didn't need any more reminders that he was an outcast.

"What the hell were you trying to prove in there?" He knew this was Coach Scottie reprimanding him. He didn't even need to turn around to recognize that tone. "What were you trying to prove in there, huh? What do you have to say for yourself?"

Gus shrugged his shoulders. He couldn't understand what was going on. It was all happening so fast. "Well until you have some answers for me, you're suspended. Get your stuff." Coach Scottie quickly darted out, trying to conceal the rest of his anger from the team.

Gus was confused but he would have to figure all of this out later. He got up off the pool deck, quickly headed to the lockers where his training gear was and tried to quickly disappear.

"How did you do that?" the familiar voice said from behind. Gus turned around. It was the maintenance man.

"Do what?"

"I saw you. I saw you standing right in front of me. But how? You were still in the pool. I looked back over the footage, and you were still in the pool. No one came to get you until I signaled the lifeguards."

"What do you mean? That's crazy," Gus dismissed.

"It is, but you did it. How were you in there but also in front of me at the same time?" Gus was floored. The man repeated again, "How did you do that?"

Gus couldn't possibly answer. He was too infuriated by the fact that everyone must have seen him jump and noticed him not getting out of the pool, but it took a stranger who worked there that he had never spoken with to signal the lifeguards to save him.

He was Black, the only Black swimmer, but that shouldn't have meant he was invisible. Gus grabbed his stuff and quickly dashed out without answering the man. He couldn't ask for his name; he just knew he had to get the hell out of there now. But he did wonder what really happened back there. *How did I do that?*

11

Together Again

Prue knew it was time for her to go back. She cringed when she set the parking brake, and she cringed even more as she walked inside the building. She cringed further when she passed the elevator and elected to take the four flights of stairs. She didn't know what to make of the experience she had one week ago of being trapped in an elevator, plunging to her own death, so she wasn't taking any chances.

She paused, held her breath, and then walked through the doors of suite 105, leading to the weekly grief and loss support group. She remembered the plants which she was convinced were fake, the nearly bare walls with oddly positioned elitist art that you would expect to find in a counseling room. She remembered the carpeted wool flooring, the white sofa set, and chairs, and the foldable black ones she preferred to sit in as they were the closest to the door. She saw the rather large aquarium housing the rainbow goldfish she was sure had passed, how ironic for a grief and loss support group.

She took her seat, hoping that this time would be better than the last. She had managed to busy herself this week with distractions. The distractions kept her from feeling her feelings, at least not directly. She focused on tasks around the house she could do, shows on streaming channels she could watch, cooking recipes she could try, music she could allow herself to fade away to, and that supernatural experience she had that day driving on the road, the day she should have crashed and died. Unanswered questions allowed herself to get lost in an abyss of philosophical debate and morbid curiosity. Anything was better than remembering that he was gone. Anything.

She saw him walking in and taking his seat a few chairs away. He looked a little different than the last time she saw him, he walked with a slight limp and when he placed his duffel bag down, she noticed it had a nautical logo on it and an image of a sapphire. He was wearing shorts, or possibly swim trunks, that had the sapphire emblem too. Bandages were around his ankle, his left wrist and elbow.

She tried to look around so it wasn't apparent to anyone that her eye was fixated on him, but their eyes met nonetheless. Gus noticed her, his expression changing from increasing discomfort to a warm smirk. The other group members had managed to fill up nearly all of the open seating, unlike the last meeting.

Mx. Thomas greeted them, "Good evening and thank you all for coming today to our weekly grief and loss support group. We are all here because we have lost someone close to us, someone that meant a lot to us, and we're trying to grapple with it and figure out a way to get through it. Some of us want to just get over it. Some of us just want to ignore it. Some of us just want to forget all about it and move on.

"The way to move on, or get over it, is to get through it. You get through it one day at a time, one moment at a time, and the moments add up to the days, that add up to the weeks that add up to the months where you find yourself a different you, a stronger you, a you that has accepted this loss. You'll still feel it, but you won't allow it to consume you. You find a way to acknowledge that those feelings are there, but you don't stop living your life forever. You find a way to continue on for them and for you."

"But how do you do that?" a group member asked. "How do you do that when you miss them so much, when they should still be here if it wasn't for...one thing?"

"I wonder that too," responded a different group member. "This all sounds good. But how do you actually do this? I miss my daughter every day. She should be here. She was only fourteen. She shouldn't have been killed that morning."

Mx. Thomas chimed in, "There are no perfect answers. We do what we have to do. The loss is real, it's real to feel sad, to feel that pain. We weren't meant to experience loss like this. How have some of you dealt with your loss?"

Another group member raised her hand. "My name is Lynn. My best friend was killed in a car accident. It didn't make any sense. It still doesn't. She had her whole life ahead of her. I felt really sad for a long time, and I still do. But I remember what she stood for and that helps me. She wouldn't want me to just stay sad and depressed and live there. She would be sad and depressed that her death made me feel that way. So, I keep moving on, doing things I know we enjoyed honoring her."

"That sounds incredible, Lynn. I want to thank you for sharing and showing us a way to deal and cope with painful loss. Does anyone else have any suggestions?"

Another group member who was wearing a nametag that said Shawn spoke up, "I pray. I pray each and every day for God to help take the pain away. I lost my brother to a drug overdose a few years ago. It was really sudden and caught me and our family by surprise. He was only 26. We didn't have the best relationship, but I felt a lot of guilt because maybe if I had been around more, he could have done better in his life."

"Your brother's decisions have nothing to do with you," the words immediately departed from Gus's caramel lips. Too bad he didn't quite believe them.

"Thanks. Logically I know that but it feels like I am responsible."

"Each of us have to make our own decisions. We are only responsible for the decisions we make. We can't live in a place, feeling other people's guilt for the decisions they chose to make. That keeps us feeling bad for things completely out of our control and causes us to blame ourselves instead of looking at what the problem really is in the first place."

"I guess you have a point, Gus."

"That was a very thoughtful thing you just shared, Gus," said Mx. Thomas. "Have you found anything that has helped you dealing with your loss?"

"I can't really say. I lost my older brother to suicide ten years ago. I found him. My mom was never the same. Neither was I. I think the thing I try to do is put it out of my mind and swim. When I swim, it's like he's with me and it helps me get through it." He looked down at the sapphire emblem on his shorts.

"That's often something that helps us with the pain, finding places, things, activities that help us feel closer to the one we lost. Just because we can't see them, doesn't mean they aren't still here and with us. We can feel them sometimes even more when they aren't right in front of us."

Prue allowed those words to echo and repeat in her mind over and over again. *Just because we can't see them, doesn't mean they aren't still here.* This provided her comfort for her own loss, but also furthered her sadness as she didn't have a place or an item that she could use to feel closer to Kaleb. She didn't have a place they had gone together or a teddy bear or t-shirt or jersey he had given her. She could listen to his voice online and scroll through his social media, but those lacked the personal connection she needed to help her get through her own grief.

The words escaped her, "What do you do if you can't do that though, if you don't have something you can do to connect you with the person?"

Gus turned toward her. "I'd think about it but I wouldn't think too hard. Allow the spirit to guide you." The two exchanged a warm look. Prue felt seen by Gus, a young man that she didn't know but seemed to get her. Gus appeared to feel seen by Prue, his racial identity not being in question.

Suddenly, the counseling door swung open, Devon, rushing in late for group. Spotting one of the last open seats, he dashed past the group members when all of a sudden he accidentally tripped over someone's foot, his fall knocking over a nearby table and the long metallic quartz crystal lamp heading directly towards Prue. Frazzled, Prue flailed up her hands to brace for the impact, her hands sensing a familiar tingling sensation escaping from her fingertips and the palm of her hand, closing her eyes.

Moments ensued, devoid of movement and sound. Finally, she opened her eyes. Everything in the room was frozen still. Everything and everyone in the room had stopped. The crystal lamp was still headed towards her face. The expressions of the other group members were frozen, their bodies were frozen in time, their eyes still, no motion. A loud groaning on the floor was the only motion which began to stir Prue. It was coming from Devon who was now dusting off his clothes and checking his body for injuries. Then Prue noticed Gus who appeared frozen but was more so bewildered, as he was able to move around despite the shock of it all.

"What the hell's going on?" Gus gasped.

Devon picked himself off the floor and then he too realized that everything was still. "What's wrong with everyone?"

Gus exclaimed, "Did you do that?" pointing at Prue. "How did you do that?"

Prue appeared paralyzed, unclear what to make of this. She slowly stood up out of her seat, moving like a zombie sat to move into another seat away from the lamp. She didn't understand what had just happened. She didn't know what she did, she didn't know how she did it and she couldn't understand why it was now happening a second time.

"Is she frozen too?" Devon asked Gus.

"She seems more confused than anything," Gus responded.

The three were immediately shook by the sounds of the lamp falling, crystal glass shattering to the ground followed by a few screams and select curse words.

"Hey, how did you get over there?" Shawn asked Devon, expecting him to be on the floor instead of standing up.

Devon and Gus looked at each other, shocked, surprised, amazed in a trance. The other group members looked at them, as well as at Prue who seemed to them to have magically jumped from one seat to another in a blink of an eye. The group looked at Devon, Prue, and Gus as if they were aliens. Prue couldn't take another moment of this. She quickly grabbed her stuff and charged out of the room. Seconds later, Devon and Gus came to their senses and quickly followed after her.

Prue again elected to take the stairs, forced to accept that the nightmare she had of the elevator crash actually happened. But how could it have? She remembered the light, the fireflies that floated around her, holding Devon and Gus's hand as they held on for dear life. She remembered the light was so bright, she couldn't see anything else anymore and then abruptly it was all over.

Devon and Gus finally caught up to her outside the building. The parking lot was dark, light emanating from the high parking lot poles provided a faint amber tint along with a flickering light from a nearby corner store.

"Wait up!" Devon exclaimed.

"Where are you going? What was that?" Gus asked.

Prue stopped. "I don't know. I don't know what's happening."

Instantly, Devon noticed a glimmer out of the corner of his eye. It was a Camaro. He stood still, trying to concentrate. Something was speaking to him. A young man wearing a Morehouse college shirt walked up, opened the door, started his V8 engine, and drove off. A few moments passed by before Devon was able to connect his thoughts.. He turned towards Prue and Gus, "One of you have a ride?"

Gus and Prue exchanged looks. "Obviously it'll have to be her car," Gus said.

Prue took her car keys out of her purse. "Why? Don't you have your own car?"

"No time," Devon said. "We've got to follow that car before it's too late. Is this your car?" Devon pointed to the Ford Focus.

Again, Prue and Gus exchanged looks.

"Look guys. We don't have time for looks." He grabbed the keys from Prue's hand. "Get in the car and let's go."

12

On the Run

"This was a mistake," Prue shouted while trying to cover her eyes from this unfolding tragedy. They had made the decision to give Gus her car keys to drive so Devon could focus on whatever it was he was looking for.

"Exactly, why are we just aimlessly driving?" Gus agreed.

"Because we have to find that guy. License Plate P01," Devon exclaimed, with a tone as if the others clearly understood the importance of this.

"Right, License Plate P01, 'cause that makes all the sense in the world. Clearly don't need any more details than that," snickered Gus.

"Look, this will all make sense if we can find him. If she can do this magic stuff with her hands, this thing I saw may be a real thing too."

"Everyone has just gone nuts," said Gus, who was trying to drive while also following Devon's random and impulsive requests to change directions, often halfway into the intersection.

"Could you try to focus on the road, Gus? I'm still making payments on this," Prue retorted.

"Right, give the guy with the limp leg the car to drive and make sudden overly excessive demands. All good here." The gang could easily read his sarcasm, but were robbed of time to respond. They were speeding, doing about 65 in a 35mph residential area, but Devon was determined to catch the car before it was too late.

They were, however, not the only car on the road. They had to swerve past several cars, speed through quickly approaching red lights, and try to read signs that were barely visible under the streetlights. All of a sudden, they were inches from plowing into a blue Chevrolet. Instinctively, Prue threw up her hands and instantly everything was frozen.

"Whoo-hoo. That is super fun," Gus cheered.

Panicking, Prue had started to learn that in these moments, she could do something with her hands that allowed her to magically freeze time. Even the time on her phone and car stood still. Only Prue, Gus and Devon remained in motion. She couldn't understand why she was suddenly able to do this, but this being her third time using these mysterious powers, she was at least able to understand she couldn't freeze time for very long, barely 30 seconds at most.

"Gus, you have to back up and hurry before we start moving again." Without much hesitation, he followed her instructions. Still, he was in awe of what he was witnessing, and it made him think more about his own experience in the pool.

Gus maneuvered the car to a different lane to continue down the same direction. Devon stopped him. "Wait. With his- I mean her magic power, we can cover more ground to see where the car is since everything is still."

"I don't think it works that way," replied Gus. "It doesn't seem to last long enough for that and how can we drive if all the other cars are frozen too? Plus, she seems to need to do this hand thing in order for it to work."

While Devon was still talking time caught up with itself, all of the cars suddenly moving around them, startling Gus who was just getting used to the cars being still. The trio was alerted by car horns and bright headlights in their faces, reminding them they were not alone on the road anymore.

"Why are we doing all of this anyways? What's
going on?" Gus asked.

Devon paused. "I think I saw something that either
already happened or is supposed to happen. I don't think it
already happened yet, but I'm not sure."

Prue looked at him but the moment she took her eyes
off the road, she became queasy. Gus was driving at a faster
speed, and with the anxiety of what they were doing and
trying to process this new magic power she had, it was too
much to ask her not to lose it right here, right now.

"You think you have a magical power too? Well,
what did you see?" Gus asked.

"That guy in the red Camaro getting pulled over by
the police and then murdered by them."

Gus was horrified, knowing this possibility with dark
skinned members of his community, something he couldn't
personally relate to with his skin tone but knew was real.
And in moments like this, he never knew what to say, aware
of the privilege he walks with as a mixed-race person. He
was so lost in his thoughts that he inadvertently ended up
driving directly into a wooden bus-stop bench, but in the nick
of time, Prue threw up her hands freezing time once again.

"That is a pretty nifty power there," said Gus. "I'm
guessing by how you're reacting that this is all new for you."

"Of course it's new. Magic doesn't really exist," Prue
blurted out.

"I don't think you've been paying very much
attention then tonight." Gus pointed in front of them, their
car frozen in midair heading towards the bus stop. "It seems
real to me," he chuckled. Gus immediately started the car and
backed it up, ready to go in a different direction when Devon
told him to stop once more.

"Wait, here it is." Devon looked around. There, above
the bus-stop, he saw the 30th and University Street sign. He
recognized where they were. Devon jumped out of the car.
Gus and Prue went after him. It didn't take Devon long to
find him but the scene didn't seem to be quite how he had

remembered it. When he saw his premonition, he was watching the police already interacting with the young man, but the Camaro was currently at a red light a block away headed towards them.

"Where are the police?" Devon muttered to himself. He looked around. "Where would the police be sitting at right now?"

"Wait, what are you thinking? We are going to stop the police somehow? How could we do that? We would get killed too," Gus said.

"Not with her power." Devon looked at Prue. "If she can do her hand thing, she can freeze time and that may help save his life."

"Hold on. You want to use me because of some magical power you think I have?"

"I don't think you have it. I know you have it and so do you. We literally wouldn't be standing here right now watching everything be frozen if you didn't. The problem is now the light isn't turning green because everything is still frozen. Can you do something about that?" Devon asked.

"Are you crazy? I just learned that I can freeze time for the first time in my life and that magic may actually be real, although I have no idea why me or why now, and you want me to see if I can turn a red-light green?"

"You don't have to get all dramatic. I just need you to unfreeze time so that the car can go."

"Devon, with time frozen, we may be able to walk around to see if there is a squad car parked somewhere and then..."

"And then what..." Prue interrupted Gus.

Time had caught up with itself. The red light had turned green and the car being driven by the young man was headed straight their way. The gang split up on different sides of the street, running to see if they could find where the police car could be to avoid Devon's premonition from coming true. Suddenly, Gus spotted it.

"There," Gus pointed behind a boarded building. "Prue, can you freeze time from here?"

Prue threw up her hands, but nothing happened. The squad car had started moving and was now behind the young man's Camaro, his siren blaring. Prue flailed her hands again, still nothing. They were running out of time. The car was about to pass them with the police already on its tail. Prue didn't know what to do.

"Prue, do something!" Gus yelled.

She flailed her hands like she had in the car earlier that night but nothing happened. The guys exchanged expressions of disappointment and regret. They didn't know how to help her, but Devon was not about to wait for Prue to figure this out. Without a moment's notice, he ran into the middle of the road, the car seconds from crashing into him.

"Wait..." Prue yelled afterwards. The panic, the worry… she could see the headlights getting brighter and illuminating the shadow of Devon. She threw her hands up and closed her eyes. She expected to hear the crash, Devon screaming, tires screeching, but she heard nothing. She opened her eyes. Time had stopped.

Devon breathed a sigh of relief. He tried to hide it from the two, but Prue and Gus could tell he was glad he found a way to help Prue summon her inner power. At the moment though, he was more concerned about what to do next. They didn't have a plan to save this man. Devon could only think of how to stop the police but he had no idea how they could save this man from being killed tonight, so he could walk away the way Dwayne never could.

"Now what do we do?" Gus asked.

Prue could still hear other cars at a faraway distance, the engines roaring speeding by, the sound of metal braking on asphalt. She now had an idea. She used both of her hands to freeze time. Was it possible if she used only one hand, she could freeze what she wanted while unfreezing the things she wanted to stay in motion? She didn't know, but she knew she had to give it a try.

She took a chance and went closer toward the car, telling herself that she wanted the car to continue moving, but the squad car to stay frozen. If the car continues moving, it may give the young man a good chance to get away from the police and drive away free.

She took a breath, closed her eyes, and imagined the car with the young man continuing to move forward and flailed only her left hand. She couldn't tell who was more surprised, herself for actually hearing the car continuing to drive off, Gus from the gasp that he made, or Devon who seemed frozen in shock, standing to the side of where the car was, watching as the squad car was still frozen in time.

"Are you just going to stand there or can we get back to the car?" Prue exclaimed, knowing full well the answer, and for the first time in a while, feeling something good.

With a smirk, Gus rushed back to the car, Devon stumbling a few seconds behind. Only a few seconds after they closed the car doors, time caught up with itself again. The three tried to hide under the console, peeking out of the rearview mirror to see when it would be safe.

The squad car appeared to slow down and then come to a complete stop, sirens still blaring. Lt. Hunter was in the driver's seat scratching his head, his partner also seeming bewildered. His partner reviewed their computer monitors while Lt. Hunter used his flashlight to survey the scene. With nothing and no one in sight, the two had no choice but to give up. The police officers turned off their sirens and with great hesitation drove off.

Prue, Devon, and Gus took a collective sigh of relief and got into their seats. This impromptu plan had worked.

"So, you mean to tell me that you have premonitions and can see the future, meanwhile she can freeze time and selectively unfreeze time as well?" Gus said in amazement.

Prue and Devon, two people unlikely to ever be in the same room, much less have a conversation, were now connected in a unique experience.

"I don't get it. I don't get it," Devon said.

"I guess the question is Gus, what can you do?" Prue smirked.

Gus snickered. "Guess you'll have to wait and see."

Prue and Gus chuckled while Devon felt temporary relief. They had just saved this young man from being killed tonight. But Devon knew this was not over. As long as Lt. Hunter was out there, more people who looked like him would be at risk.

While Prue and Gus celebrated their success, Devon was a million miles away. That's because his mind was. He started out in the car with them, but, as he had experienced this feeling before, suddenly, he found himself in a place far, far away, seeing and experiencing what would happen next.

13

Second Chances

It was the next morning. The sky was foggy, blue peaks teasing layers of the grey-tinted sky, overcast with shuffles of charcoal and a slight glimmer of the sun trying to rise.

Gus could tell this was an omen of the type of day it would be, undoubtedly a sign from his late brother David, laughing on the irony of this day. With streamers up on the Greek-like Antiqua columns, royal blue, silver, and golden balloons with colorful banners flew, this day had all the makings of a five-year old's birthday celebration. Gus was half expecting a magician to jump out of the podium on the stage with a teeny tiny rabbit to pull out of his hat.

They were in the most exquisite, exclusive, republican-type country club, the kind Gus detested because he always was the center of attention, like he didn't belong. And he didn't. He didn't quite look like them. Parts of him did, but no one accepts one part. They either see you or they don't. They don't see half of you. But these people did. They looked you right in the face with their fancy martini glasses, hedge fund children, name brand clothes like Gucci and Giorgio Armani that cost more than his first car, and they only see the part of you they want.

The podium and the center stage were cloaked in white. The ridiculously large columns, the glossy ceramic flooring, the podium, ivory and as white as snow. The outdoor seating on the artificial turf matched perfectly. So many people sitting and standing around, undoubtedly bragging about the parts of their lives they can use to impress people and make themselves look and feel better, meanwhile hiding all the parts of their lives that don't.

Several people close to Gus's age intentionally had their eyes glued to their phones, scrolling through social media so they wouldn't have to look up and have a meaningful conversation with someone right in front of them. An age of society where we prefer to share our deepest, darkest secrets through a computer screen with someone we've never seen, talked to or met before.

Gus knew his place. When he got close enough to finally read the sign, he knew the part he had to play today, after all, this was supposed to be a celebration. It was ten years since his older brother, David, took his life. Gus remembered it so well. But today wasn't about that, today was about acknowledging his accomplishments, his passion and dedication as they launched the 10th annual David Brooks Scholarship to help disadvantaged athletes achieve their dreams of Olympic gold and success.

Gus didn't understand how this scholarship fund came to be. His brother wasn't exactly disadvantaged. The white side of their family had all the money and happily gave it to support his athletics the way they always did, but with strings. It was such a habit, the strings were unspoken; their mother knew what she had to do to keep the cash flowing since she couldn't do this on her own, and didn't want to accept the reality they lived in.

Without a father in his life, it was only he and his mother, and that relationship was fractured beyond reconciliation as each day Gus's presence was only a reminder of what his mother had lost. Each day he grew to look more and more like the man that left her for another woman, due to the loss of his brother being too much to bare, and him being reminded of that each and every day he was with her.

Not that he needed excuses. Before his brother committed suicide, their father was already lost in the game of drugs, sex, and affairs with anything that could wear a skirt. That didn't stop his mother from trying to find healing in the arms and pants of the closest man that even slightly resembled him.

The cycle of family trauma is real, but at the moment, none of it mattered as it was Gus's job to stand to the side of the podium, look bereaved still, as if he couldn't move on with his life. He stood there to show the white side of himself and use the Black side of his heritage to inspire feelings of guilt to donate to the Sapphire Elite Athletic and Swim club and to give poor Black students free scholarships to enter the sport and excel in aquatics.

This experience of being on display felt like he was being used, and he was, because the upper-class whites would feel guilty enough to use their privilege to support the foundation, and then feel less guilty for the system they continue to perpetuate that keeps out Black athletes. They are more tolerant to biracial athletes because they can still pass, the way Gus could when he slicked his hair back, or if he didn't open his mouth, or if he changed his clothes. But Gus knew of many athletes that were not biracial, that were Black with two Black parents and they didn't have access, they didn't have the privilege he had.

"Gus, will you fix your hair, please? They are about to announce us on stage," his mother's voice interrupted his thoughts. And pure to her character, she tried to take away the things that forced the world to acknowledge him as half Black.

He stumbled around, a quick lick of his hand to his hair hoping it would do enough to shut his mother up. It didn't, but he was already disappearing. He was wearing his suit and tie, the one he kept in the very back of his closet. He only had two, one for occasions like this and the other from the funeral. He vowed to never ever wear that one ever again. He could see Mrs. Johansen and Mr. Thompson, co-owners of the country club approaching him. It was time to put on a show.

"How are you doing, Gus? I hear you had quite the accident a few weeks ago," Mr. Thompson started.

"I hope it's not affecting your performance. The trials are only a few weeks away. You're going to want to honor your brother. My, if he were here, he would be so proud of you and he'd tell you to focus, let absolutely nothing get in your way."

"That sounds exactly like him, Mrs. Johansen. David would never let anything get in his way. He used to talk all the time about his mentality. Fearless. Never ever give up." Gus could feel the dozens of knots in his stomach. Nothing could prepare him for moments like these when he'd be forced to acknowledge David's death, the uncomfortable conversations as folks always talked about his achievements and multiple awards but winced over and silently ignored what led to his death.

"Yes, sir. David was always about higher achievement no matter what." Something in his tone, he knew, gave what he was really feeling away.

Mr. Thompson fixated his gaze on Gus, shifting his eyes downward to look deep into Gus's eyes. "You know boy, you should be lucky that you are here. Not everyone is so privileged to have the opportunities you have and to be standing here today. David was an incredible role model and continues to be for so many today."

Gus could feel others' eyes on him, watching him to see if he would entertain. He could see his mother rushing towards him in a frenzy. "You're absolutely right. I am privileged to be here and very thankful for the opportunities you and the country club have given to me and my family. My brother's legacy continues to shine on through all of us."

"Very good, boy. Now this is a party and celebration. Mrs. Johansen, let's take our seats."

Gus could hear the voice on the microphone telling everyone the program was starting and advising everyone to take their seats. Gus used this as his cue to escape. It was time. He walked briskly, not in a way to gather attention, but in a way that appeared he had to take a phone call that he had been trying to answer for a half hour. Although he had been to the country club many times, he still felt awkward and uncomfortable being there. He wanted to punch Mr. Thompson straight through his teeth, but knew he'd be responsible for the denture costs and would lose his spot on the Sapphire team. Old white money, his favorite.

Still walking briskly, he found the bathroom, distant enough away from the event that he could potentially not be recognized, but not far enough away that he couldn't hear what was being said on the microphone. He wanted to lose it right there. All morning, he could feel the feelings bubbling up. He tried to subside them by reminding himself why he was there, that this was contingent on his academic scholarship, but also good appearances. He had had enough. He reached in his pocket for his slice of happiness. In his hands, he found it. He thought he could go without it and get through this day without it, but he felt that was a lost hope.

He went to start his normal process to inject it, but he felt inside it wasn't right. Despite the irony of the day, he knew that this didn't commemorate David at all. This day was about honoring his work in the pool and the various sacrifices he made to reach his success. Even if it ended on that rope in his room, he knew this wasn't right.

If only he could get to the pool, his calm place, his safe place. He could see it now. The tranquil blue in the water. That feeling of calmness and serenity. The silence of the aquatic center, only hearing the back strokes he took. He could see the 20-meter platform up overhead. The aquatic center was empty, the way he liked it. He had a way of going to this place even when there were hundreds of people there. He could always do something that made it seem like he was the only one in the room. But that never lasted long.

As he would go to take his high jump, he'd hear the familiar voice. "Gussy, you're never going to beat my jump." He knew it was David. Sometimes the voice changed, where it seemed like David was younger than he remembered on that fatal day. Always, Gus had to turn around. And when he did, he knew he'd get lost, but it was better than being where he really was.

He saw twelve-year-old David rushing to climb up the ladder to the platform to beat Gus at doing the 10-meter jump. This was always his favorite until that day in middle school when Jason Chadwick decided to bully him for being too old to still like that jump.

David was on fire. Two jumps in a row that were pure perfection. Gus just found himself standing in awe, studying his older brother, trying to figure out how to be just like him, how to be better than him. Gus would never find the answer.

. Gus moved to the platform, his tiny body feeling so light and diving deeper than he had before, getting lost in the waves in the ocean. Hearing the pelicans above. Seeing the sun setting below the ocean waves.

"Look out for the green tint of the sun before it completely disappears. I always love that. It's so magical."

Gus ran back to the sand, chasing after David. The two sat on the beach, digging their toes deep into the sand, looking at the isolated beach with coral and seaweed at their heels. It was peaceful as they stared into the sunset waiting for that green tint that David loved so much. Gus was surprised that he hadn't noticed earlier that they were no longer at the pool in the Sapphire Club but instead they were at David's favorite place, Emerald Beach. He also just started to realize that when he first saw his brother, he was twelve, but the brother he was looking at looked like the age he was shortly before-

Gus couldn't see himself, but he could tell he felt older than moments ago, yet not as old as he felt in real life. But it felt like real life. He could feel the sand between his fingers, the bareness of the cold sand between his toes. He reached out and pointed at his brother.

David looked suspiciously at him, pointed back at him and began tickling his armpits. Gus both hated and loved this. David was the only person who knew his funny places. He would never tell this to another living soul. This moment felt so real.

Too real. In fact, it was a memory of something that happened. Gus remembered being on this beach with David the day before he took his life. Staring at this sunset, he could remember he felt something was off about David. He should have been so happy. He was moving through his goals to make it to the Olympics, doing what he loved to do, making Mommy and Daddy proud. But he didn't seem happy. He seemed lost. Gus wanted to say something, but he felt he couldn't. It felt like his mouth didn't work. He tried but nothing could come out.

"Gus, do you ever feel like blah, like no matter what you do, you're still not happy?"

Gus wanted to answer, but Gus had figured out what this was. Gus had moved from being in his body to observing himself sitting with his brother. He knew what he wanted to do now, but the Gus in this memory would have had no knowledge of what was about to happen. He hopelessly watched himself and the words he would say. "What? Are you crazy? You have everything you should want. Just be happy." He watched himself push his brother in the sand, kick him, and then run off, hoping David would take chase. He didn't look back.

Gus never saw the look on David's face until now. While younger Gus was running away, hoping David would take chase, David was picking himself up off the sand, hair messy with coral reef, and for the first time, Gus could now see David fighting back tears. He took a few moments, but he got himself up and went chasing after his little brother, playing the part he knew he had to play as the older brother.

Gus was horrified. Watching now, he had no idea that this was what was going on with his brother. The next day, he would find his brother hanging from his bedroom ceiling fan, his limp body still attached to the fan that continued turning. Gus was so paralyzed; he instantly was outside himself and became numb. The love, admiration and respect he had for his brother made him freeze, instantly.

He was in his last year of high school. After seeing his brother like this, everything became locked away, out of his mind, compartmentalized, so much so that he had totally forgotten about this memory until this moment. But he wasn't just going to lay down now and not be there for him. He could do something now to change this.

Gus fought as hard as he could to get back into his body. He was watching this now, maybe he could do or say something to stop his brother from what he would do the very next day. Gus tried to pound his way back into his body. He tried to shout out to David, tell him to stop, tell him he loved him. He tried to shout out to himself, telling him to turn around, look at your brother, look at what you did, he's hurting and needs you now.

But nothing worked. And in a sudden flash, he saw the green tint that his brother was looking for in the evening sky.

"Wait, what?"

He was awoken by the coldness of the bathroom floor. It took him a few moments to orient himself. The echoes of the announcer bounced off the bathroom walls. He knew where he was now. He was back at the Country Club scholarship foundation, ten years after this memory.

Had he been in the bathroom that whole time? Never mind that, he had to figure out how to go back to that memory. If he could, maybe he could have another chance to repeat it and save his brother. Maybe he could change everything. Maybe his brother would still be alive today. He had to figure out how to get back to that time and to that moment one more time and reverse what he had done, for a second chance at life.

14

Where it All Began...

She knew that she had to go back to where it all began. She didn't have a place she could go that felt like him. She didn't have a place she could go that allowed her to reminisce of her moments with him and the times they shared together. She didn't have anything she could hold that he had given her. She didn't have any place that was his and hers alone that she could go to feel connected to him. The afterschool program could have been a good place to go but because of how he left, the injury he sustained there causing him to file for disability, those memories were more poignant than the positive ones he shared there. Besides, the high school would be full of photographs, memorials, and she couldn't deal with that right now. It would be all too overwhelming right now. So, she knew what she had to do. She got in her car, tears streaming down her face, and she went back, where it all began.

It must have taken her three hours to drive as far as the Stone Mountain area. She didn't care. She had one thing on her mind and that was making her way to where he last was with blood shot eyes that she didn't care to hide anymore from anyone. Driving faster than she had ever before, unafraid of crashing and ending it all.

She wanted to be near him. She wanted to be wherever he was. The music was blaring through her speakers, she had her corduroy teddy bear in the backseat with the letter she wrote to him. She didn't know if he could read where he was right now but she had to give it a try. She signed it the way she had started ending her messages to him on social media, "Always and Forever –".

Prue had reached a point she just didn't care about anything anymore. Kaleb was gone and the world had no rhyme or reason to it without him. What did it say about God that he would do such a thing? End his life at a young age, at this time in his life with his own teenage prodigy son? He had so much more of his life to give.

Prue would have given anything to go back in time and have stopped that day from happening. If she could have just gone back that morning and convinced him to never get in that aircraft. The hundreds of times she replayed that scenario in her head, she found something to stop him from getting into the aircraft- faking a bomb scare, sleeping with one of the pilots so he couldn't wake up on time, hiding the aircraft keys, figuring out how to cancel the scholarship college tour they were flying off to see, hiding their cellphones, vandalizing the aircraft so it couldn't move, sending an anonymous tip that there was a problem with the aircraft, personally getting in the way until she had to be escorted off the tarmac. She didn't care. He would be alive. They all would be alive. She could figure the rest out later.

She had finally arrived. She parked her car at the beginning of the trail, patted her face, covered her sunken eyes and knew it was time. She opened her car door, took a breath of the fresh air, and felt the warmness of the sun overhead. She saw the high hills, the dirt pavement and the path that was hers to take. She took a step forward and started the next part of her journey.

Fifteen minutes later, it was to her own surprise that she continued her walk, hiking up the trail overlooking the city. The far-away businesses and upscale neighborhoods were far in the distance. She continued her hike, one step at a time, holding the bear and the note, noticing the incline and trying her best to distract herself. She knew if she concentrated on what brought her there, she wouldn't be able to make it. The emotion would overtake her.

Further along, she passed by a very large, oak tree comprised of twisting branches that stretched for what appeared miles. Her steps passed over patches of grass that looked maintained but then began reaching parts that seemed to have died off. Yet another section appeared to stand out with markings and pieces of fiber, plastic, and metal fragments. as if blown about from the wind. It seemed as if a big boulder had crashed into it, but it had to have been stronger to create those types of indentations. And then she saw it and froze in her steps. Her insides wanted to scream and burst open. She knew this was the spot where it had all started, where she and the world had lost him, Kaleb, the most incredible man and inspirational leader to the next generation. The pain had awoken.

Realizing where she was, she couldn't feel her feet anymore, the pain so strong it knocked her off her feet to the bare ground. Touching the very ground she knew was his last resting place, her tears violently exploded from her face where every organ in her body could feel this tension and every bellow of this cry. On her knees, she wept like never before, unsure if anyone was watching and unfazed if they were. She didn't give a fuck. She couldn't give any less of a fuck.

Kaleb was gone, there was no pain greater than this, no pain more intense, nothing more that could make her die inside. The essence of her soul was already on fire and ever since he left, she had been experiencing a slow, tantalizing, agonizing burn inch by inch, until her eyes were black with soot and fingertips turning to ash.

There was a beautiful sun over her head. The hills that were cascading, a light breeze in the air, not a cloud in the sky. This would have been a lovely spot, overlooking the view of the city, if this wasn't the place the airplane crashed, killing them all instantly.

To think this was such a beautiful day, one he may have enjoyed in this very spot if he was alive to stand here and see it. Prue's brain refused to accept that he was gone. She kept racking her brain to figure out a way she could reverse it. How could she determine how this happened so she could go back and do something? Because this couldn't be the way his story was supposed to end. This couldn't be the final chapter.

Out of the corner of her eye, she noticed a piece of paper blowing ever so gently in the breeze. It was now caught in a small bush a few feet from her sneakers. She kneeled down to pick it up before a harder breeze nearly blew it away. Grasping its edges, she noticed it was a receipt. Most of the words appeared faded but she could still read the words, *New Beginning 824 Inspiration Way*. She could just barely make out an image of a book with its pages open, as if one was flipping through it. Suddenly, a strange feeling took over her.

She got up to her feet, wiped her pants, returned to the ground once more to kiss it and then left the teddy bear with the enclosed letter on his final resting place next to the indentations in the boulder. She didn't want to leave him here. She didn't want this spot to just be a typical spot that folks hiked past. She wanted everyone to know that this was the spot where he last was. She wanted this spot to be somewhere where people could pay their respects, somewhere where people could send him off with love so that wherever he was, he could see that we all love him, current tense and that we would never ever forget him, always and forever.

45 minutes later, after a few failed attempts, she finally found what she was looking for. She parked her car and walked to the front of the storefront until she finally saw it. *New Beginnings Bookstore* with the logo she saw on the receipt. It was located at *824 Inspiration Way, Bayside.*

Standing in front of the bookstore, she was afraid to go in. She found this receipt, but what was she thinking, driving aimlessly to a strange place she'd never been? The logical side of her wanted to get back in her car and drive home, but something deep inside of her told her to walk up closer to the store and open the door. Normally she would have hesitated, but for some reason, she felt calm and serene. She looked at the beautiful books in the window, sitting on individual stands lining the inside of the large window case in the converted Victorian house.

Before she even opened the door, one book immediately caught her eye. It was a thick, heavy-looking, leather-bound antique book, with golden pages and markings on it that appeared ancient. She couldn't make out what kind of book it was, but something about how the sun shined on it made her decide to go into the store and pick it up from the window. It looked like it was in a language she didn't understand. It had a cursive and elaborate fancy font, perhaps Italian, that made the title hard to read.

Prue's curiosity took over. She allowed her fingers to fumble through the pages. The page titles looked a little scary to her, *"How to Invoke Love"*, *"Setting Someone Free"*, *"Finding What's Lost"*, *"Redemption"* but her eyes paused when she saw *"Time Travel Spell"*. She was holding a spell book. She was holding an ancient spell book that had a spell to travel back in time. What was she getting herself into? Was this real? Was this the answer she had been anxiously searching for? Was this what she could do to bring back Kaleb?

15

The Book of Spirits Past

Prue waited for the guys to show up in her loft. She was so anxious she could barely sit down. She sat for a moment, then hopped back up, then tried to sit again. She finally gave in to the feelings in her legs to just pace. What was taking the boys so long to get here? She had texted them her address and told them it was an emergency two hours ago. It was now almost 1am. MEN!

Two knocks at her front door. *FINALLY.* She rushed to open the door to find only Gus standing there.

"Hey, wow your place looks nice. You did this yourself?" Though she wasn't a wife, Prue enjoyed keeping her place nice and tidy. She polished her cherry wood furniture twice a week, swept and mopped her wooden floors weekly, kept her fridge full of food and a variety of baked goods on the dining room table. Her grandfather clock struck. "Oh, is that him?"

"Oh no, that's just my clock," Prue explained.

"You have a grandfather clock? How old are you?" Prue rolled her eyes at his sense of humor. "Yum, these look good. You bake too?" Gus grabbed a double chocolate cheesecake muffin, no plate, no paper towel and clearly leaving crumbs all over the table. "Yum, this is a nice getup. You have some milk?"

"Clearly I'm the maid."

"Hey, who told you to serve me chocolate muffins?"
She found herself rolling her eyes again and searching for a
plate, napkin, and a glass of milk for Gus. Sitting at the
dining room table provided a great view of the first floor.
Her television hanging on the wall, Victorian style furniture
with accent pillows and tall vivacious bamboo palms in each
corner. Butterflies were on several of the walls and art
depicting nature and calm ocean waves at the beach.

Gus noticed while scarfing his second muffin the
picture of a twisted tree with great force. "So, what's the
emergency, magic power lady? C'mon, gotta get you to roll
your eyes a third time."

A smirk fell across her face. "Where is Devon?"

"I don't know. We can text him again or you can just
tell me what's burning so we can put out the fire."

Prue walked to the living room sofa and picked up
the book, bringing it over to Gus and placing it on the table.
"This is the emergency." She opened the book to the time
travel spell.

"What is this?" Gus eyed the spell, moving the book
closer to him.

"I'm not sure. I went to a bookstore and..."

"You pick up spell books from bookstores?"

"No, of course not. Before I met you guys, I never
even thought this stuff was real, but we have seen magic
happen already with our own eyes."

"Yes, we have, but it wasn't found in some old
smelly book from Harry Potter."

Prue paced the floor.

"Look, what did you think I would say when you
showed us this?"

"I would think you would have said, 'Let's give it a
try.'"

"Why would I say that? This looks like demon stuff."

"This isn't an evil spell, it's just a spell so I can go
back in time..."

"Why do you want to go back in time?" Gus asked her, raising his brow.

"I have my reasons."

"So why don't you just say the spell then yourself?"

"Because the spell looks like it coincidentally needs three people, see how it's written? Plus, it's probably more powerful that way."

"So, you want me to trust you to say a spell that could do Satan-only-knows-what to us, but you don't want to tell us why you want to go back in time?"

Prue abruptly stopped pacing, her back towards Gus. "Because if I go back in time, maybe I can save him from being killed."

Gus paused.

"I know that probably sounds crazy to you, but this spell looks like we can go back in time, I don't know how, I'm not even sure if it would work."

Gus stood up. "What do we need to do to see if it works?"

Prue looked puzzled. One moment ago, Gus was calling this evil, now suddenly he seemed on board. "I don't know. There are other spells here. Maybe we could try a different one to see if it even works. If it does, then that could mean the time travel spell could work too."

Gus flipped through a few pages then returned to the time travel spell. "Yeah, but the time travel spell looks the most complicated. It has a lot of ingredients that don't even look like they're in English."

Prue snickered. "Don't worry. I'll do my research to help decode the ingredients."

"Then let's find a spell that we can try, a simple one so we can see if it's even worth the trouble."

"Wait. You're down for saying this spell?"

"Don't push your luck. If this first spell works, I'm in, but you still have to convince Devon if you want the spell to work." Gus's fingers stopped at a page called the *Awakening Spell.* "How about this one?" Prue inched closer towards the book to read the spell. "It looks like a simple spell to help read other people's thoughts. Should be harmless enough," Gus said. "It looks like it only lasts 24 hours and the worst that could happen is we learn just how much people love my gorgeous smile."

Prue laughed, "Right because that's what everyone will be thinking about."

"Obviously," Gus concluded.

"So, what do we need to say this spell?"

"Do you have any purple or blue candles?" Gus asked.

Prue paced and then suddenly went upstairs. Seconds later she returned with matches and four purple candles.

"Great, then looks like that's all we need. You may want to turn the TV off, Columbo."

Prue had a comeback on the ready, like how would he even know who Columbo was, how old was he? But she was too excited to try this new spell. It brought her closer to seeing if she really could go back in time to save Kaleb, to save them all.

She turned off the television and lit two candles, passing the match over to Gus to light the other two. They arranged them in an arc so they could still read the spell in the book. Prue had started referring to the book as the Book of Spirits Past, as the book seemed to develop a mind of its own, at times acting on its own accord. The candle flames danced, synchronized in a rhythm no one could hear.

"Okay, let's do this. Looks like we need to hold hands and repeat the spell at the same time, cool?" Standing closer to him, Prue noticed Gus was actually a bit taller than her, standing a little over six feet. "Prue?"

"Yes." Prue felt the anxiety in her chest and took a deep breath in and out. Gus reached out his hand to grab hers, the two exchanged a wondering glance and then read the spell together:

"Give us the gift to see inside the mind, thoughts that others can't hide behind. Our ears are open to hear the

The two stood holding each other's hands waiting for something to happen but nothing. They looked around, seeking any sign that they had read the spell correctly for confirmation it had worked.

"Gee, that was fun. What's for dinner?" Gus broke the tension.

"Gus, that's not the least bit funny. That should have worked."

"Yeah, but it didn't. Probably for the best anyways."

Prue shook her head and blew out the candles. For a moment, everything was dark. *Oh, God. Now I will never get to stop him from dying.*

"Dying? Who died?" Gus asked.

"What? What are you talking about?" Prue searched the room for the light.

"You said you wouldn't get to stop him from dying. Who?"

"I didn't say anything." Prue switched on the hallway light upstairs and then returned downstairs to find the living room light.

Gee, she lives in this fancy ass loft and she can't find the light in her own place. Who is she sucking?

"Excuse me. I'm not sucking anybody. The light is usually on down here until I get ready to go upstairs, thank you very much."

Gus was unsure what to say. "What are you talking about?"

Prue stood a few feet from Gus, a frustrated look on her face. "What do you mean what am I talking about? Did you just get crazy after one spell?" *The cute ones are always crazy*, she thought to herself.

"Well at least you have one thing right, I am cute."

It took the two of them a moment to realize what had just happened.

"You're reading my thoughts? Oh, this is very bad," Gus said.

"That's great! That means the spell worked. Wow. The spell worked!! Oh, my God!!" Prue exclaimed, nearly jumping up from newfound hope, joy and excitement.

"Yeah, but it wasn't supposed to work on us, I mean not us reading each other's thoughts."

"Why? So that I won't learn how much you think about sex?"

"Yes and stay out of my head." Gus flipped through the pages. *Is there a spell here that blocks Prue from reading my mind?*

Prue rolled her eyes in her normal fashion. *Well, when you find it, let me know. But until then, we've got to start decoding the time travel spell.*

Gus turned towards her. *And maybe then you can tell me who you are travelling back in time to save before it's too late.*

Suddenly Prue and Gus heard knocking on the front door. Prue rushed to the door to open it. There was Devon standing there in a panic, "I need your help."

16

The Power of Three

It was 3:17 am. They had been sitting in the car for the last two and a half hours, bored, tired, and hungry. Hidden by the darkness of the midnight sky, as they watched the rustic traffic lights swinging overhead, casting their valiant colors onto the streets that were as shiny as silk. The neighborhood was as still as could be, minus the occasional car passing by, causing momentary interruption before all was once again movement free.

The world was different at night. The parked cars spoke to each other in only the way they could, the random squeak and occasional alarm as a loud frequency passed by. The architecture and landscape of the various size buildings had a narrative to read, but the organic community art and graffiti on the buildings themselves told a story of its own.

A clock melting away on a tree branch, a light bulb finally sharing its light as it swung in the distance, sand falling through a broken hourglass. Behind each piece of art was a story to be told and lessons to be learned. Even as

Prue, Devon and Gus saw the image of Ahmaud Arbery defaced for the second time in a row. These signified the harsh lessons the world was still trying to learn but most people hardly see what is right in front of them.

Why are we here? Gus thought.

Prue responded using a language only the two of them could understand, *Because he's worried that the same thing will happen again.*

When did he start caring about other people? This is madness, Gus replied, causing Prue and Gus to chuckle.

Devon looked at them strangely. "What's so funny?"

Both replied simultaneously, "Nothing."

Devon could sense something was going on but his focus was waiting to catch the next unprovoked attack. "I wish I could have seen the time, but I just know it's supposed to happen tonight." They had found themselves in the same spot they were in last time, right above the 30th and University sign. They witnessed the bus-stop they were just at not long ago when Prue used her powers to save the young man from being killed by the police. "There must be something wrong. I'm going to get out."

"Wait. Are you sure it was here again? We were here last time," Gus asked.

"I know what I saw, and it was here."

"Isn't that coincidental though, two in the same spot?" Gus retorted.

"I don't understand it yet but I saw him running and…we aren't going to lose any more Black lives to the police. That's all I know," Devon said before he jumped out of the car.

"We should probably follow him since you have the active power." *So jealous mine isn't that cool.* Prue rolled her eyes. "What? I know you heard that," Gus snickered.

With all this stillness, both were worried getting out of the car would awaken the neighborhood but they had little choice. Gus could hear Devon's thoughts and knew he didn't have a plan again so he clearly was going to need their help.

Both could hear how worried he was that he needed to save this man, they just couldn't tell why.

The two got out of the car and followed quickly behind Devon. Devon seemed like he was on a mission. He was trying to retrace his footsteps. He had seen all this before in his last premonition, trying to stop the senseless murder before another one occurred. No more on his watch. After losing Dwayne, that was enough. That was more than enough. They looked around but didn't sense any movement aside from *Roberto's Taco-Shop*, casting its bright colorful lights from its drive thru window.

"I'm hungry. Let's stop by there," Gus said.

"Are you always hungry?" Prue asked.

"Not always. I do have to sleep right?"

Gus was starting to grow on Prue and it seemed the feeling was mutual. Devon, on the other hand, the serious one, the militant, was not feeling this in the slightest. "Can you two shut up and just look out for the guy?"

"Ouch. Someone woke up on the wrong side of the bed," Gus said deflecting with his usual humor. "Well, I'm headed to get carne asada fries. Prue, want a burrito?" Gus asked as he started walking ahead towards the taco shop. In that moment, a young Black man walked out of the taco shop holding a brown bag, wearing a black hoodie and gray sweatpants, now crossing the empty street.

"That's him!" Devon shouted.

The man overheard, clearly not suspecting anyone to be outside. He turned around, startled. "What the fuck?"

Devon approached him, but the man took a few steps back. "Hey. This is going to sound crazy but we should probably drive you home."

"What the fuck man? No thanks. I don't do the homo stuff," the man replied.

Devon's face tightened. "What the fuck? No. The police are out here and…"

"And...?"

"And something could happen to you if you don't come with us," Devon's voice sounded uncertain.

"Man, get the fuck outta my face."

Devon looked at Prue, "Will you just freeze him?"

Prue was shocked at this ill-fated plan Devon seemed to conspire at a moment's notice. Nonetheless, she opened her hands, but unsurprisingly nothing happened. She looked around, all eyes focused on her and she tried again. Nothing happened once more. The man shifted his eyes towards Devon. "Um, okay. You on some weird shit. Deuces." And he took off running.

"Oh shit. We have to get him," Devon said.

He really didn't think this through at all, did he? Gus thought.

Clearly, no.

Devon studied the two. "Why are you two looking at each other like that? What the fuck is going on?"

"A very sad excuse of a plan backfiring which doesn't surprise me since you plotted it on an empty stomach."

Prue smirked. "He means what did you think would happen telling him that something would happen to him if he didn't come with us? That sounds crazy."

"Look. We don't have time for this right now and of all times for you to lose your power."

"She didn't lose it. She's just not scared," Gus replied. Prue was surprised she hadn't realized this herself. "Didn't you pay attention? Each time you have frozen time you were afraid." He turned to Devon, "It's not a bunny she's pulling out of a hat, Devon."

Devon shook his head. Suddenly, the bright flash of red and blue lights awoke the night sky and disturbed its peace, followed by the siren. They could even feel it's vibration in the ground. It wasn't far away.

"Where is that sound coming from?" Devon asked. The lights pointed them in the direction to the right. It was the same direction the man was running off too.

"We have to go after him." Devon chased after. Prue and Gus took off after him, trying to keep up but everything was so dark, they might as well have been blind. They could hear footsteps running.

Not again. This can't happen again, Prue and Gus could hear Devon think. They ran closer, passing Kansas Street, Florida, Maple, and finally arriving at Palmdale. Devon could barely see the man trying to elude the tall white police officer chasing him. There was a second officer running behind him, but Devon immediately recognized Lt. Hunter and his partner Sgt. James who he had seen before. The officers were gaining on the man who was trying his hardest to lose them by jumping over a few nearby fences.

Devon shouted, "Prue, try it again."

Prue was out of breath; she felt like she was a mile behind him and couldn't see where Gus was. She opened her hands but still nothing. "Dude, you have to!" Devon shouted.

Gus caught up to Prue and placed his hand on her shoulder. Suddenly anger erupted in her at hearing Devon misgender her again despite helping him earlier. She could feel the rage instantly try to take her over like a flash of electricity charging through her veins. When she opened her hands this time, she did the most unexpected thing.

The house that was in front of them literally blew up. Parts of the house wall, bricks, plaster, and bark from the nearby tree exploded in miniature pieces. Shards of windowpane flew through the air, several shards hitting the parked cars in front triggering their two distinct alarms.

Lt. Hunter and Sgt. James looked back and for a moment, even the man stopped running, frozen in place. Devon appeared stupefied. Prue's face couldn't appear any less lifeless. After the initial shock, the man turned around and continued to run trying to dodge the police. But Lt. Hunter wouldn't let up.

"We have to do something. They're too far ahead of us." Gus and Prue were still aghast. Devon marched over to them and slapped them both. Gus appeared too deep into thought to feel anything.

"GUS!!!" Devon grabbed his hand and immediately Devon, Gus and Prue were four blocks ahead, in front of the man that was now headed towards them. The trio could see that Lt. Hunter was hot on his trail.

"Where the hell are we? How the fuck did we get here?" *How are we going to stop this motherfucker?* Devon thought.

"I think I know how we can stop him," Prue said. Devon looked surprised. "If I freeze him again, that should give him enough time to run away."

"Yeah, but now you're blowing stuff up," Gus said.

"Okay, so not perfect, but they're coming this way and we have to stop the officer from getting him because we know what will happen if he does."

"Why is he after him anyways?" Gus asked pointedly to Devon. "Is he a criminal or something?"

"Why he got to be a criminal? Because he's Black?" Devon countered.

"Clearly no," responded Gus.

"Clearly no," mocked Devon. "What would you know anyways, pretty boy? What would you know about being Black?" The two stepped closer to each other, the tension building.

Prue had to do something, "Guys this isn't the time for this. We have to work together. Gus, why don't you try to distract the police and I'll see if I can freeze them?"

With great hesitance, Gus went jogging back towards the direction they came from, hoping to get closer to the police officer to distract him. He didn't know how he would, but he'd figure it out later. All he could think about though was that stupid Devon who had the audacity to question his Blackness just because he had light skin. It made him so mad. First, he can't fit in with the fancy pants at the scholarship foundation because he's too dark and now he can fit in with regular Black folks on a dark street corner because he's too light. He had been running for a few minutes so he was shocked to find himself running into Devon again who was directly in front of him.

Devon took a double take. "What are you doing here? I just saw you go that direction," pointing behind Gus.

"Clearly no," Gus mocked Devon mocking him. "Duh, why did you follow me?"

Devon grew irritated. "You must be high or something. Why would I follow you? I was right here, you just left." Gus seemed perplexed which only added to his confusion when he saw Prue still there. He knew she couldn't have beat him. Gus looked as though he wanted to sneer but he reframed and took off to running again. He could still feel all the anger in him though, *How dare Devon embarrass him like that and say that to him? Especially in front of a girl.*

He had been running for the past two minutes now, wondering when he'd see the police officer, hoping it wasn't too late. Like clockwork, he ran right back into Devon again as if he had been running in front of him and merely turned around. The two were seconds from a fist fight.

"What the fuck are you doing, Gus?" If the car alarms and the random explosion didn't wake up the neighborhood, Devon's loud baritone voice would.

"What the fuck are you doing, Devon? As usual you're fucking up another plan. Wait, I forgot, you never have one."

Prue finally caught sight of the officer and opened her hands. Nothing happened.

"Great, she has no powers now. Thanks to you, dumbass," Devon shouted at Gus.

"Dumbass? Clearly no, you stupid ass motherfucker," Gus retorted.

The two were ready to fight when Prue felt something strange crawling on her leg. She looked down but she didn't see anything. But she could still feel it. She had been ignoring this feeling of lightness, as if she was floating but she could see her feet were well on the ground. She also didn't feel cold even though she should have.

Devon was moments from projecting all frustration with the police at Gus who was more than happy to return the favor by pounding him for days of troubles that Devon had nothing to do with. Stepping forward, Devon took a swing at Gus with his right fist, but his punch missed. Gus fiercely threw a blow towards Devon but also couldn't connect. Devon went to push Gus but instead he ended up falling down on his stomach, his hand sliding through him. Stunned, the two had no choice but to scratch their heads.

"We aren't really here. Our bodies are over there." Prue pointed blocks back. "I can see from the traffic lights that we are laying down in the streets." The guys looked at her in disbelief.

"What? How can we be here but over there? Are we dead?" Devon asked with a lower tone.

"No. You just learned my power, asswipe. I can astral project. I've done it a few times now, but I've never brought people with me," Gus explained.

"Just like I have never blown up a house before," Prue smirked.

"Why is this happening?" Gus asked.

"I think it has something to do with us being together, it makes our powers stronger. When I blew up the house, your hand was on my shoulder. And when we were running trying to get here, then all of a sudden we were here. Kind of like the elevator accident."

"That was real?" Devon asked.

"I didn't think it was real either, but I guess it was," Gus replied.

"How does your power work?"

"I'm not really sure."

"I wonder if it's connected with how you feel or something you're thinking," Prue inquired.

"I really don't-" Gus stopped himself. It actually began to make sense, why he kept running but every time he ran, he ended up back in front of Devon. "It must be connected with what I'm thinking about. I was thinking of beating the life out of Devon. I was running the opposite way, but I kept ending up in front of him."

"That must be the trick. Gus, imagine us back over there in our bodies." Gus closed his eyes, and to his own surprise woke up inside his body again, getting himself off the ground.

"Gee, that was weird." Dusting himself off he realized Devon and Prue weren't moving. "Prue? Devon?" Gus shook them trying to wake them but his actions were futile. What had he done? Did he kill them? Gun shots penetrated the sky. *Oh no. Where were they?*

Like a lightning bolt, he was suddenly in front of them again, happy to see they both were intact. "Whoa. I thought you guys were hurt. Gee, why didn't you guys come with me?"

"You just disappeared man," Devon said.

"Gus, take our hands." Prue held her hand out. Devon hesitantly followed. "Now just think about returning us back to our bodies on the street." Gus grabbed both of their hands and thought about returning to their bodies lying on the cold asphalt. They closed their eyes and when they opened them, Prue, Devon and Gus had returned back in their bodies again. Prue swatting off the ants crawling on her legs and Devon trying to make sense of all of this.

"Okay, let's go. We have to head over to that direction but I don't know how to get there in enough time without you astral projecting."

"We don't need to," Gus said mysteriously.

"What do you mean?" Prue asked.

Gus swiftly pulled something dark out of his back pant pocket and aimed it at Prue. Instantly, she flailed her hands and jumped. The car alarms ceased. The neighbors that were peeking outside their windows were frozen. The siren lights stayed stuck on red.

"Great, I'm glad that worked." Gus chuckled as Prue and Devon realized he had pulled out his phone.

"You had me thinking that was a gun and it was just your fucking phone?"

"You're welcome, now let's go find them."

Gus ran in the lead, Prue and Devon trailing behind. They arrived to where the man was jumping over yet another fence, frozen in midair, Lt. Hunter only feet behind him, Sgt. James nowhere in sight. Gus's plan seemed to work but they had lost time having to run here versus astral projecting. This was consequential. If they had astral projected, Prue wouldn't have been able to use her powers.

At just the right angle and spot, she thought to use the same gesture as before to unfreeze the man so he could continue to run and get away without further interference. The scene unfroze, Lt. Hunter running into her and nearly pushing her down to get to the man.

"Stop!" yelled Lt. Hunter. He pointed a gun at the man who was now crouched behind the building, wearing his hoody over his head to conceal his face. His eyes looked in fear of his life, not as calm as he was moments ago when they first met him at the taco shop. The man looked close to tears, fidgeting, panicking.

He placed his hand in his left pocket and took out a square object. Lt. Hunter fired his bullet. Prue couldn't control herself, she panicked, the cool sensation taking over. When she opened her eyes, she couldn't believe what she saw. In midair the bullet stayed frozen inches from the man. She had frozen time again.

"Oh, my God."

Instinctively, Devon ran up to the bullet to move it. The bullet was extremely hot, scolding his fingers at the touch, but he managed to throw it away, far into the night sky. "Unfreeze him."

Prue tried again, focusing, and thinking only about the man she wanted to unfreeze. Her arms and legs shook from the effort, adrenaline racing through her veins. She

114

closed her eyes, made her one-handed gesture, and heard his footsteps running by. Second later, she could hear a door slam. He was one of the lucky ones, he made it home.

"We have to hide," Gus demanded.

"Hide? Now I can kick this motherfucker," Devon shouted.

"Devon, let's go. It's going to unfreeze any second." Devon reluctantly followed behind Gus and Prue, hiding in the shrubs where they couldn't be seen, something Prue had experience with.

When time caught up with itself, it left Lt. Hunter infuriated, in a daze and beside himself. "What the fuck?" he said. *I let that nigger get away. These niggers need to be stopped.*

Prue and Gus slowly looked at each other, understanding the full impact of the spell they cast. Now they were able to see inside the minds of monsters who secretly hated them because they were Black and would do anything to make their lives harder, even going so far as to murder them for the color of their skin. They were also relieved that only two of them had this gift right then, hating to imagine what Devon would do if he had heard this. Lt. Hunter walked away back to his squad car in defeat.

"Same police officer. Same area. I wonder what he wants. Why is he targeting these people?" Devon asked.

Prue and Gus were too full of anger and animosity to answer. Too full of sorrow for their generation, all the ones before and all the ones after that would have to experience and deal with this never-ending fight for the right to live, walk home and breathe while Black.

17

Hell Hath No Fury or Justice

"No Justice, No Peace. No Justice, No Peace. No Justice, No Peace! Black Lives Matter! Black Lives Matter!!" The crowd shouted from the very top of their lungs, shoving their signs high into the air, yelling, screaming, revolting, fighting for the right to walk home safely, drive home safely, live.

They stood in front of the Police Department, large groups of melanated people, with beautiful rich skin, inner strength, depth, beauty, and resilience that no man could overthrow. So much beautiful melanin that Devon had rarely seen altogether before. The crowd yelled, watching the police officers looking from their highbrow headquarter windows several feet off the ground.

The protestors fiercely shoved to the sky their picket signs, showing the faces of the countless victims. Ahmaud Arbery, Amir Locke, Daunte Wright, Andre Hill, Manuel Ellis, Breonna Taylor and Dwayne Harris, innocent Black people who lost their lives by the hands of a police officer or justice vigilante.

Devon couldn't stand much more. The group chanted, "No Justice, No Peace!" and "Defund the Police." These were more than words being yelled with every available fiber in their body. The group sought liberation and freedom and stood together in solidarity against the common threat to achieve that.

Devon recognized Mrs. Harris a short distance away, near a few of Dwayne's cousins and Derek, who had been left traumatized since the killing. Survivor's guilt, he continued to feel that it should have been him.

Fighting back her tears, Mrs. Harris held up the signs showing her late son in the air, raising it as high as she could to the man upstairs, yelling, "We demand accountability. Justice and accountability."

All this yelling and shouting wasn't doing anything. It wasn't bringing Dwayne back. It wasn't bringing any of these people back as the police just stood watching inside, safe in their glass tower behind their blue badges. Devon was sick of it. He was nearly foaming at the mouth with seething fury.

All these people standing here, speaking the truth, but nothing would be done. Even in Dwayne's case, they knew who the murders were, but here they were, back at the police department about to harm other innocent Black people, what the fuck was that? There was no trial. There were no charges. Paid leave was a sentence? Paid leave to sit their smelly asses in their recliners and scratch their balls while watching football and NCIS?

He could feel the black smog rapidly expanding within him, starting to spread its wings and turn into something which he couldn't control. And he knew he was running out of time. His thoughts were running into each other, tripping and falling but cascading in a direction he was losing control.

And then no more. Devon was outraged, he could no longer contain the pollution eating him up inside. He had to set it free. The energy was too much. He had seen this too many times. He had seen the images over and over on repeat on the news, on social media. Images of Black men fighting for their lives, one after another after another after another, with all of them ending up dead.

He had seen his brother's neck being knelt on until he was dead. He had seen his brother being shot while running in fear. He had seen his brother being pulled over and trying to explain to the police that he didn't understand what was going on and being shot dead in cold blood. Something in Devon snapped. Never no more.

He knelt down, seeped his hands into the ground and pulled up the biggest rocks he could throw. Feeling the anger pounding in his hand, throbbing, pulsating, deeper in his veins, he launched the rocks straight towards the glass ivory tower. He watched those rocks break the glass panels and shatter their shatterproof window. He watched the aghast looks on the police officers faces as they witnessed the unthinkable falling.

The crowd was in an uproar. If the justice system wasn't going to provide justice, if the law wasn't going to right a wrong, they would do it their way. Taking Devon's lead, the people got on the ground and found rocks to heave at the Police Department. Several stood shouting and lunging towards the police station.

Panic filled the air, protestors screaming at the top of their lungs. They broke the glass windows of the squad cars, attacked the windows and doors of the front of the Police Station. They catapulted more rocks into the air, releasing the fear that had been instilled in them since they learned what it meant to be Black and that the police protect and serve only the select few.

Although the front doors were locked, police officers had somehow emerged around the crowd and were demanding them to calm down, their weapons pointed at them. All Devon could see however was the face of Lt. Hunter, who had murdered his friend, his brother. All officers now looked like Lt. Hunter. If they didn't say anything against him, they all might as well be Lt. Hunter. He wasn't going to take it anymore.

Devon took a step back, found two more heavy rocks under foot, and hurtled them forward, trying to aim directly for the officers' faces. The officers bent down, several held their shields, appearing to retreat. Seconds later, officers surrounded the growing crowd with fog horns, demanding everyone to get back.

They followed this up with tear gas, burning the eyes of all the protestors now writhing in pain. Gun shots shortly followed. People ran as fast as they could anywhere, they saw an opening out. A heavyset older woman was slumped over a bush, noticeably hurt but people continued tumbling past. Devon could barely see; the tear gas burning his face and eyes but he had to save her.

He tried to get through the crowd. His senses told him someone was behind him. He couldn't care, he had to get to her. Just as he reached her, two police officers came and helped him get her off the ground. Devon wanted to kill them in their own blood right now, but these officers seemed different. They seemed more concerned with helping her than trying to cause anyone harm. The siren sounded, nearer to his ears. Together, Devon and the two officers helped the older woman inside the ambulance.

Worrying about Mrs. Harris, Devon quickly left the older woman in their hands to find her. He wanted to make sure she was safe too. Over his dead body would he let anything happen to her. She had been through enough. Looking around, all he could see was the thick haze caused by the tear gas and the revolt for justice. He saw shouting, he saw fighting, he saw piercing silver objects moving through the air.

Several people had been shot by bean bag rounds, holding their chests, holding their heads, lost and confused. Devon continued looking through the crowd for Mrs. Harris, he had to protect her, to make sure she was okay. Suddenly, he felt something behind him jerk his hands together. Instantly, he knew what that cold, metal object on his wrist was. Isn't it something, the feeling of liberation when you break yourself free of the system until the system turns around and chains you again?

18

Two Times a Virgin

There were only two hours left before the spell would wear off and Prue was determined to use this to her own advantage. She had finally healed enough where she could go out on a date with a man she had been casually chatting with online. She was ready and her body was especially ready. The urges were penetrating through her, much like a virgin being ever so gently stroked, touched for the first time.

Prue wanted a man inside her, completely inside, all the way inside her, deep, penetrating her walls with firmness and dominance, forcing her to submit and her begging him to stop. She yearned for this experience, legs open, eyes tearing up, holding on for dear life to the bed sheets, biting her pillow, trying to muffle her screams, the spanking of his hand on her ass, the sound of their bodies' clapping as the nights efforts leads to them both sweating in a mad frenzy with no other possible end but to feel his hard cock shooting all of his hot, wet cum inside of her. She grieved, she mourned, but she still wanted this. She wanted to feel a man's wetness once he ejaculated into her. She wanted it now.

Dominic texted that he was downstairs waiting in her driveway. Not entirely the type of guy she would usually see, but he had his qualities. He was employed, had a charming, beautiful smile, a full head of dark, thick, gorgeous, silky hair, was only about an inch shorter than her, and if she leaned, she could barely notice the height discrepancy. He stood with his olive glowing tan skin, his last name was Amici, an official Italian name. He enjoyed Italian cooking and was taking her to an authentic Italian restaurant.

For their first date, Prue had decided to wear a thin, shear, mesh dress shaped enough to show off her slight curves and short enough to emphasize proportions that her body had never seen before. And by the looks of Dom when she approached the passenger side, he wanted to see more. Dom seemed nice enough, he was good-looking, clever, witty, and attentive. They drove off to Alexanders, ordered together the capellini pomodoro, crostini with fresh tomato, basil, garlic and balsamic, and la dolce vita for dessert and he actually paid the bill. She knew she would pay him back in other ways.

When the dinner was over, she knew she wanted him to come inside so she could thank him. He seemed intrigued. He never exactly claimed to be a gentleman. His animal instincts awoke once they were alone together under the faint luminescence of the wall sconces and the TV light. He chased her around the dining room, she enjoyed being caught and captured. He picked her up and took her up the stairs into her bedroom.

With his lips against hers, she could feel his warm embrace, his tongue meeting hers and the way he kissed her felt so different and unlike anything she had felt before. She felt like a woman, a real woman. He kissed her with such passion, like she had never seen before. She had never experienced this even in the park. Her job was to tease the faceless men and as they approached, there was no contact, she could only get on her knees and satisfy them. But here, Dom had his hands all over her. He rubbed her soft insides. He kissed her soft lips.

Prue worried that her chin fuzz would detour him, but it didn't. He kissed her nonetheless and she herself could tell how aroused he was getting. But it felt sensual, it felt passion-full, it didn't feel like it was just so she would please him for him to then hurry out of the door before anyone showed up.

Dom had told her earlier in their messages that he found Black women extremely attractive and that he had a thing for trans women. He said he had never been with a trans woman that had a pussy. These two things made her feel rather uncomfortable. She wondered if this was the trade-off now that she was herself, being able to go out on dates with men instead of just hiding out in parks to get men's attention but only getting said dates because of a fetish that these men had. Why couldn't she just be seen as the woman she was?

They made out, him rubbing her make-up all over his face. It was apparent, brown make-up on Italian olive skin. He didn't care. He wanted to kiss her, he wanted to touch her down there. And she wanted to see what this bulge was in his pants. This was her first date, but old habits die hard. She wouldn't have to wait long. He could barely control himself.

In the next few moments, he unzipped his pants and took them off, revealing his pulsating, hard Italian circumcised cock. And she enjoyed it and admired the image of it before taking him. She instantly got to her knees and began his ascent to heaven. He moaned, he moaned like he had never been pleasured this way before. He moaned as if he had never reached this place of ecstasy before. He wanted to stop her. He could tell he was so close, and he didn't want to. He wanted to enjoy more of her.

He picked her off the floor and began taking her dress off, rubbing his hands between her soft pussy lips. That's what he wanted. He wanted to see it and he wanted to put his fingers inside of it and he wanted to suck it, and so he did. He placed her on her bed, lying her on her stomach so he could use his tongue to explore her.

Prue laid back unsure of what to feel. She was more nervous than anything that he would find something peculiar that would without a doubt prove her vagina wasn't as worthy for entering as a cisgender woman's. Dominic seemed satiated with her enjoyment and excitement. She had never had this experience before; she was always the one on her knees happily pleasing a man until he came. She never received, anything. She was afraid he internalized how women's vaginas work from watching hours upon hours of porn videos. She was afraid he expected her to squirt hot gooey cum all over his face. Her anxiety got the best of her, and she pulled him up.

He was on top of her, looking now at her completely nude, her breasts, her waistline, her soft, hairless pussy, and he wanted to be inside of her. She was nervous. She didn't know if she was wet enough but she had placed some lubrication inside and dilated just before they left. He kissed her and slapped her pussy with his throbbing hardon. This hurt a bit for Prue, her pussy was ultra-sensitive. It had never been entered by a man, and he was going to be the first. This would be her second chance at losing her virginity.

Dom was on top of her, kissing her and trying to stick it in. Prue began to worry when it didn't feel like she was opening enough. She tried to calm herself, but she was getting scared. What if her vagina wasn't working? What if she didn't know or couldn't learn how to do this? Doing it the other way seemed so easy.

Dom rested his penis and continued passionately kissing her. She could feel something happening below. Her new body seemed to enjoy this level of intimacy and his warm tongue. She rubbed his cock in her hands to keep him warm and hard and opened her legs, helping guide Dominic inside. And when she felt him finally opening her walls and entering her to the point he was undoubtedly inside, she just about lost her mind. He felt so good deep inside of her. And then he began fucking her hard. Her body began to shake from enjoyment and volts of pleasure. The entire bedroom shook with them.

Dom learned the grooves of her body. He learned how to change pace from fucking her slow and deep, to fast and harder. She tried to tell him to slow down but he was already too far gone to hear her. He continued, taking her soul mercilessly, kissing her, going as deep inside of her as he could, making her body violently shake, awakening the demon inside. She was so wet; she could feel herself enjoying his meat inside of her and calling her his bitch. She liked when he called her his bitch, his nasty slut. She wanted to be.

He grabbed her breasts and sucked on them while turning her pussy out. She knew this was how this was supposed to be, the way it was supposed to be all along. She cupped his warm testicles in her hands and cuddled them. She wanted every drop of his sperm to fill her up. She wanted to completely drain him inside of her. Her pussy wanted him to fill every hole in her soul. She held on to him, her legs wrapped around his waist, and she thrust herself deeper onto his erect cock.

Dom couldn't take it anymore. She heard him plea, "You're gonna make me cum." That's exactly what she wanted, just like what she wanted all those years cloaked in moonlight in the forest. With a satisfying, animalistic male groan that seemed to speak to the gods of ecstasy, she felt his several bursts of soothing hot fiery cum shoot inside of her pussy like a dam that burst, followed by his final four thrusts. She knew he had received his halo and she had certainly repaid dinner.

With the little energy he had left, he rolled over to the other side of her bed, first resting, trying to catch his breath, and then admiring her through the illuminance shining through her bedroom curtains. *Wow, she feels just like a woman.* Prue's identity felt validated in this moment. She was over the moon that she was able to meet with him in the final hours to hear this thought before the Awakening Spell ended. *Too bad she still looks kinda like a man.*

Her newfound joy completely fell away. She could see it and she wondered if others could see it, and apparently they did. There were times she looked into the mirror and saw herself, but still many times where she instead saw the person she had been known to be all those years, trapped. But after this, she knew it was time for her to start the next phase of her journey, FFS, facial feminization surgery.

She would never be satisfied with only being half seen. She needed to be completely seen as the woman she was, by others and most importantly by herself. She knew she was that beautiful woman that had always been inside, and it was time to set her free.

19

Fuel Meets Fire

Buzz. Buzz. Prue woke up frantically, immediately jolted by the sound of her phone and the flashing light. She nearly fell off the corner of her bed. Prue hurriedly searched through her room for the source of the light before Dom woke up from his slumber. Success. She found it. Wiping sleep away from the crust of her auburn eyes, she found a text from Devon, *I'm at the county jailhouse. Please bail me out.*

3am-Prue was trying to gather her thoughts, trying to convince them to just tell her point-blank period what they needed. 3am-Prue was trying to arrange an appointment with 9am-Prue that was ordinarily articulate, well-groomed, organized, and put together, but she was shit out of luck.

Tiptoeing around her own room, she quietly found clothes to throw on and then a new pair of panties as Dominic was still sleeping on hers. She looked at his soft skin, the feeling she had never had before, having a man sleep over. He felt much cuddlier and more comforting than her teddy bear.

Okay, time to focus. No time to think. She had to figure out how to slip out of her own house and quietly start her car without awakening him. Although she wasn't 9am-Prue yet, she had managed to chat with 6am-Prue who had arrived at an idea and a few minutes later, she was pulling

126

out of her garage, Dom oblivious in his slumber while her bedroom fan blocked out any sound of her garage opening and her car driving away.

Thirty minutes later, she pulled up to the dark jailhouse parking lot and once inside, was escorted inside to the sheriff who gave her the information she needed to bail Devon out. A costly sum of $5,000 to which she cursed the day she ever laid eyes on his tall, dark, Jamaican maleness. With great hesitation, she signed her name for the bond and soon after was taken to his holding cell.

For the first time, they were alone, aside from a snoring transient a few cells back. Devon sure had a lot of nerve asking her for help and why did she even bother helping him, a man that would refuse to see her? But this arguing in her head was pointless now, she had already posted his bail and clearly had to take him home.

She approached Devon's cell. He was lying on the bunk in his cell, a moment where he actually appeared human. A moment where she could see the hurt on his face, as if he reverted to his child-self once she came in to rescue him. He sat up on his bunk, not wanting to look her in the face, avoiding all eye contact, wanting to hide the parts of him he never wanted seen. Prue could relate.

After a few moments, Prue broke the silence. "So, I posted your bail. $5,000. Wanna tell me why I had to post that?"

Continuing to look away, Devon replied, "I'd really rather not."

"Of course. I mean, wake me up at 3am without any reason, just so I can drive here in the cold to save you."

"Look, I didn't need to be saved, especially by you."

Prue could feel the heat rising in her chest. "Yet, you texted me. Why didn't you text someone else then?"

"Because I couldn't think of anyone else that quickly that could have helped me, and your number was the first one I saw."

"Sure, chosen by default."

Devon began shuffling around and then finally stopped and looked directly at her, their eyes meeting. "Look, I don't have anything against you."

"You sure fooled me."

"I just don't understand you, what you are."

"What I am?" Prue felt the branches snapping her very last nerve.

"I don't know if I should address you as a boy or a girl, this is all very new to me."

"Well, let me help you." Prue stood up. "I'm a woman. Always have been, always will be."

"You say that so easy, but you weren't born that way," Devon snapped back.

"Yes, I was."

"You know what I mean. You were born with the same parts I have."

"So? That wasn't my fault. Do you know how many times I wished that wasn't the case? I can't help how I was born. Something clearly went wrong, but this is who I am, whether I had the same parts as you or not."

"Had?" Devon inquired.

"I don't know what the big deal is. What difference does it make to you or any of these other Black men that I was born in a man's body? I am NOT A MAN," she postured, hands on her hips.

"Because we aren't taught to look at gender like this. It's not something you just decide to change."

"But I didn't just decide to change it. There are millions of transgender folks in this world, many who realize very early that they are put in the wrong body. Millions. What, we are all lying to you?"

"Look, why are you getting so mad at me? It's not my damn fault."

"Because you're part of the problem. People like you try to erase millions of trans identities."

"I'm not erasing shit. I'm just saying no one is taught that you just decide what your gender is."

“Then we need to start teaching them then, everyone.”

Devon was growing impatient, “Look, I don’t think you’re lying but it’s hard to understand. You look halfway one way, but you sound and act another way. It’s confusing. If someone sees me with you, they’ll think I’m gay or some shit.”

“Are you?”

“Fuck no.”

“Then what’s the problem? You care so much about what other people think, you allow that to dictate your life, everything you want to do.” Prue stood firmly in her truth, feeling all of the strength in her voice as she never had before. “I am a woman. Address me as a woman at all times. And despite the fact that I may have a harder journey, I feel sorry for you. Guys who aimlessly go by what everyone else expects for them, it’s pathetic and a sad life. I’d rather be my own person any day.”

Devon scuffed, and threw her a scolding look, “Fuck off. I am not the fucking problem. I just want a real woman.”

“Well baby, there’s no realer than right here.” Prue grabbed her purse that was sitting on the bench. “We need to go. We have serious work to do.”

Devon was bewildered, “Work? What work?”

Prue looked him deep in his eyes. “We have to travel back in time.”

“The fuck?”

Prue headed towards the door, “Anyone smell fish?”

20

If at First You Don't Succeed...

He received the text message about 25 minutes ago but was already at her place within the first five. This was what he had been waiting for. Since he saw his brother that day on the beach and he saw the look on his face when he pushed him over and ran away, Gus craved to relive that moment again, to go back in time and save him. To say whatever he needed to say to have stopped David from taking his life that next morning. He knew he had to go back. He'd figure out what he needed to say later but he had to return to that moment.

Gus knocked on Prue's door for the third time but Prue still didn't answer. Instead, an unfamiliar, Italian man did. Gus was caught by surprise. "Who are you?"

"Um, I'm Dominic. Who are you?" The two sized each other up.

"I'm Gus. Where is Prue?"

"I don't know. She slipped out early this morning to do something. How do you know her?" Dominic's phone rang before Gus could come up with an answer. "Look I have to go. Tell her I'll see her later." He walked past Gus and headed to his car parked in the driveway.

Gus felt a burning sensation in his stomach and he felt relieved of it once he saw Dominic's car drive off. Gus's attention was swiftly diverted as he noticed the open Book of Spirits Past on the dining room table.

As he inched closer, he noticed the book was open to the time travel spell. He wondered if Dominic had seen this before he had left or if Prue had left it open during her research. He could hardly wait for Prue and Devon to arrive. There was another page attached to the time travel spell but he didn't have the patience to read it. He wanted to say the spell now and see if it worked, if it took him back through time ten years ago to save David from his own demise.

Gus was so full of excitement and anticipation, he tried to distract himself, wash her leftover dishes, take out her trash, but ten minutes later he was still antsy and decided that he could wait no longer. Standing over the Book of Spirits Past, he read the cypher Prue created to decode the spell ingredients and then he searched the house to gather the items together. A few rosemary twigs, three blue candles, two mandrakes, a slice of guava and passionfruit, three drops of peppermint, and a crushed amethyst in a wooden bowl.

He organized the candles similar to the way they were depicted in the Book of Spirits Past and followed the directions. Gently, he used a pocketknife to poke his index finger so that a few drops of blood would bleed into the bowl, and he said the magic words:

"Blood to Blood, Soul to Soul, Spirit to Spirit; the steps I walked, may I travel again; take me back through time, where I can unwind, and walk where I once walked again."

The wooden bowl began boiling over, fog mysteriously rising from the concoction of the ingredients and the magical words Gus had allowed to emanate from his lips. Rapidly growing around him, the dining room was now completely consumed, robbing Gus of all sight and sound.

Shortly after, he began to feel this spinning sensation, as if he was moving or floating away. Suddenly there was a loud burst, like he had leapt forward or jumped the highest he ever had in his life. His blood was rushing. His senses were on high alert. His legs felt shaky. He felt he was moving at the speed of a jet blindfolded high above the western skies.

Gradually, the fog began to dissipate, and he could hear more familiar sounds. Once the fog cleared, Gus found himself standing in the middle of a beautiful promenade in a luxurious park. He could see the luscious forest trees with heavy widening branches and the wooden oak benches and the children's swings and the vibrant green grass.

The park was full of people, all unfamiliar to Gus, causing Gus to pause and wonder. Where was he? Did the spell actually work? Had he gone back in time? But the people didn't look much different than they did in his own time, the cars, their clothing. Had the spell backfired? Had he done something wrong?

Gus walked around, studying the park, wondering where he was and what time he was in now. Everyone seemed normal, they seemed happy and cheerful, polite. *Just great,* he thought to himself, realizing that he was in such a rush, he had no idea how to return to his own time to fix this calamity.

He was just about to kick himself when something made him look up and pause. A man was not too far away that kept his attention and something about him seemed very familiar. As quickly as he saw him, the man took chase after his golden retriever. Gus's instincts told him to follow the man, so Gus ran after.

A nearby stranger was able to help wrangle his dog so the man could take hold of him. Gus could overhear the man thanking the stranger. That's when the feeling in his chest started. It felt warm, it felt calm, but it also felt anxious and scared.

Hearing the man's voice sent Gus into a tailspin, and when he stepped closer to the man and was just a few feet from him, he saw it in his eyes, he saw something in his face and the pieces finally came together for him; it was David. He had nearly missed it, David didn't grow his hair that way and David hadn't lived to be this man's age, this man appeared to be in his late thirties. Who would have known what David would have looked like at that age?

Gus initially was puzzled, but the moment he saw his eyes, it all came back, it didn't matter that he looked different, was older, had different hair, that was his older brother David. Gus was overcome with emotion, there was no possible way he could hold it back. He ran up to the man, jumping fully into his arms like a great big child.

"Oh, my God. It's you. I've missed you. I've missed you so much. All these years." Gus just had to let out all the emotion. At last, he was finally holding his older brother again and he was alive, they both were.

He couldn't understand how he cast a spell to go back in time but ended up seeing David's future self instead that was never able to actually exist. He didn't care about the logistics though. All that mattered was he was holding his big brother again. The man held Gus loosely and seemed more startled and befuddled. "I have missed you for so long. I can't believe I finally get to see you again."

The man gave Gus two pats on the back before finally speaking. "Mister, I'm really sorry but I think you have me confused with someone else."

Gus laughed it off. "Funny, jokester man."

"I'm sorry, mister. I don't know who you are and you're scaring my son."

Gus backed up from David, stunned and in disbelief that his own brother didn't seem to recognize him. "David, that's not funny. This is no time for jokes."

"I'm sorry, mister. My name is Thomas, not David."

Gus couldn't believe what he was hearing. "What do you mean your name is Thomas? You think I don't know my own brother? What's going on? Have you hit your head? You don't have a son."

A young man, around the age of fourteen approached them. "Dad, what's going on? Who's this weirdo?"

"Nothing, Gus. This man just seems to have made a mistake."

Gus was astonished, "Gus?"

"Yes, mister?" the fourteen-year-old answered.

Gus was sure he was quickly losing his mind. He cast a spell to go back in time only to somehow go to a future where his brother never lived, to have a son he wasn't old enough to have and for him to be named after him. The mystery only continued as Gus examined the fourteen-year-old, his jaw nearly falling to the floor when he recognized a scar on his forehead, identical to the one he incurred during his car accident several weeks ago.

"Wait –this doesn't make any sense?" he uttered. Was this fourteen-year-old somehow him? It couldn't be. He didn't look like him, but David didn't quite look like David either, I mean Thomas. Nothing was making sense and Gus's head was only starting to ache more.

"Mister, I'm sorry that we couldn't help you, but I hope you find the person you're looking for. I'm sure he's missing you just as much as you are." Thomas turned to his son, "Let's go, Gus."

Both of them walked off with their dog, leaving Gus standing in dismay, paralyzed in bewilderment. He stood back and watched them both go off, happy and joking with each other, similar to how they did as brothers, now they were doing it as father and son.

Gus came to understand the feeling within his chest, he realized that he didn't go back in time. He went into the wrong time, a different time, a different plane of existence where David wasn't his older brother, but this time was his father. What did that mean? He couldn't imagine David as anyone other than his older brother, but he adored the comfort of knowing that even in another life, he and his brother were still connected, one way or the other, together again.

He wrestled with the feeling of running after them but knowing he couldn't. This wasn't the life that he was meant to go back to, this wasn't his time. He was supposed to go forward. Now would have been a good time to have read that attached page. He didn't know how to go forward and didn't have a return spell, but he would leave this David alone, knowing that Thomas and Gus had their own life and destiny to fulfill, but he would not give up on saving the David from his own time that he had lost for one more chance at life

Out of the corner of his eye, he noticed a silver string that was very sparkly and peculiar. It looked a little far out of reach. He had remembered seeing this before that day in the Sapphire Club. Maybe this was his way back. Gus went down to his knees to try to grab it. Holding it in his hands, he was surprised to see the string was somehow attached to him, but he couldn't see how. A gentle tug led to no avail so he pulled harder.

All of a sudden, Gus found himself falling through a colorfully broken glass sky. Multiple lives and spirits passing by, Gus could feel his heart in his throat, the blood rushing to his brain falling upside down with a thunder as he awaited the plummet to his final destination.

21

Ready, Set, Lift Off

He continued his descent, falling quickly and with great trepidation, spiraling down from greater heights faster than his brain could think nor his eyes to perceive, feeling the wind between his hair until he fell right back to his body, his soul floating momentarily above Prue and Devon who were kneeling over him, trying to shake him from his unconscious state.

Like lightning, Gus jumped back into his body and leaped forward, Prue was relieved that Gus hadn't died on her living room floor. "Gus are you okay? What happened?"

"Bro? What the hell happened?" Devon interrogated. Gus appeared in a fleeting daze but in the next few moments, he was able to find his sanity and return to his friends. Devon looked over to the Book of Spirits past, still on the table, opened at the page Gus had read the spell. He turned towards Prue. "Is that the book you were telling me about?"

"Yes, Devon," Prue answered.

"Does that stuff really work?"

"The hell it does!" Gus shouted. "I just saw my dead brother in another life as my father."

"Oh wow. One spell made this kid that delusional. Oh, fuck no."

"I'm not delusional!" Gus exclaimed. "I saw my older brother who died in high school suddenly in another life in his freaking thirties and I looked right at myself, only fourteen and this time his son." Gus began to tear up. Prue rushed over to his side.

"How is that even possible?" Devon asked. "Did you read that time travel spell? Weren't you supposed to go back in time?"

"I don't know how it happened, but it happened. I got to see my brother again. But he didn't recognize me."

Prue gave Gus a warm hug. "I can't imagine what you're feeling right now."

Gus looked her deep in the browns of her eyes, "It makes me feel like I want to try the spell again to make sure I go to the right David this time. The David I saw was living another life." Gus paused.

"You think your brother is living in some other time loop?" Devon inquired.

"I know that he is. I saw him. He and I are living there, existing there together."

"No, my half nigga. You are here in front of me."

"Why can't I be both? Maybe somehow a part of me is with him now. I don't understand it, but I know what I saw and I know what I felt."

Prue comforted Gus, "I don't think we have to know all the answers." Prue's voice seemed to mildly calm down overly suspicious and cynical Devon, his crossfires ready to load at any moment.

"It makes me happy that he is living in some other plane. Living, still existing, and we are doing that together. I feel a little less lost without him now because I know we are still kinda together. But I still want to save the David from my time, in this life and I think we all need to read the spell to do it, not just me, but for each of us who have lost someone."

"How does a spell like that even work? We all lost someone at different times," Devon remarked. "Besides, how do I even know this witchcraft stuff is real?"

Prue postured to Devon. "Well Gus just cast a spell and clearly something happened. You could cast your own spell."

Devon was astonished. "I could cast my own spell?"

Prue walked over to the book, turning the pages as she spoke. "Well, the book seems pretty organized, it has lots of spells to choose from. So far, I've been studying it and it has love spells, love potions, spells to quench your heart's desires..."

"You are such a girl," Devon rolled his eyes. "I don't need a love spell. This isn't a romance novel or the Hallmark channel." Gus snickered.

"Then what do you want?" Prue asked him.

Devon thought for a moment. Gus sitting down at the dining room table and Prue sitting next to him, Devon walked over to the book. Suddenly, it began flipping pages as if something invisible were turning them. "Whoa. What was that?" Devon nearly squealed in panic.

"Oh, sometimes it does that." Prue approached the book and noticed it had turned to a page called *Heart's Desire*. "Looks like you need a little love in your life after all," Prue giggled.

"Makes sense. When I got here, the book was already opened to the Time Travel spell," Gus interjected.

"But I didn't have the book open."

"Maybe your *friend* opened it," Gus retorted.

Prue's cheeks were of a dark mahogany, but even still she could feel her cheeks burning red.

"What friend?" Devon said defensively.

"Anyways, I think the book turns to spells that it thinks we need or can help us." Prue read the spell under her breath. "Except, this one looks like you have to fill in the blanks."

"Fill in the blanks?"

"What are you a parakeet?" Gus joked.

"Shut up before it's round two," Devon objected.

"Here it looks like you have to finish the spell:

Devon pondered for a long moment in contemplation. What did he really want? What did he really need? If he was going to go along with all this, this was his chance, his opportunity to see if this magic was for good or Satan's workshop. He was having premonitions that were bad, but he used them to protect innocent people, something good. But if he could make his own wish, what could he do so that he wouldn't have to keep relying on his visions to protect them, so that more goodness could be in the world? The answer appeared.

"But before you do anything," Prue interrupted, "I'm going to cast a protection spell so that if anything else weird happens, we will be safe and okay here."

Prue walked over to the book and commanded it, "Find me the protection spell." Nothing happened. She held her hand over the book and said it once more, "Find me the protection spell." Still nothing happened.

The guys tried to hide their chuckle. She looked over at them. "It was worth a try." Prue flipped through the book, passing the lovebirds potion, turning from the past life spell, ignoring the deflection, projection and magnification spell, and the invisibility cloak until she finally reached what she was looking for.

She moved with a quickness, it was clear to the guys that she had used her time wisely to study up on the book and all of its secrets. She took three white candles, arranged them in a triangle, one a few feet from the front door, one near the garage door and the other by the kitchen entry way. "This spell should protect us in here from anything trying to get to us." She lit her candles, set fire to a bundle of sage that smelled God-awful, threw around some handfuls of a mysterious oil, and read the spell.

The boys were amazed to see what a quick study she had become. They half expected ghosts or angels to appear around them, floating, playing their harps and trumpets. "Now, we should be good to go. Are you ready to say your wish, Devon?" Prue asked.

Devon nodded his head. He searched for the page again, but as before, the pages flew as if they had wings, right to the spell he was looking for. He hesitated, a bit of fear in his voice that he wanted to keep hidden from Prue and Gus.

Prue and Gus were flabbergasted by his wish, followed by a loud explosion outside. Prue and Gus leapt over to the living room window when suddenly the TV hanging on the wall magically turned on, flipping channels, as it did the pages, until resting on the local news station. The news headline read breaking news, as the reporter in the field announced, "This just in, the world is in chaos as all police officers have suddenly vanished from the world. No more police stations. No one protecting our houses and homes. The world has gone mad."

Prue, Gus and Devon stared at each other until Devon ran out of the house, needing to see with his own eyes the effects of his spell. Running down the street, he reached a cul-de-sac where he saw Prue's neighbors arguing with each other. Devon attempted to run across the street when he was nearly hit by a car, the driver crashing into another parked car alongside the road.

140

As Devon watched, the driver exited his car, a beer bottle in his hand. He walked over to the barely conscious driver, whose window was already rolled down, and without notice sucker punched him in the face. From Devon's right, he could hear someone firing a gun. They appeared to be on the top of a building. Immediately the neighbors got to the ground.

Prue chased after Devon, "What the hell is going on?"

"I—I don't know. This shouldn't have been what happened. The spell must have gone wrong somehow. See? It must be evil."

"Don't blame the magic. You asked for no policing. How do you know this isn't what no policing looks like?"

"Because the community should take care of itself, that's why. The community wouldn't act like this. I mean this is crazy. People have common sense, and we still have laws."

"But who's enforcing them?" Prue noticed several men watching her from no more than 50 feet away. She didn't look any different than usual, but these three men were watching her, studying her. She could feel their eyes on her like she was an animal or worse, prey.

She nudged Devon to come back to the house, but he was unfazed. He couldn't accept what was before his very eyes. "I'm getting out of here." Briskly, she began moving back towards her house. The three men that were in the opposite direction drew nearer to her, following.

Devon was too much in a daze to notice. Prue sped up but she was no match for two of the men. One of them had drifted off, but two of them were hot on her tail. Frantically, she took off, running as fast as she could, fear stifling her throat. The men ran faster, yelling, "Tranny! Faggot! Tranny!"

Prue knew these words very well, she hated them, and she had to run. She had to get away from these men that clearly saw who she was and were taking chase to cause her harm. Obliviously, Devon was astonished when he finally turned around to see Prue wasn't next to him, and from a distance could see two guys chasing after her. Without hesitation, he went racing after them, his fists balled up, senses raised, ready to attack.

After what felt like an eternity, Prue finally made it to her doorway and slammed the door shut, startling Gus who was still watching the news trying to understand what was happening around them. "What's wrong?" he asked, puzzled.

Prue appeared comatose; she was there but she was not there. She felt only a few strings were holding her pieces together. She was terrified. She was embarrassed. She was ashamed. No matter what she did, the world would never see her as the beautiful young woman she was. There would always be people that saw what she had been forced to be for so many long years. Gus drew closer to her, taking her to the couch, holding her. Feeling his warm embrace was the permission she needed to fall apart.

Seconds later, they heard the pounding on the front door. The two predators had caught up to her and were determined to get inside. Pounding continued and then mysteriously ceased, tears streaming down Prue's face. Gus tried to look over his shoulder. The door suddenly opened. To Gus's surprise, Devon walked through the doorframe, rushing over to Prue's side. "Are you okay? Did they do anything to you?"

"Who? Do what? Who were those guys?" Gus asked.

In Gus's arms, Prue began to tremble and shake. Suddenly three red bricks crashed through the living room window, glass shattering all over the kitchen counters and floor. The thunderous shouts of protestors followed. The predators had increased with more people, yelling "Faggot, Tranny! An abomination."

Prue had fallen apart, Gus was beside himself, trying to understand what was happening while Devon was in attack and protect mode. He leapt up, searching for anything in the house to use to beat the protestors senseless. Almost magnetic, like it couldn't bear to part from the window frame, the broken shard pieces began swimming through the air, piecing back together the window until the kitchen floor was clean of any shiny pieces and the window was intact again.

Gus and Devon were in a state of shock. Devon looked twice, three times at the window, almost like he couldn't believe what he had just seen, but he had seen it. He went to the floor to prove to himself that in fact three bricks had been thrown in but before his eyes the bricks began disappearing and seconds later had completely faded away.

"I can't take much more," Gus sheepishly said.

Unfazed by the window repairing itself, the two guys who had become the ring leaders of the violent protestors were trying to force the door in. Inside, Gus and Devon could smell the smoke embers filling up the vents, Devon could see the garden shrubs underneath the kitchen window set ablaze. But as the flames tried to grab hold of the building, the walls, the soil underneath her house, the fire would not hold. The protestors tried again, over and over to set the house on fire but like an igloo, the house refused. The protection spell Prue had cast had been protecting them, but no one knew how long it would last.

"What are we going to do?" Gus panicked. Leaning towards Prue, "I know you're in there. We need you now. Help us figure out what to do."

Trying to find herself again, she uttered, "We must go. We have to use the time travel spell now if we are going to get out of this."

"But how does that change what's happening now?" Devon asked.

"If we go back in time, maybe the changes we will make will have prevented this from happening. At the very least, we can go back in time to the moment before you said this spell to prevent you from saying it in the first place."

Having everything to lose, the three hurried up and located the ingredients Gus had just used for the time travel spell. Gus grabbed the candles upstairs. Prue took the sprigs of rosemary and crushed amethyst and Devon watched silently, panicking to himself in case this spell didn't work. He looked through the book for a return spell or a reverse spell, but he couldn't find one. The Book of Spirits Past continued to flip back to the addendum to the time travel spell, but much like Gus, he had no patience to read it. Even his own spell that he had read only moments ago appeared to have vanished. He watched the words disappear in front of his very eyes.

The three stood in position, Devon trying to go with the flow as it appeared Prue and Gus were more familiar with this. Gus began saying the spell but abruptly stopped, realizing his error. "I forgot to prick my finger."

"Prick what?" Devon sighed.

"Don't be nervous," Gus said.

"I'm not nervous. I don't know where that knife has been."

"It's going to be in your finger in a few seconds." Gus walked over to Devon and before Devon's reflexes could respond, he had already pricked his finger and was squeezing it into the wooden bowl.

"Ouch. What the f----?"

"Your reflexes are a joke, man," Gus laughed.

Gus pricked Prue's finger next and then before he started again at the spell, Prue interrupted. "Let's grab the book this time so that we can say the return spell when we need it."

"But I didn't find a return spell," Devon said.

But Prue couldn't hear him. Pounding resumed at the door, this time with a louder, larger, and angrier crowd yelling, "Faggot! Tranny! Kill him!" The windows had been broken again and particles were flying again in midair to repair it again. They could smell an odd gas filling the house and then miraculously disappearing and turning into daisies and orchids suspended in air before falling to the floor. They were running out of time. The three put their hands together,

144

Book of Spirits Past in Prue's other hand and started to say the spell at once.

"Wait," Prue interrupted. "Gus, I think you have to go first." Gus looked surprised. "You lost your brother years before we lost the people we did. We are going to go back to your time first and then see how we can catch up to the rest of them."

Gus nodded in agreement. Holding each other's hands, standing in position, they read the words to the time travel spell and hoped with all their will that it would take them to where they needed to go.

"Blood to Blood, Soul to Soul, Spirit to Spirit; the steps I walked, may I travel again; take me back through time, where I can unwind, and walk where I once walked again."

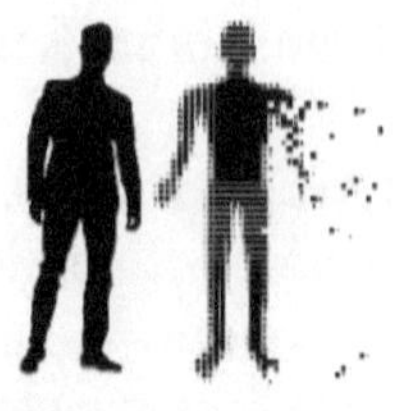

22

Journey to the Past

It was a bright, sunny evening. Without even opening his eyes, he could see the beauty and the calmness in the ocean as the waves bounced from one side of the beach to the other. The fresh scent in the air. The sand between his toes. The pelicans flying overhead, on a cloudless evening as the sun began to set, day turning to dusk, twice becomes twilight.

The trio was afraid to open their eyes to find out if their wish was granted, if their spell worked, if they were rescued from the present and back in time to save the ones they loved. They didn't know if it worked but before ever opening their eyes, they knew wherever they were, it was safe. It was calm. It was tranquil.

In sync, the trio decide to take the chance, and they opened their eyes. Speechless, Prue, Devon and Gus found themselves in the dunes of a sandy beach, waves ripping calmly, hardly anyone in a mile's distance, this piece of paradise to themselves. They held on for dear life, hoping this moment would not be but a dream.

Gus walked around, slowly separating from the bunch. This seemed very familiar to him. A voice in him was calling him to remember. As he sought out into the distance, he could start to make out two figures that appeared almost like shadows. It was hard to see with the sun setting between his line of vision. Prue and Devon stood back, watching Gus as he continued to move forward.

He was trying to remember, but there was no need. From behind the shrubs, peering out through his line of sight, he was able to make out the image of two young boys sitting on the beach, their feet in the sand, surrounded by coral reef. One looked a bit bigger than the other, but it took him until he saw the younger one kick and push the bigger one down in the sand then run away that Gus understood what he was watching. He had seen this very scene when he had astral projected to this memory during David's 10th Annual Scholarship Foundation.

He saw what he had done and he recognized the look in his brother's face as he ran off and expected his brother to chase him. Remembering the guilt and shame that he felt knowing he was part of the reason why his brother decided to take his life. Gus couldn't sit idly by and just watch. That day he wanted to take over and tell his brother how wrong he was, that he understood him, that he loved him, that he'd always love him, and now was his chance.

Gus busted out of the shrubs, racing after himself. He saw his feet moving faster than his body could. Suddenly, his younger self turned around, ominously stopping Gus in place. And before Gus could utter a word, Gus watched his younger self vanish in thin air, a smirk on his face as the child Gus said goodbye. Out of everything they had already done that day, this should not have been so hypnotizing, but it was.

Scratching his head, Gus began to feel different, lighter. Everything he saw seemed different. He felt as if he were laying down, but he knew he was standing up. Gus didn't have time to think about this now. This was the moment he had been fighting for, that day at the beach when his brother was trying to confide in him and Gus acted like an insensitive dickwad. The Gus he was ten years ago would have had no idea, but this Gus did. He ran to his older brother.

"Wait!!!" He approached him, out of breath and sat down. The sight of his older brother living and breathing again immediately brought tears to Gus's eyes to which he couldn't hide.

"What's wrong with you?" David asked.

"Don't listen to me. Don't listen to whatever I just said. I love you. I'm here for you. You can tell me anything. I will always be here for you. I will do whatever I can for you. Please don't go away."

David seemed baffled and clearly caught off guard. "What's wrong with you? Did you slip and fall on your head?" he chuckled.

"David, I'm serious. I'm not joking. I love you. You can tell me anything and I will always be here for you, just don't leave me again."

"Again?"

Gus's thoughts were racing into each other at a disastrous speed. Now that he was finally here, he wasn't sure if he could say anything about what happened, how he got here. He doubted his older brother would believe that one day he met two people, and, in an elevator accident, he mysteriously was given powers that allowed him to transport out of his body along with his two friends. One who can freeze time with her hands and the other one that can see the future.

He found it hard to believe that his brother could believe that a magical spell in a magical book mysteriously found at an out of the way bookstore could send them back in time ten years to save him. He wasn't even sure if this was the moment his brother had decided to end his life and he didn't want to give him any ideas. Not knowing what to say and being afraid that he would say something that would change the future in an even worst way, he said only what he could.

"Yeah. I just wouldn't want something to happen to you. You're my older brother. I love you. I will move heaven and earth for you, always."

David smiled. "I love you too." The two embraced. Gus was wrapped up in arms that he had wished for, for ten whole years, that he could feel again.

"Is there anything that you want to talk about or tell me about?"

"Not really," David replied matter-of-factly.

"Are you sure? I mean, I'm here and I'll always be here for you."

"Gussy, I got it. Stop acting weird," his brother said, slightly annoyed.

"Okay, just wanted to check. Well, let's get outta here."

"Wait," he stopped. "We haven't seen it yet." Gus knew what he was talking about. They looked ahead, both enjoying the gentle waves, the pelicans flying in the distance, and the sunset as it touched the waters. And then it happened, the slight green tint as the sun set over the waves of the beach, saying goodnight.

Gus's heart was full. He had done the unthinkable, he had gone back through time to save his brother. His brother knew now that he was here for him, he would always be here for him, and that there would be no need for him to take his own life. Together at last. They had succeeded.

23

Surprise, Surprise

"Oh, my God. Oh, my God. Oh, my God, it worked." Gus was buzzing with such excitement, jumping up and down, higher than he ever could before. "Why do you guys look strange?"

Prue and Devon laughed. "I think you may have that backwards," Devon chuckled.

Gus stopped jumping.

"Because you look about ten years younger," said Prue.

Devon could hardly contain his laughter. "Looks like the way the spell works, not only do we see our past selves, but we become them."

Gus was awestruck, but he cared more that his brother was okay. They could figure out how to return him to his late twenties later. "It doesn't matter. Oh, my freaking God, it worked. The spell worked. My brother is alive. We did it!!"

"Not so fast there Sherlock. Is this the day that you lost him?" Devon asked.

Gus paused. "Well, no, but..."

"Then it may not be over then."

"What the fuck do you mean? I just talked to him. I just talked him out of it."

"Are you even old enough to swear?" snickered Devon. Gus went over to punch Devon, but his reach only made it to Devon's arm, and he could tell by Devon's laughter that the blow was a soft one.

It seemed going back in time, he truly became his old self, his strengths or lack thereof. Maybe when he saw the original version of himself, when they locked eyes, something about that meant only one of them could live at a time, causing the original version to fade away. This seemed different than when Gus astral projected. He could watch but he couldn't interfere and change anything.

"The question now is, how do we get back? Prue do you have the book?" asked Devon. She held open her hand.

"Is this a joke?" asked Gus. "That can't be the book. Where are all the pages?"

The pages looked bare. In their own time, The Book of Spirits Past was a large, leather-bound, extensive book full of spells, writings, and enchantments. This book, however, looked like the CliffsNotes version. It had the same front cover and some familiar writings, but flipping through its thin pages, Prue could tell it would be little help to return them to their own time or move them to the next time period. They could hear footsteps approaching followed by the baritone of David.

"Quick. You two have to go."

"Go?" They both looked at each other.

"I have no idea how to explain the two of you, especially since I now look ten years younger, or am ten years younger here, or whatever the fuck is happening."

Prue and Devon didn't know what to do next. Prue knew they needed a return spell to get back to their own time, and she knew she needed to find or come up with a new spell to help them accelerate through time to get to where she and Devon lost their friends. But time wasn't on their side. They had to go quick.

24

The Way it Never Was

"Are you just gonna keep following me?" Prue glanced at Devon as she continued walking off into the late evening, dusk setting across the skies.

"Pretty much. Ten years ago, I wasn't in this city. I'm not from here so you're the best choice I've got for a place to stay." Devon followed her.

Prue stopped. "So, I guess that means you kinda need me…again," she snickered.

"Don't get used to it," Devon sneered. "So, what's your plan anyways?"

"We are going back to where I lived ten years ago. I lived with my mom in our two-bedroom apartment in the inner city. It's gotta be like 25 minutes from here."

"Walking?" Devon questioned.

"Surely you can hang for 25 minutes. I mean, we just traveled from the present to the past, casting protection spells and eradicating police all over the world. Surely walking for 25 minutes should be easy," she chuckled and continued onward.

Devon had little choice but to follow. Walking for over 40 minutes, Devon nearly lost all hope they would make it to a place they could sleep for the night. He was becoming more disappointed that during the time travel, they didn't teleport money that they could have used to book a hotel.

In the pitch black of the night, Prue was lost, never walking from Emerald Beach to her childhood home. Luckily, once they made it to the Lakeview Branch Library, she knew they were only blocks from home. The streets were busy with an air of nostalgia surrounding her. She knew things were different but they still seemed more or less the same. The cars looked a little older than her current time but not too far off.

The tall, leaning palm trees were fuller but they were the same trees she knew. The pockets of people on each corner were hardly any different than the crowds of people she passed in her own time. She was so immersed in her own sentiment that she didn't recognize Devon's surprise as they passed the 30th Street and University sign.

"Wait, you live near here? Or, lived?"

She stopped. "What?" Devon gestured to the sign.

Unshaken by Devon's surprise, Prue answered, "Oh, yes, I don't live far." Prue's focus was following her instincts, retracing the steps she had taken many, many times for many, many years. But this time, she walked them not as Doug, but finally as the woman she had always been, and with all people, Devon.

If a boy like Devon had noticed her years ago, she surely would have had a grand mal seizure and died slowly and truly over and over again. She was only used to meeting boys like Devon in the depths of the local park after dark where the cars would park under the moonlight, and she'd tempt the faceless men under the midnight trees with the moon gleaming as she swallowed one after the other, draining their souls.

They were almost there. She could see the light emanating from her upstairs bathroom window. This was the nightlight she turned on once it turned 9pm and until she went to bed. She stopped.

Devon abruptly stopped with her. "Why are we stopping?"

Prue was at a loss for words. She was worried that she would find herself in there and she remembered what happened when Gus ran into himself earlier that day. He became, and took the full image of, who he was at that time. She never wanted to see or feel that again. She didn't want anyone else to see it, especially not Devon. She clamored for an excuse, "Because if anyone is in there, how are we going to get in? We can't just walk in and announce that we are from the future. We need a plan."

"I thought this was your plan?"

"Well plans change."

Devon grew impatient. "Then what are we going to do now?"

Prue tried to immerse herself into this new time that they were in now. It was ten years ago from the day they had left. What was going on in her life at this time? What was her life like now? She had found her apartment, but she knew she couldn't go inside without the risk of changing into her old self. Then it came to her. "I used to rent out the garage below, that garage," she said while pointing. "I wonder if I'm renting it now."

"Huh?"

She ran across the street and braced herself, standing in front of a large forest green, wooden door. She looked around the edges to see if she could locate anything. If it had a padlock, this would tell her she was renting it out still. If it didn't, then they were shit out of luck. Devon soon followed behind her. Blind without light, she felt around the lower corners of the garage entry. The left side yielded no luck but on the right side she could feel something hard.

It was a flash of light from a car turning onto their street that gave her the answer she needed. Before her was the iron, black padlock that still had her initials inscribed into it. She felt relieved. "Yes, here it is."

"But what now? How are you going to open it?"

"Open it? Oh no…" Her relief was short-lived. She had completely forgotten she still had to open it. She turned it over where she could see numbers. "I don't remember what the code is." She got off the ground, ready to give up.

"You can't give up so easily. We just got here," said Devon. "Just think, 'ten years ago' is now today. Breathe, and like muscle memory, just enter the combination."

Prue took a deep breath in and followed Devon's instructions. She didn't overanalyze it. She just walked up to the lock and entered the numbers that felt right for her and like magic it opened. She stood back, amazed. Devon helped to manually pull the garage door forward to open it. Prue used to be able to do this with no problem but since she's been on HRT, the door was heavier than she remembered. Quietly they walked in and closed the garage door as to not alert past-Prue, who likely could feel the vibration of the garage door from the ceiling to the upstairs floor.

There was total darkness. She had forgotten what was inside until she ran into a heavy piece of furniture. Then she knew exactly what to do. She headed to her right, calmly feeling around the darkness until she found it. And then there was light. The garage was full of furniture. A dining room table, two futons, two nightstands, two lamps, various boxes stacked on top of each other in the back, and a large white contraption in the left corner end of the room.

"Wow. This is your garage?" Devon was astonished.

"It was my lair," she smirked. Devon looked at her, surprised and amused. "This was where I brought my 'dates' so that they wouldn't know exactly where I lived and no one else would have to see them."

"Awe, very risky but nice taste."

"Thanks. Some of this belonged to an old friend of mine who now lives in Atlanta. He moved there after he retired from our local school district as superintendent."

Devon looked around, finding solace in that they wouldn't have to worry about where they could sleep, at least tonight. He stopped once his eyes spotted the large contraption. "What is this thing?" He moved toward it and opened the door. It looked like a closet except it had a few round holes cut out that were not too particularly wide but were perfectly circular. He looked up and noticed the monitor in the center of the backboard at about eye level.

"Um, I don't think you want to know what that is."

"Is this what I think it is?" He entered the contraption. Prue entered from the other side. "This is a gloryhole." Prue looked down. "You don't have to be ashamed. It looks nice. Very creative."

Prue had a perplexed expression across her lips. "Thanks."

"Well, I guess we better settle in." He plopped himself onto the couch and turned on the old-fashioned television screen. On the screen appeared two guys fucking the same girl, one in her ass and the other in her vagina. Devon hadn't expected this. He didn't know what to think, but he clearly liked what he saw.

Prue could feel tension between her genitals. She had recognized this feeling before. "Maybe, let's turn this off," Devon said. He stood up, popped out the DVD and looked to see if there were others nearby. Prue tried to pretend not to notice the bulge in his sweatpants. He tried to ignore it as well.

He finally stopped when he saw the movie, The Notebook. "You would have this, wouldn't you?" with a smirk across his face.

"Hey, nothing wrong with a rom-com."

Devon rolled his eyes. They sat on opposite ends of the two-seater couch, staying in their own territory. Prue got up only to turn off the bright light, leaving them with only the ambiance provided by the movie screen.

"I just don't get you." He turned towards Prue. "You're you..."

Prue looked confused. "Of course, I am me. And you are you," she snickered.

"No. You act like a typical girl. The dumb things you say. The way you dress. The way you act." Prue nodded. "I don't get it. I mean, this doesn't seem like it's an act."

156

"Because it isn't."

"I'm really just confused. The way I feel when I'm around you, it's just like I'm with any other girl." Prue inched closer to his side of the barrier. "You shouldn't act like this, be this way if you were born a man. YOU WERE BORN A MAN. But you don't act like one, you don't seem like one." He placed his hand in her hands. "You don't feel like one." There was a pause. "I just don't know what to think. You're not even like a gay guy or something so I'd know what to do with you. It's just like who you are."

Prue sat back. "What would you do if I were a gay guy?"

Devon looked at her directly in her face, "If I were horny as fuck, I'd let you suck me off, I'd bend you over and then I wouldn't ever see you again."

"Why?"

"Because I'm not fucking gay!"

Prue softened her voice. "But you are bi, that's a real thing and there's nothing wrong with it."

Devon turned away from her. "I don't consider myself bi. That only happens if I absolutely have no other options."

"You can call it whatever you want, but there's nothing wrong with it."

"Hey, I've got nothing against gay guys. That's just not me."

Prue nodded her head, knowing it didn't make sense to argue with Devon about his sexuality right now. But she was relieved to see that they both had something in common. It took a while for her to accept herself as who she really was, so she could understand that Devon was fighting his own level of acceptance still and would have his own valid experience, even if different than the one she presumed.

"I'm not trying to upset you."

"I know. Besides I'm not a guy so it really doesn't apply to me."

"Have you been this way your whole life?" Devon inquisitively asked.

She faced the adjacent wall, trying to avoid all possible eye-contact. "I've known since I was about four years old that something was wrong. People didn't believe me. My mother didn't believe me. The doctors didn't believe me, but I knew that something was wrong. I could tell my body was trying to betray me, it did things I didn't ask it to do, things I didn't want, things I never wanted. It was a way that I never ever wanted and knew didn't belong to me but as a little girl, I could do nothing but just watch it happen."

Devon connected to what Prue was doing, looking away kept her feelings from bursting out. Seeing her and hearing her this way gave him vision to see into her soul for the first time, as if he were seeing her the way she really was for the very first time.

She tried to hold back the emotion, but it still bled out, "I was a hostage in my own body, a body that never felt like mine. I had problems all through school because everyone wanted me to be something I never was. I was born to be a man but that was never who I was, that was never my destiny. I got into fights at school, boys didn't like me, girls didn't like me, and all this time I knew that something needed to happen so that I could finally be myself. But I couldn't until just earlier this year."

Devon sat closer, leaning on the adjacent pillow. "What happened earlier this year?"

"I started the first of several surgeries so that the real me, the me that I've always known was there, would come out for everyone to see."

"What kind of surgeries?"

"The 'male' parts of me that never belonged to me, they have been removed. Now no one can question if I am a woman. They can question all they like, but none of it matters."

Devon didn't know what to say. He could tell that this was really important to her and he was overcome with this need to protect her. "I don't know what you're going through. Honestly, I've never been good talking about emotions like this. It's probably why I act the way I do most of the times..."

"You mean like a dick, rude, arrogant, cocky..."

"That's enough adjectives for the day, Prue." They chuckled. "Since I lost Dwayne, I lost everything that kept me together. He had so much to live for. He was a good guy; he wasn't up to nothing. He always kept it straight and narrow...and then one day two police officers have nothing better to do but take his life away from him just because he was Black and because they could."

Prue empathized. "I totally understand how you feel. The day I lost Kaleb, I felt that same anger, pain, helplessness. He is...was...continues to be a great man. He didn't deserve to lose his life that day and certainly not in that way. It's heartbreaking, unfathomable pain to wake up one day and everything is different than it was yesterday. One thing and all of its changed forever."

"Isn't that why we are doing what we are doing though? To go back and change this to make it better?"

"I used to believe there was a God that did that, but he left me a long time ago." Prue could feel the words burning the inside of her throat.

"I don't know about that."

"What do you mean?"

"Well, look around. We are here now, aren't we? Something had to give us these powers to do all this crazy shit. We certainly didn't do it ourselves. Call it God or some other divine energy, something's working with us to guide us and help us be okay."

"Then why didn't it do it for Kaleb and your friend Dwayne?" Prue crossed her arms.

"I really don't know. But maybe with a little luck we can find out tomorrow. We've already saved one guy. Maybe we can save Kaleb next and see what happens, especially when we get back to our own time."

For the first time in a long time, Prue felt a sense of peace beckoning at her front door. She hadn't felt this in a long time since she lost Kaleb. When she lost Kaleb, out came her steady faith with God and sense with the world and in came doubt, suspicion, and feeling utterly and completely lost in a world that just seemed to grow colder and colder each moment.

When she lost Kaleb, she lost the view of the world where everything could somehow work out in the end. There was no way that this could ever be okay. It felt no matter how hard you try and however good you try to live your life, you still end up paying the price.

"I guess I just don't want you to give up yet. Don't give up. If you need to believe in something now to keep going, believe in us." Prue was beside herself. The narcissistic, pompous, misgendering douchebag was somehow becoming a caring, compassionate gentleman with an empathizing heart and feelings. "Let's go to bed."

The two stood up and began pulling out the futon so that they could sleep tonight. Prue went around the side to find the comforters and the extra pillows. Together, they made their bed and it was time. Both fully clothed, lying next to each other, faces in opposite directions with a moat of pillows between them, they still felt as though they might as well have been naked.

"I'm sorry what happened to your friend," Prue said, breaking the silence. "I wish I knew what to say. I've been so busy in my own pain; I couldn't see yours."

Devon turned around and placed his hand around her. The two faced the same direction, unable to see each other but feeling intimately intwined on a deeper level that didn't require sight, words or sound. "I couldn't see your pain either. But we can get through this together."

Laying with this man felt different than the last time she laid with a man. She liked the feeling of Dominic, the experience of revealing her new body and being seen as the woman she was. But there was something different here. Not

160

only did it feel like Devon was beginning to see her as a woman, but he was seeing into her, he was emotionally connected to her.

For the first time, she felt there was a man she could rely on, count on. She remembered how he had run to come after her when those guys were chasing her. She felt his warm embrace around her hips as they lay in the dark pretending to find sleep when they were both replaying the events that led them to this very moment.

"Devon..." she said with regret in her voice.

"Yeah?"

"What will you do tomorrow if you see the real me?" two tears swelling in her eyes, the coolness grazing her cheek.

"I'm seeing the real you now. Good night."

25

Mirror, Mirror on the Wall

She was awoken by the sounds of snoring and a sudden shuffle of the garage door opening. She immediately winced and prepared for whatever lie she needed to tell to explain why she was down there. But as she laid there, nothing happened. Devon's hand was still on her side and he seemed even closer to her than last night. Here she was lying next to a tall, handsome, intelligent, college educated Black man that had a soul and a face and saw her as she really was. She clearly had to have been dreaming.

Prue didn't want to wake him, but out of habit, felt she needed to get up and check her hair and her face. She gently slid out of his grip and found it interesting how much lighter she felt. She felt different. She couldn't explain it. Sunlight streamed in from the cracks between the garage door frame. She headed towards the mirror and was immediately dumbfounded.

From the other side of the mirror, she saw an image she never wanted to see again. She saw the image of a teenage boy with short hair, a thin body, and something in her pants that she had long said goodbye to and never wanted to have and feel again. Instantly, she fell to the floor, engulfed in tears. The fall caused Devon to stir. He turned over to find she was no longer in the bed with him.

"Prue, what's going on? What's wrong?" She immediately crept behind the couch as he began to wake up. "Are you okay?" He stood up in his morning glory.

"No! Stop! Please!"

"Talk to me. What's going on?"

Prue knew what must have happened. Past-Prue must have come down to the garage to entertain someone and that's when she must have become him again. She began sobbing. Devon understood immediately. He didn't know when but he knew that there was a chance that he would see the Prue from ten years ago and he would be even more confused. And so, he was. "It's okay, Prue. I already know. You don't have to hide."

Prue continued crying.

"You don't have to cry either. This is just the past." He took a few steps closer to her. "This is all temporary. We are just here so that we can change the future. That's the only reason we are here, to save our friends. But I need you to do that."

Once again, Prue heard his words and somehow found the calmness in the sea she needed to hang on and pull herself free. She didn't have her hair. She didn't have her make-up. She didn't have her fancy perfume, but those weren't the things that made her. She didn't need those things to be strong. She didn't need those things to be beautiful. She didn't need those things to fully become the beautiful woman she was.

"Now what I need you to do is get up and let's start working on a spell to accelerate time so we can get to your friend next. Is that okay?"

Her face being wet was okay. She was sitting in her own power and was now ready to get off the floor. Prue got up. She wasn't hiding anymore. She was right in front of him. "Now you see the real me."

"No. I saw the real you last night and you're still in there. I'm not afraid."

She began to pick her face off the floor and move through the emotions she was feeling so she could get back to the job she came to do, to save Kaleb. He was more important than seeing herself as the boy she never was and was never meant to be. "I'm going to look through the Book of Spirits Past and see if there is anything in there that can, in the slightest, give us a hint to creating an acceleration spell."

Her voice was lower, but Devon still recognized the intonations and fluctuations. He still saw her in there even though she looked different. She had her same mannerisms, her same body postures, and way of speech. Even though he was seeing a different person, he knew she was still in there. But he finally could understand, at this time of her life she felt trapped.

He could see her trying to get out, trying to fly away, trying to spread her wings, but she was being held back. And he wondered if this is what transgender people felt. He never had to think of his gender. He knew he was a man, that was a silly question to him. He was born with a penis, he liked it, he liked being attracted to women, he liked being seen as a strong, intelligent man. He never thought about these things.

But this Sunday morning, he thought about these things. He thought about what it would feel like to be trapped, to have no way to get out on your own without the help of other people writing letters and insurance covering surgeries just so you can finally be yourself, see yourself, feel free. Freedom. He said he was unafraid, but he was scared inside, because whatever it was he felt last night, he still felt this Sunday morning even though she was still trapped inside herself. And now all he wanted was to set her free.

26

The Day that Repeated Itself

Gus was overwhelmed with excitement, something he hadn't felt in years. Here he was, sitting downstairs at his old kitchen table with his mother, whom for once didn't look like she had been crying all day. His father, whom he hadn't seen in years, was surprisingly sitting at the table and didn't smell the slightest of alcohol. And most of all, his older brother David was indeed alive and eating all the silver dollar pancakes covered with strawberry syrup.

This was the family he remembered on this beautiful Sunday morning with the sunrise above, peeking through each window, a cheerfulness in his step, a feeling that all was finally right in the world. Laughing, joking, this all felt so real. He wondered to himself just what would happen if instead of returning to the present, he got to relive these years the way it should have been. He would have more time with his brother now than if he sped forward ten years, losing all the memories, laughs, experiences, moments along the way.

He wondered what his brother would look like when he returned to reality, what David's life would be like. Clearly, he'd be famous, his face on every bran and frosted flakes cereal box cheesing. He'd be the most famous and successful Olympic swimmer with drop-dead gorgeous models hanging on his every word, medals, and awards all over his fancy house, dripping in gold. How he envied him.

Why in the world would David want to take himself away from all this? A question Gus never could answer, and it brought too much pain to even fathom. He would show him around. He would go back to his regular time and find that they were the best of friends. He would go forward in time to find that David was happy, and he was still loved and that he was there for him and that -

"Hey goofball. You're hogging the strawberry syrup. Give it up or it will be your ass."

Gus beamed from ear to ear. "Right. Because you should be eating all of this before your swim meet. You know you have your trials coming up," Gus replied while passing the syrup his brother craved that Gus started to only love after he had passed.

"Swim meet? Oh yeah."

"Of course, our son is going to take us all the way to gold, make the Brooks name proud. Make something of himself," their father interjected.

"Oh Dad. I'm just going to try my best. I'm sure that will be enough."

"Wrong. Your best is not enough. You have to be better, greater. This isn't your sport. It's the white man's sport," his father said.

"Oh Michael, will you relax? Let the boy eat in peace." This was a tone from his mother that Gus had completely forgotten. She sounded relaxed, happy, elated.

"Thanks, Mom. No, Dad's right. I have to be the best. That's what you guys taught me."

"That's right, son. Failure is not an option," his father happily serenaded.

There were two loud blows of a car horn outside. The family directed their eyes to Gus who was so enamored in his breakfast that he hadn't noticed.

"Gus?" his mother asked. "Aren't you going to get your stuff?"

"Huh?" looking up from his hash browns and sunny side up eggs.

"It's time for you to go. I hope you're ready for your meet today too."

Gus nearly choked on the sausage now stuck in his windpipe. "What meet?"

"Are you kidding?" his mom asked. "It's your trials for varsity swimming. You've been only talking about it all month."

Gus was lost. He didn't know what was happening. He had forgotten he was back in time and had a role he was supposed to play, a life there of his own. He had forgotten all of this. His life had completely changed that day when he came back home and found his brother hanging from the ceiling fan. He completely forgot about varsity swim because he decided that he wasn't going to do it anymore. It took him six years to decide that he was going to try out again and he only really immersed himself into swimming because it helped him feel close to David. Stammering to find the path he was to take now, he tried to play to his role. "Oh, right. I guess I should get my stuff."

He went to clear his plate, but his mother stopped him. "What are you doing? I'll take care of that. Since when do you clean your own plate anyways, Gus?"

He looked up at her. "Oh, I don't know. Since I graduated high school, Mom." He immediately regretted his words since in this time he was still a junior in high school.

"Gus, are you feeling okay?" His mother went over to feel his forehead. "Maybe you should stay home, try out another time."

"Are you out of your goddamn mind, Maureen?" his father pummeled. "He's going to trials today. He's not going to have another chance until the summer of next year and then he'll be too old. These white kids started out years ago, Maureen! What are you trying to do to him?"

"But honey-"

Gus interrupted, "Dad's right. I'll go get my stuff." Gus started up the stairs then suddenly started to feel this mysterious feeling in his stomach. It was so strong, strong enough for him to come back down the stairs and return to the kitchen. "Hey Mom, Dad, where are you guys going?"

"To David's meet of course," said his father quite matter-of-factly.

"Oh!" Gus replied.

"We talked about this," his mother said. "This is a very important meet for David. But we will make sure we make it to as many of your meets as we can this year, if they don't overlap with David's, okay?"

Gus felt a different feeling rising in his upper body, one he had almost completely forgotten. Moments like these where he remembered how his family lifted David up and made it crystal clear that he was their favorite. In the past, these were moments where Gus would get angry and jealous and say negative things to David because he felt insignificant, that he would never be enough. But now, he knew better. He knew what those feelings were and where they belonged, so he didn't give them to David. It wasn't his fault. He knew that now. "And David, where will you be?"

"He'll obviously be at the Olympic Trials. Seriously Gus, are you okay?" his mother asked. The horn honked a third time. "Hurry up. Go grab your things. Dad and I are leaving with David right after you in the next fifteen."

"Actually, Mom," David interjected, "Stacy is going to drive me there. I've been looking for my lucky swim trunks and I can't go without them."

Gus fixed his gaze on David.

"David, are you serious? You're going to miss the trials," his mother panicked.

"I won't, Mom. I just need to get those first. Failure isn't an option remember?"

"Boy, you better get out of here or you're not going to make that varsity team and you really won't like me when I'm through with you," his father squarely addressed Gus, giving him the chills as he always did any time he raised his voice like that.

Gus hurried up the stairs, befuddled by his racing thoughts. A part of him wanted to go to his varsity meet, knowing that his brother would be alive when he returned this time, but the other part of him wanted to stay just to make sure that he had done what he came to do and to make sure his brother had changed his mind.

Two more honks followed by some yelling of choice words from his ride outside. Gus had to get a grip. He had talked to his brother, told him he loved him, told him he'd always be there for him if he needed to talk. His brother wasn't going to kill himself again. Not this time.

Gus was still unsettled in his spirit. He wanted to ignore the warm, strange feeling inside, but it only continued to intensify. He had to do something. He needed a reason to stay home, even though he would face hell from his father. An idea came to him. He entered his childhood bathroom, the car stickers still on the wall, and stuck three fingers to the back of his throat, hoping this would save him. Seconds later, he felt the most magnificent breakfast he'd eaten in ten years come out of his mouth in reverse and spray all over the toilet bowl. He moaned so loudly that even his ride outside could hear him puking his brains out.

"Gus? What the..." he could hear his parents say as they marched up the stairs through the hallway. Gus didn't have much time for planning. He grabbed the old thermometer he used to use to get out of biology class and raised it to the bathroom lightbulb. He could hear his parents' footsteps approaching.

"Gus, oh no, are you sick?" his mother asked, grabbing a warm towel. Gus stayed bending over the toilet bowl while knowing his mother would look for the thermometer conveniently placed on the countertop, assuming he had just taken his temperature. "Oh no, this is 100.4. You're not going swimming today. You're going to stay right here," his mother went to comfort him.

Gus slowly got off the toilet bowl, took the medicine his mother gave him and then went off to his room, slipping quietly under his Cullen Jones bedspread and matching covers. His brother's bedroom was right next to his. He waited until his parents sounded like they were about ready to leave, then he ran to look under the door as he could see and hear them from two nearby mirrors at the front and end of the hallway. A few minutes later, he heard his parents closing the door and starting the old Subaru outside. Once he saw the car driving off, he pressed his ears close to the wall so he could hear everything happening in David's room.

At first, he couldn't hear anything. *Maybe David's already left.* After fifteen minutes, this answer didn't seem to satisfy him. Gus leapt out of his covers, opened his door and… *Oh shit!*

All of a sudden, the strangest thing was spinning on the floor outside his room, emitting shards of metaphysical light from another world. It looked like pieces of the floor had been burned away by a colorful acid and the spinning spiral stood in its place, almost like a tunnel of some kind to a new dimension. Gus had no idea what the heck this was. He had never seen anything like this.

Curiously, he bent down to take a closer look. He could feel the wind through his hair and upper body, trying to suck him into it. He grabbed on to his bedroom doorknob to keep him from being pulled in. The winds grew harder. Gus's sock was totally absorbed, he watched it be sucked into another realm for all he knew. Gus had to hold on. He had to find a way out of this.

Holding on for dear life, he held on to the doorknob, positioned his feet against the door…he had one chance to do this, and miraculously he swung himself to the other side of the hallway. He breathed a sigh of relief as he realized it worked. He didn't know what kind of magic this was but whatever it was would have to wait, he had to check on David.

He went to approach his brother's door, being mindful not to get sucked into the portal in the hallway, but suddenly became more paralyzed by something different, fear. He remembered what happened the last time he opened his brother's door, all those years ago. He remembered what he found, he remembered how he felt. He was alone again, just like he was now. He couldn't seem to open the door. He had his hand on the doorknob, but he was too afraid to open it.

All the emotion seemed to return, the memories he didn't want to remember and had to forget. But he had to do this. He had come so far. He had to open this door; it was just one door. He had to open it. The fear was too much. What was the big deal? He had said what he needed to say to him. He had done what he was supposed to do. Gus stopped this inner critical dialogue within himself and decided to just do what he knew he had to. He calmed the voices in his mind, took a breath, braced himself and opened the door. And there he found his brother. *Idiot.* Listening to his music with his headphones.

"David, what are you doing? Aren't you going to your trials?" David didn't seem fazed at all that his little brother had just barged through the door unannounced. A stark difference than all the years before. David moved very slowly, seemingly distracted by something that was happening in his own mind. Gus moved nearer. "David? Are you okay?"

David was looking right at him but only this second time did he finally remove his headphones. "Yeah. Of course."

"What's really going on? Have you been smoking something?"

David made little effort to lie, "Yeah. So?"

"Oh no, is that what led you to doing it?" Gus believed he had thought this to himself.

"Led me to doing what?" David asked as he rolled up his next blunt.

"Oh, nothing," Gus tried to cover it up.

"You're not a good liar either," David chuckled.

"David, you can't do stuff like this. You're going to blow your chances at the Olympics."

"Gee, thanks, Dad," David laughed, licking the paper. "What if I don't want to go to the Olympics, okay? What if I don't want this grand plan that everyone has already picked out for me?"

Gus took a step back. He was shocked by what his brother was saying. He had been about swimming since Gus could remember. A part of Gus thought this was the weed talking, but another part of Gus knew this could be a side of David that he never got to see, much like when they were at Emerald Beach yesterday and all those years ago. He looked his brother in his eyes, "What do you want to do?"

David took a pause. "I don't know. I really don't, but I know this isn't it. This was fun before, but now it's all about competitions and titles and proving that we are worthy to the whites. That's not why I did it."

"Okay," Gus spoke in a voice that was completely unfamiliar to David, a voice David never had the opportunity to meet, "So what else makes you happy?"

David was bewildered. "I... I like video games. I like computers."

"Okay, well that's a start. That's something. You've found that out, maybe there's more or maybe there's something there that you'd really like. No one says you have to have all the answers right now."

"Are you kidding? Dad says that all the time. That we need to have all the answers now, a master plan so we can prove how worthy we are, that we are better than all the white people, not including Mom of course. We aren't white enough to be accepted by the white people in the Olympics, and we aren't Black enough to be accepted by the Black community either."

"David, that's not important right now. Forget what Dad says," Gus sat down next to his brother. "You have to do what makes you happy. This is your life. I'd rather you be happy with what you're doing than following a path not meant for you that was designed for, and by, someone else."

David appeared dumbfounded. "Who are you? You don't talk like this. Have *you* been smoking something?"

Gus laughed. "No. It's like I said at the beach yesterday. I love you. I'll always be here for you."

"Yeah, but you sound like I'm the younger brother. I'm supposed to teach you this shit, tell you what to do, inspire you to do and be better."

"Don't worry, you did. You will, I guess you always have." Gus reached over to give his brother a hug. "I think you should talk to someone about what's going on, like a therapist or a support group."

"Dumpster fire, no thanks. I'm not going to one of those things. Those things are for crazy people."

Gus smirked. "I know why you might think that, but that's not true. They can actually really help you out a lot, help you feel better connecting with other people who have experienced loss, gone through shared experiences, learned how to get through it and to cope." Gus himself was surprised by the words that were coming out of his mouth. Surely, he had to thank their group facilitator Mx. Thomas when he returned.

"Have you been to something like that before?" David sheepishly asked.

"Yeah, I have."

David paused, "Why did you go?"

Gus turned away from him. Never in a million years had he imagined he'd have the opportunity to say this, "Because I lost someone I loved very much. He meant a lot to me. I said the wrong thing and I never got to see him again and fix it, or tell him I love him, or make it right. I let him down." Gus tried to fight back the tears in his eyes, using his sleeve to end their departure.

David stood stunned. "Don't put that kind of pressure on yourself."

Gus turned around.

"If he went away, it probably had nothing to do with you. It was probably something he had going on in himself. It wouldn't have mattered what you said to him. If he made up his mind, he made up his mind."

Gus was astonished. The weird feeling in his stomach had been released and the tears were now coming down like a waterfall. David wrapped his arms around Gus and pulled him into a warm embrace, one Gus had longed for, for such a long time. "I'm sure he knew that you loved him and he probably wouldn't want you to feel responsible for something he decided to do." Gus was breaking down. And then came the sucker punch. "Even if he was your gay, male lover."

"What?" David laughed, lightening the moment and lifting his brother's spirits. "Whatever."

"Well at least the roles are correct now. I'm the older brother, you're the younger brother, that's all there is to it." David rubbed his brother's frizzy hair.

"Just for the record, I'm not gay."

"Right, sure. Our secret, my nizzle." The two chuckled.

"You've got to tell Mom and Dad. They are waiting at the trials."

"You're right. Let's go. I'll drive and you can help me figure out how to break the news to them after the trials."

"Good idea." Gus held onto his older brother for a long time.

He never had this moment with him but it was the moment he had so desperately longed for after all these years. This time, he wouldn't need to see his brother buried in a casket wearing a suit he knew his brother would despise. This time his father wouldn't have to buy the ugly, itchy suit that he never wanted to wear again that was hidden in the back of his closet. He was here, holding his brother, telling his brother that he loved him and nothing could take this moment away. Now he had finally found peace.

27

Like Sand in the Hourglass...

Gus could not have been happier. He and David made it on time to David's Olympic trials at the Sapphire Elite Athletic and Swim Club. They would come up with some lie on why Gus was feeling much better the moment they saw their parents. David was in the locker room changing without his lucky swim trunks, which he later confessed never existed.

For the first time, Gus was eager to see his brother doing phenomenally and blowing all the other competitors out the water. He was proud to share the same last name. He was going to be his biggest cheerleader.

As Gus looked through the stadium seats to find his parents, most specifically his father, who stood out due to being one of the only Black men there, Gus saw a familiar stranger out of the corner of his eye. He tried to follow him but there were a lot of people there and great fanfare as the Olympic swimmers for the U.S. team would be announced today. Unfortunately, he lost him but Gus was so elated with the festivities and excitement from watching his brother, he brushed it off and continued heading towards where he believed his parents would be.

He saw the familiar stranger again, he seemed to be pointing towards the adjacent stadium used for regular swim meets. It was large and white but these aristocratic folks only used the very best for the Olympic swim trials. That beautiful, gorgeous, freshwater pool with eucalyptus steam jet packs and a sauna were of no use for today. Poor rich white folks. Gus headed through the double doors over to the adjacent stadium and was indefinitely surprised.

"Devon, where have you been? Where's Prue? Who's this?" Gus asked without spending much time looking at the guy that was standing next to Devon.

Prue looked embarrassed; she knew she looked nothing like herself but it still hurt to hear.

"This is Prue," Devon tried to politely use his words carefully. "We travelled back in time to before she was able to transition."

"Oh," Gus said. Prue looked awkward and felt as small as an ant.

"Prue used a soul-searching spell which led us to you."

"Wow, this magic stuff is fucking cool," Gus was beaming ear to ear.

"Anyways, we have to go," said Devon.

"Go? Go? No. I just saved my brother. I figured out why he killed himself. He's going to be okay now."

"That's great Gus, but if he's going to be okay, you should be able to go back now."

Gus hesitated. "No. If I go back, all the years forward, we would miss everything in the middle. I would have no memory of it."

"I understand what you're saying but..."

"Are you okay? You don't sound like yourself," Gus interrupted.

Devon smirked. "Yes, I know. Look, I'm glad you saved your brother. That's great. That's why we came. But now Prue and I need to save the people we love, and we can't do that without you."

Gus looked at his feet. He knew they were right. Without the help of those two, he would have never been able to travel back in time to this moment to save his brother and give him a second chance at life. Still, he was ashamed, looking bashfully at his feet he admitted his selfish thoughts. "But I don't want to leave."

"I know you don't, Gus. But Kaleb needs me." Prue stepped in. "He died before his time and he is counting on me to help save him and all those other people on that airplane. Just like we helped you to save your brother, they deserve a second chance at life too." Gus was quiet. He felt the sorrow of leaving and the fear that this would all just be a dream.

"Gus, if this worked, you will see him again when we get back. And if not, maybe we can write a spell to send you back here for good," Devon suggested.

"I'm just being selfish," Gus admitted. He tried to bring himself together. "What do we have to do now?"

"You're okay?" Devon asked.

"Yes. You guys helped me save my brother, something I never would have been able to do without you. I owe you guys. So, what do we have to do next?"

"We have to say the acceleration spell," Devon said.

"Acceleration?" Gus asked.

"We are already back in time so the words we used to get here wouldn't work, they would just send us back further. We need to go forward, not backwards. We also don't have the Book of Spirits Past like we did before, nor the same ingredients, so I had to make a few adjustments," Prue explained.

"Okay. Whatever you need," Gus said.

"Okay guys. I took the liberty to write a new spell but we are going to need a few things. Something we can use as a portal, and some natural earthy ingredients. Something calm and tranquil."

Gus didn't need to think. He knew the calmest, most tranquil and serene place they could use. "How about the swimming pool?" They looked to what was right next to them, the rather large swimming pool that stretched about nearly two yards and had a fresh scent of eucalyptus.

"Oh, that's a good idea. We can use this as a portal," said Prue.

"A portal?" Gus asked.

"A time portal. It's something we can use that transports us to a different time. They usually open when you do something that changes or alters time or destiny," Prue advised.

Gus questioned, "What does a time portal look like?" Devon looked at Gus.

"It could be anything really. It has a force that tries to pull you back. Sometimes it's something in the walls, like a missing brick that if you fall through the wall, it takes you to another dimension. Sometimes a spinning tunnel, or in our case, a swimming pool."

Gus's mind raced to when he left his room to go to his brother's room, but instead ran into the weird spinning thing in the floor that tried to suck him in. "Okay. We can jump from here."

"Jump?" Devon asked frantically.

"Yes. We are going to say the spell together, and I prepared a potion that should help us." She pulled out a vial that had a blue silvery liquid in it. "Okay." She threw it into the pool. Within seconds, the quiet pool waters turned into roaring rivers. Steam soaring above, the sound of mighty rivers and a strong wind filled the gymnasium. "Are you guys ready?"

They could hardly hear her over the wind. Gus looked over the distance to see if anyone could see them and to take one last glance to see if he could see his brother just one last time. The three held hands and Prue, who had memorized the spell, trusted her heart with all her might to take her where she needed to go and began:

"Soul to Soul, Spirit to Spirit, give me wings to fly; take me forward through time to unwind that fateful day.

Make what was once yesterday today."

The swimming pool water turned a light, translucent blue and silver, shrouds of white light emerging from the crashing waves inside. Gus said goodbye to his brother in his heart, unsure of what he would find when they returned, but now there was only one thing left to do, jump. Holding their breath, all three took one large leap inside, Prue hoping her spell wouldn't fail her and her heart would guide their path forward. Out of the darkness and into the light.

28

Taking Flight

The park was still, the occasional breeze blowing through the leaves of tree branches. The sun was on the other side of overcast skies, trying to shine its way through. Beautiful, tall, forest green Ficus trees lined the street pavements and luscious green lawns.

Antique historical buildings lived here, mostly used as museums that housed centuries of knowledge and piqued interest. This included the Railroad Museum, the Natural History Museum, the Science and Technology Center, the Aviation Center, the Jefferson Observatory, the WWII Monument, the Automotive and Car Museum, the Archives, the Museum of Man, the Museum of Us.

Alluring steps descended below, leading to miles and miles of more elegance. Places to gather, food trucks, artists painting faces and henna tattoos. Vendors selling popcorn, sportswear, memorabilia, taco-on-a-stick, and deep-fried Oreos to name a few.

There were musicians performing with their top hat out, dollar bills and silver coins inside. Others dancing and performing, inciting the crowd's attention to enhance their tips while performing magic tricks. Pigeons fighting for breadcrumbs, homeless folks hidden in plain sight, a gentleman pacing back and forth having conversations with people only he could see.

The majestic Moreton Bay Fig tree with its twisted colorful broad branches, so full of force, so full of majestic energy and spirit. It sat at the center of the promenade, taller than all others, surrounded by an exquisite water fountain, shooting water out at various angles simultaneously with its ever-changing colors. Turning from a beautiful baby blue to an amber glow to a warm light, and a magenta before returning to a clear translucent color. The colors seemed to morph into one another like a mood ring, a beautiful bronze and golden light aura surrounding the fountain.

The waters began to heighten and rise, the amazing golden light above the fountain and the tree meeting the fountain below. The waters became a storm of bioluminescence, crashing into the fountain's waves with such power and force.

Suddenly Prue, Devon and Gus emerged from the other side and landed feet first on the ceramic tile ground. Prue was the first to gather her bearings. She almost immediately recognized this place as Plaza de Balboa, the largest historical park in the city.

"Whoa. Did we really just come out of that thing?" Gus exclaimed in awe, looking around to see if anyone noticed.

"Welcome back, Prue," Devon said noticing that she looked more like herself this time. They all did, even Gus was closer to his age.

"What year are we in now?"

The breeze picked up, blowing newspapers and trash their way. Trying to fix her hair and make-up just right, they were all completely drenched in the glowing water. She shook her head, hoping her hair wouldn't shrivel up as Black hair does when it's exposed to water. She looked around for a mirror, any mirror when she noticed a newspaper page snug under her shoe. She bent down to retrieve it and she noticed the date. Her eyes couldn't believe it. "We need to go."

"Go?" Gus asked. "Where are we?"

"We are at Plaza de Balboa. It's one of my favorite places to come to calm my mind but we'll have to talk about that another time. We returned to the very day his accident happens. We have to stop it."

A nearby bell tower rang seven times, each ring separated by a brief pause.

"Oh no," Prue exclaimed.

"What's wrong?" Devon asked.

"It's 7am. We have to get to him. His accident happens in this hour. This very hour!"

"Okay, okay. Where is he? Where do we need to go?" Devon asked.

"We need to get to Stone Mountain."

"Okay," Devon said.

"Wait that's about an hour away. We won't get there in time," Gus said.

"We have to get there in time. We have to."

"Gus, I have an idea," Devon interjected. "Why don't you astral project us there, like you did that one night?"

"What? I don't even know how I did that?"

"Yes, you do. You just have to think of where you want to go and take us there."

"Yeah, but I don't know where we are going. I can't see it to imagine taking us there."

Gus had a point, meanwhile Prue had an idea of her own. She reached for her phone in her pocket, it was time to research. But she couldn't. When she entered his name in the search engine, nothing about the accident came up. Everything continued to read as if he was still in the present tense. The accident hadn't happened yet.

"What are you doing now?" Gus asked.

"I'm going to pull up the airport they left from. If you can see pictures of it, you can imagine teleporting us there."

"Prue," Gus paused, "What if I can't do it? I only did it once."

Prue looked at Gus, placing her hand on his shoulder. "You have to. You are our only hope. We need to get to the James Dean Airport."

"Do you know which flight? Which terminal?" Gus asked.

"No."

"You're not giving me much to go on, Prue."

"I know, but I trust you." Prue glanced at Devon. "I have faith that we haven't come this far to only be forced to stop now. I need you to believe."

Gus felt the pressure, but he understood. He studied the pictures of the James Dean Airport in Prue's phone, trying to imagine the three of them there, inside the airport, trying to imagine them landing there, their feet on the ground safely. It was so difficult, there were many pictures and this was over 50 miles away. He knew he had to try, that he couldn't give up. He would do his very best. His best would have to be enough. He held Prue and Devon's hands, closed his eyes and took flight.

*   *   *

"Does this count?" Gus asked.

Prue, Devon and Gus were standing in the middle of the tarmac, planes with their large logos and flashy designs in each direction, several people in uniform rushing towards them presumably thinking they broke some security clearance, or simply to arrest them after seeing three magical beings just appear in the middle of a tarmac blocking planes from departing.

"We need to get out of here," uttered Devon.

"Hey though, I got us here. Props for me."

"Later, Gus," Devon shook his head. "Do you see where they should be? Quickly, Prue."

Prue looked around. She saw probably thirty planes, but she was struggling to find the plane that they would be on, and they were running out of time. TSA was only feet away from them, she feared they would lock them up, test them, bisect them and study them like insects to find out where their magical powers emerged from. Prue needed more time. She needed to find out where their airplane was.

That's when it happened. She made up her mind. In this moment, it was time to feel calm. She could smell the jet fuel, hear the airplanes revving their engines, and the yelling of the workers coming to take her and her friends away. She closed her eyes and she opened her hands. Everything froze. The birds in the sky, the revving of the engines sound ceased. The yelling of the workers coming to escort them away, security frozen in their steps. Not a single sound could they hear.

"Oh, my God. You are getting so good at that," Gus said in amazement.

"But you weren't angry?" Devon noted.

"I don't have time to be angry. I need to be calm and figure out where they are."

She ran inside the closest airport entrance door, looking for anything that could help her figure out where Kaleb was. And with success, she found exactly what she was looking for. Locating the flight information display system, the information was staring right at her. Kaleb's plane had taken off fifteen minutes ago. It was now 7:21 am.

Devon and Gus had caught up with Prue inside. They were in awe of a sight they had never seen before. The door must have been open because everyone inside the airport terminals were frozen as well, you could hear a pin drop. The boys marveled their magical abilities that seemed to have no bounds or limitations.

"What did you find out?" Gus asked

"They left fifteen minutes ago." Prue pouted but would not stand in defeat. "Gus, I need you to try again." She pulled out her phone but realized again this would be in vain. The accident hadn't happened yet so she wouldn't be able to find a picture of the airplane to show Gus, and without an image, he wouldn't be able to transport them there. Gus needed to know what the plane looked like inside and there was no way she could show that to him now. But she knew what it looked like.

"What do you need me to do?" Gus asked.

Prue looked up for a moment and then directly in Gus's eyes. "I think I need us to switch powers."

"Switch powers?" Gus was flabbergasted.

"Here, hold my hand." Prue reached out her hand.

With great skepticism, Gus hesitantly placed his hand in hers. She could feel the fear running through her, wanting to shake her up. She wanted to scream, jump out of her skin even as she needed this to work. There wasn't a spell or a potion in the Book of Spirits Past that she had read that taught her how to switch powers, so she was about to find out if her time studying the book was worth it.

Holding Gus's hand in hers, she voiced the spell that came to mind:

"Sharing with you what's mine, giving to you what's now

yours, as we cross the great divide, we exchange our

powers before our time."

Suddenly, a round, bright, glowing particle emerged from Prue and was floating over her head, followed by a round, silver, shiny orb which appeared to be floating above Gus. The two looked up, Gus in a state of shock, both anxiously watching to see what would happen next.

The two floating orbs appeared to be gyrating and as if they were going to fuse into each other when suddenly a third round, amber colored orb emerged, dancing over Devon's head. Prue and Gus were aghast, Devon perplexed, noticing the expressions on his two friends faces as they looked at him.

"What's wrong with you two?" he asked. He then realized they weren't really looking at him but something above him. He moved his eyes to where they were fixated, and he saw it. He paused, "What the fuck is that?"

Prue could hardly utter the words, "I think that's your power."

Devon was defiant. "My power? How is that my power? I didn't say the spell."

Their powers were now dancing in the air above them, and all but Gus's appeared free to move around. It was as if something seemed to be holding Gus's back. Prue was able to spot it, it appeared there was a silver translucent string attached to Gus that kept the power connected to him.

"Gus, your power is attached to this silver string. What is that?"

"Silver string? I have no idea. What does that mean?" asked Gus.

"I don't know. Your power is somehow attached to you. I think the string has to break to release it and we are running out of time."

"Oh the string. I remember seeing a string when I saw David in the other realm. I pulled the string and that's what brought me back to you guys."

"Well right now it's stopping us from switching powers." Prue felt panic instantly rising in her.

"Let's hold hands again. We seem to be stronger together when we touch. But I really hope nothing bad happens if we break the string." Gus had a look of melancholy.

"It should be okay and we can just rewind time again if we need to," said Prue.

Gus and Prue held their hands together hoping to free Gus from the silver string to allow their powers to switch. They held on to each other, first looking above their heads and then alas finally at each other. Prue could see the fear in his eyes, and Gus could see it in hers. And then the silver string broke from Gus, their powers jumping into each other, breaking apart their grip, flying to the ground.

"Oh, my God. Did you just make that spell up on the fly? You just make up spells on the fly like that now?" Gus was hysterical as he picked himself off the tarmac. "Did we just see what happened? Did that really happen?"

Suddenly a flash came to him. Fire, flames everywhere. Something large was burning. He could see thick black smoke. Gus gasped.

Prue's hands were shaky, but she had to try it. She flailed her hands, and nothing happened. A mixture of joy and sorrow filled her. She had grown used to her powers as if they had become a part of her. Gus tried to extend his hands to mimic the motion he was used to seeing Prue do, but nothing happened. "I don't get it. I'm doing it like you do."

"You have to feel it, remember?" Devon asserted. "She's usually feeling anger and then she does it like this." Devon flailed his hands and suddenly there was a loud explosion. He nearly blew up the Boeing 737 that was less than thirty feet away, setting it ablaze with a roaring and vengeful fire. The blaze was moving swiftly even though everything else had remained frozen. "Oh, my God."

"Oh, my God," Gus exclaimed. "You have her power. You weren't even in the spell."

Devon was panicking, "Shit, we have to put out that fire." He gestured his hands, placing them over his forehead when suddenly the three could hear the TSA officers screaming at them again and the sound of the planes revving their engines. Everything was unfrozen.

The TSA officers that were after them stopped, turned around to see the blaze and then ran to the aircraft to help evacuate anyone onboard. Other airport staff seemed to run out of the airport to also assist in evacuation and calming the fire.

"Open your hands again," Prue pled. She went behind Devon. "Feel the fear inside…" she put her hands over his and gestured "…and release it."

Once again, everything was frozen and still. Devon let out a deep sigh before they ran over to the burning aircraft. "Now focus on the passengers. Feel your desire to free the people that are still in here, feel your fear that if you don't do something, you will let them down, and allow yourself to do whatever you can to help."

Devon felt this emotion, he lived in it, he resonated with it. He gestured his hands as if he could feel Prue's hands on top of his, and the individuals on the plane were unfrozen. They panicked but with Prue, Devon, and Gus's help, they were able to get off the plane, walking through the fire.

Gus, Prue and Devon took a step back. In watching the flames engulf the plane, Gus realized what he was looking at. "Devon, I just had your premonition," he said.

"What?"

"This is exactly what I just saw moments ago."

They had exchanged each other's powers, which wasn't totally part of the plan but this did mean Prue would have a chance to save Kaleb. She checked her phone. It was 7:31am. She needed to go. "Gus, Devon, hold my hand."

"What are you about to do now?"

"Your power works by seeing the place you want to go? And how do I get there? What do I need to feel?" Her eyes were already closed.

"Love," he replied. She was already ahead of them. This is one thing she had plenty of, because she loves Kaleb very much, always and forever.

"Wait..."

With her eyes closed, she remembered the recurring dreams she had been having inside the plane. She could see the pilot with his shades and headset and the cream-colored leather seats of first class. She could hear the other pilot over the intercom and feel herself inside the plane with the fog that seemed to surround and engulf them. She was there. She could see all around her. She was in the front of the aircraft, watching the pilot trying to navigate.

"Oh, my God. We are on the plane," Gus said bewildered. "No thanks to Prue. You almost forgot to grab our hands to bring us here."

"Wait, should we be up here?" Devon interrupted. "Won't we cause more confusion?"

The sound of the engine and the motor spinning overhead made it nearly impossible for anyone to hear

188

anything. Prue appeared to be in a trance. She wanted to get to Kaleb, touch Kaleb, see him alive for the first time. She inched near him, passing several passengers buckled in their seats. She could identify Kaleb from the top of his head over the back of his seat.

She stopped herself. At the tarmac, people could see them even though they had astral projected. What if he could see her now? He would panic. She didn't need him to panic. She also didn't want her and her friends causing chaos on the plane, distracting the flight attendants and passengers further leading to alarm. She had to think of something quick. She glanced at her apple watch. 7:33. With a swiftness, moving her hand from the middle portion of her bottom lip to her hip, she uttered the words three times:

"Light as a feather, clear as the sea. Cloak us with

invisibility."

Instantly, Prue, Devon and Gus appeared completely invisible. And they felt the shift on the aircraft, it felt light. Prue wasn't done. She had to find a way to land this aircraft. She knew what would happen in the next few minutes. She was almost out of time. She wanted to move closer to Kaleb, but for now, her only job was to save him.

These poor people, why did this plane crash? She tried to look out the window, but she couldn't see anything. Everything outside the window was covered in this thick gray haze. She wished she could see the other side of this fog. She didn't know how much time she had left but she knew they had to be falling right now. There wasn't a second left to spare. She looked at Kaleb texting on his phone, head down, and Marco trying to look out the window, headphones on, mentally preparing for his interview with the coaches. Prue had to give it one last shot, the words escaping from her mahogany lips:

"Out of the darkness, out of the night, turn this fog into

light."

Immediately, the thick clouds of fog that surrounded them, shed bursts of bright sunlight, seeping through the sky. She was amazed, but they now realized they were falling through the sky, only moments from where they were destined to crash and take their final breath. Prue would not give up.

"No." The first pilot immediately jolted, grabbing the control and trying to lift the aircraft up, the second pilot following suit.. Why weren't there emergency lights or sounds or something letting them know they were falling?

The pilots tried to pull the plane up, desperately trying to change its current fatal direction. All onboard were now able to see where they were headed. The look of fear on Kaleb's face Prue had never seen before and didn't ever want to see again. The shrieks, the panic from all those onboard. She was not going to let it end here.

While Devon and Gus were fiercely afraid, nearly holding each other facing their own mortality, Prue matched fear in the face with determination and sprang into action. "Devon, Gus, get it together. We need to all touch the floor of the airplane while interlocking our hands." They could barely hear her over the screams.

She grabbed them, interlocking her arms into both of theirs, touching the floor of the aircraft.

"Light as a feather, clear as the sea. Help this aircraft land safely."

She said it again.

"Light as a feather, clear as the sea. Help this aircraft land safely."

She said it one last time with one final, desperate change, as she knew their time was ending.

"Light as a feather, clear as the sea. Help us lord, don't forsake me."

They hit the ground, emitting a thunderous crash against the asphalt. All went dark. For a few seconds, things were quiet, but the air was overcome with the strong scent of motor oil. She could hear something burning. She could smell it in the air as well. Prue felt she could hardly move. She couldn't feel her legs. She tried to pull herself up, but she couldn't. Something was preventing her from moving and also stopping her from being able to see.

Out of nowhere, she felt pressure on her head. Something had fallen down but she couldn't see what it was. It couldn't end like this. "Kaleb! Devon! Gus!" she tried to yell out. She couldn't hear any response. Fear set in. She knew she had to get up. She needed to know if Kaleb was okay. Nothing seemed to move on the plane but there was a lot of sounds outside of it. She wanted to know what was going on causing all the commotion.

Suddenly, she found herself floating outside watching several cars ablaze in this hiking trail parking lot, several people crying, falling to their knees in pain. Prue knew this feeling very well. Over a dozen thick trees and bushes were also on fire, covering the hillside. Within seconds, all she could see was fiery red and orange flames, thick black smoke cloaking the sky. The fire seemed to have set a trail, starting from the planes crash. The motor oil must have drenched the path but stopped where the plane crashed.

Prue investigated the plane, which was surprisingly intact, its pelican logo still in full view. It hadn't broken apart as it did the first time, but she needed to know if Kaleb was okay, and why Devon and Gus didn't respond to her. How did she end up outside the airplane when she couldn't move? She didn't know, but she felt herself inside the plane again, without using her legs or her feet, moving but standing still.

Then she could see why she couldn't move her legs. Prue saw herself, and her body was trapped. Though the outside of the aircraft looked intact, large pieces of metal and debris had fallen inside the aircraft and was crushing her, keeping her from moving her legs. She could see blood all around her body. She didn't care. She needed to know how Kaleb was.

She could hear the sirens blaring and voices outside trying to get in. They sounded like healthcare workers trying to rescue them. So many passengers already deceased, and then she saw him. Kaleb holding Marco, their seats were broken and they weren't moving, and didn't appear to be breathing. She ran to him.

"Kaleb! KALEB! NO!" she felt the sobs and the volts of uncontrollable pain running through her veins. They had come this far and did so much for it to end the same tragic way.

"Oh, my God." Every word made her whole-body shake. It couldn't end this way. She refused to go through this again. He deserved to live. She did all of this to give him a second chance to live. This spell was supposed to work.

God, where are you? Why have you forsaken us? Prue was not going to sit around and wait for an answer. She could feel the pain enveloping her heart, her arms holding him, fully embracing Kaleb. She wanted him to know she loved him. She wanted him to know she was there. She wanted him to know that she was going to do whatever she needed to do to make it okay.

She was too distracted by her pain to notice the spinning portal outside that seemed to be emitting fine blue and silver light particles. She held him and then something strange happened. As she held him close to her, she could feel him starting to move. She felt him trying to breathe, trying to come back to life. She felt this warmth in her soul and if she didn't know better, she would swear the warm gold light was emitting from her chest.

It seemed to travel from her to Kaleb as he tried to return to her. Then, out of nowhere, she felt it travelling outside of her, moving upward and then out. Sitting there holding him, she saw her magical power floating above three twisted metallic cylinders and a silver and blue magical power orb floating next to it.

It was so beautiful and magical; it made her turn upwards when she then saw a magical orb floating over her and then flew with a quickness out of the top of the airplane. Suddenly, Prue succumbed to the pain. She wasn't holding Kaleb anymore. She couldn't feel him in her arms. But she could hear help arriving. She couldn't move her legs. She couldn't see. She couldn't move.

29

Saving Kaleb

She woke up alone in a quiet place, wearing only a hospital gown and hearing only the faint dripping of her IV bag jammed into her arm. It took her a few moments to comprehend where she was and what was happening. She last remembered feeling Kaleb in her arms and then nothingness.

The room around her was small, a tiny television mounted to the upper corner of the wall, a locked medicine cabinet to her left, a clock on the wall which showed it was half past noon. Prue tried to lift herself up but it was with great pain. Before she could investigate any further, a knock beckoned at her door.

"Ms. Fancy Pants?" The familiar antics of Gus as he calmly opened the door, Devon next to him, both wearing matching hospital gowns that couldn't properly tie in the back. "I see you're awake, Princess," joked Gus with his habitual smirk.

"Gus, how can you find it in you to have humor and jokes at a time like this?"

"Bet you wish you knew," Gus chuckled.

Devon quietly approached Prue's bedside. "How are you feeling?"

Prue sat up in her bed. "I'm feeling like I want to know if Kaleb is okay."

"He is, at least he is responsive," Devon said.

"Responsive? What does that mean? Where is he?" Prue jumped up, her bare feet already touching the cold floor, oblivious to her pain.

Devon hesitated. "I'll show you."

Devon guided Prue outside of her room, down the well-lit, chaotic, noisy hallway which to Prue felt like a twenty-mile walk. She was anxious to finally see him, to see him living and breathing as she had so desperately wanted for so long. Gus followed them, catching them right at the closed door of a room on the opposite side of the long corridor.

Devon turned towards Prue, feeling the excitement in her body trying to jump out, "You may want to prepare yourself."

"Prepare myself?"

Prue didn't have time for games or cryptic messages. She turned back the hands of time to save Kaleb, he was the whole reason she was there. Frantically she lurched the door open and immediately had to hold her breath.

There she saw Kaleb laying down flat, mostly covered in white sheets, his eyes closed, his body connected to IVs that were attached to various hospital machines each making music of their own. She recognized one as a respirator and another as a heart monitor. She could see he was breathing from the monitors, but she couldn't see him moving. He hadn't returned to her.

She stood, stunned, in the doorway. "How did this happen? We saved David. Why couldn't we save Kaleb?"

The boys didn't know what to say, Gus was particularly quiet as he felt the guilt of knowing his brother was alive, while standing over Kaleb who would probably not survive.

"He's still alive," Devon contested.

"For how long? I-I don't understand." She began pacing. "I cast the spell so that we could land safely. I cast the spell to turn the fog into light. We astral projected onto the airplane to help them land safely. Why is this happening? They were just going to visit a college for Marco." Prue fought back the tears that anxiously wanted to suffocate her face.

"And for some reason, we don't have our powers now. I wonder if it's connected," Gus inquired.

Prue sharply turned her body to Gus, animosity taking hold of her throat. "Connected to what? Because I tried to save him?"

"No. Not at all. I mean, I think because he is-" Gus looked to the floor, he didn't want to finish his sentence.

"Because he is what?" Prue demanded.

"Because he *is* still alive, might be the reason we have lost our powers," Devon interrupted. "Because we've gone back in time and changed what was supposed to happen, this may be why we have no powers. We haven't met each other yet. No meeting, no powers."

Prue scoffed. "Oh, of course. Because our powers are all that's important."

"I didn't say that or mean that at all," Devon said. "I mean that..."

Prue was incessant. "We changed Gus's future, saved David, and things turned out just fine."

"Yeah, except that weird spirally thing outside my door."

Prue was perplexed. "What are you talking about?"

"It sounds like the time warp you were talking about. Maybe it started after Gus saved David," said Devon.

"Wait, are you saying that's a bad thing?" Gus asked.

Prue snarled.

"I don't have all the answers. I just know that we don't have our powers now. We must have lost them after the crash. As long as we don't have our powers, we aren't able to change anything."

"You've gotta be fucking kidding me right now." Prue was enraged. "Kaleb is lying here fighting for his life and you two wanna argue about some fucking powers. Who the fuck cares about our powers? I don't fucking care why they're gone. None of that matters. Just get out of here, now."

The boys stood disoriented by this turn of events. They had never seen Prue like this. "Didn't you hear what I said? Get the fuck out." She rushed over to the already opened door and opened it even wider. Gus and Devon exchanged looks, their mouths nearly to the floor, and slowly walked out of the room, Prue furiously slamming the door behind them.

She walked over to Kaleb's bedside, finally getting a closer view of him. It crushed her soul to see him like this. She held his hand. It took all of her to pull herself together, but as many times as she did, she felt herself perpetually falling apart.

Suddenly, the television mounted in his larger hospital room turned on to the news, the anchor reporting, "This morning a commercial airline made an emergency landing in a hiking trail at Stone Mountain, instantly killing over twenty hikers and park-goers and setting fire to the park, causing all adjacent neighborhoods to evacuate. The passengers and crew have been transported to UCSD, their conditions are considered life-threatening. We have received word that twenty of its occupants have already been declared deceased. From the fire, an additional nine people have already lost their lives."

Prue was in shock; she couldn't believe her ears. Images of families crying, wrecked vehicles, and the blazing fire that appeared to still be burning, threatening homes and neighborhoods took over the screen. Did she do all that? She didn't mean to. How could this have happened?

Somehow in trying to save Kaleb and the other lives on that plane, they had killed over thirty others, and the number continued to grow as the fire was still ablaze. They said twenty people on the airplane had already passed away. How could this have happened? Prue was just trying to reverse and rewind time so that he would have another chance at life. She knew she couldn't live with herself being responsible for innocent lives being lost because she wanted to save him. But she wanted him to live. This was all she wanted. She wanted him to have his second chance.

She looked down at him, still holding his hand. Pointlessly trying to fight back the tears that demanded release, she spoke to him. "I am so sorry. This shouldn't be happening to you right now. You should be on a campus tour right now with your son. I'm so sorry, Kaleb. I'm trying to do everything I can. I'm going to figure this out. I'm going to figure out a way so that you can come back and everything will be okay."

As she was sitting beside him, she noticed that something looked odd. When she moved her hand down to his legs, she couldn't feel anything. She pressed the sheets down firmly and felt nothing. Instantly, she stood up and pulled the sheets back to find his legs were gone. The pain came rushing through her like a freight train. She began to dissociate, feeling everything at once so much to the point that she felt nothing at all. She knew this wasn't right, and looking at his face and his scalp, with these bruises and the scars, she knew he would hardly survive. She knew that the Kaleb everyone knew was gone.

If he survived, he wouldn't be the same man that walked onto that plane, even worse if his son was one of the twenty that had passed. He would never be the same. He may not even remember who he was or have the mental capabilities to do anything again. Prue was ashamed of herself. She knew that this wouldn't work and that she needed to fix this. She couldn't delay another second. She had to find a way to go back.

Before she exited the room, she kissed his hand and lightly kissed the top of his crown, "I don't know where you are right now but I want you to know that I love you and I'm going to make this right."

Prue found it hard to leave the room but she knew she had to. She would love him no matter what form he was in, no matter how he looked but she knew he cared about his legacy, his impact on his community, and she knew this is not what he would have wanted. He would have preferred it more the way it was before than the way Prue had changed it to become. She had to figure out a way to change what they did and try time again.

This time, they knew what to look out for, she just needed one more chance to get this right. Prue kissed Kaleb's hand, placed it down to his wrist, kissed him on the forehead and left the room while she still had her strength.

She found Devon and Gus still in the hallway. "We have to go back."

Gus looked at her. "Go back how?" he asked. "We don't have any powers."

"I think we can use a time warp," she replied. Devon and Gus quietly exchanged looks. "Over thirty people are dead because of what we did. We can't just leave it like this. And Kaleb deserves a second chance. We just need to go back to the moment we decided to..." Prue paused, she wasn't sure the exact moment they needed to go to.

"Prue, have you used a time warp before?" Devon asked.

"Well, no."

"Then how do you know that it would work?" Devon asked.

"I don't, but it has to. Either that will work or I will say another spell."

"A spell is how we got into this mess in the first place," argued Gus.

Prue stared at him. "Oh, I see. Now that we have saved your precious big brother, now the job is done. That's all you care about."

"Hey that's not fair and that's not true. I willingly left him to get you here right now. I lost all those years I could have had with him."

"Shut up. Your brother is still alive. He's probably out there right now, you can't wait to get to him."

Devon intervened. "Prue, let's just think calmly about this."

"No, I don't want to think calmly. I want to go back in time to reverse what we just did. There is a fire going on that has killed dozens of people. Did you see that?"

Devon nodded. "Yes, we saw it."

"This isn't what happened the last time."

Devon put his hand on her shoulder. "I know."

"So, we have to go back in time."

"I thought you said we have to find some crazy time warp," Gus added.

"Same thing."

"No, not the same thing," Devon said. "We have been using a lot of magic and it's worked out so far..."

"So far?" Prue shouted.

"Until today, that's my point. And we still have to go to the next future to save Dwayne." Devon paused for a second. "Actually, what day is today?" Devon looked at his wristwatch. "Scratch that."

"You're giving up on saving Dwayne?" Gus asked.

"No. He was killed tomorrow night so there's no need to use anymore magic to travel forward, least yet, to save him. I have an idea. Why don't I stay here to help save Dwayne and you two see if you can find this time warp thing that Prue is talking about?"

No one was paying attention to the loud beeping over the speakers, or the bright and colorful magical orbs that had descended and were floating above Prue, Devon and Gus's head. The orbs had begun spinning and glittering like once before until they gently fell back into them again.

"What good will that do? Don't we have to stay together?" Gus questioned. "Our powers are stronger together."

"Gus, we have no powers." Devon opened his hands and gestured when suddenly the large windowpane next to them shattered into tiny pieces. The trio stood again frozen in shock, staring at the broken window.

"Um, how did you do that? I thought you said we didn't have any powers?" Gus asked, astonished.

In a flash, suddenly Gus, was surrounded by a dry, hot, desert. He could see huge boulders, some shrubbery that looked extremely dry, and the warm, hot sweltering sun setting in the distance. He saw a bird holding a stick flying into the ground without crashing. At once, Gus was back in the hospital hallway.

"Gus, are you okay? What just happened?" Gus was in a daze.

"It looks like we have our powers back," Prue said, rolling her eyes.

Several nurses rushed past the trio heading straight to the room Prue had just left. Noticing, Prue followed after them. Standing in the doorframe, she began to hear the sounds that had been all around her. Gus and Devon knew that they needed to be there for Prue. She was having to watch Kaleb die all over again.

Gus vowed to himself to do whatever he could to help her. Each time Prue felt sensations trying to come back, she allowed herself to disappear. She wasn't there. She couldn't see this happening to Kaleb. She wouldn't.

"Prue, look at me." Prue couldn't take her eyes off the nurses trying to bring Kaleb back to life without success. "There's nothing for us here. We have to go back and try time again," said Devon.

"Let's see if we can find the time warp. I have a feeling I may know where it is," Gus escorted Prue out of the room. Tears running from her face, she was writhing in pain. "I think I saw where the time warp is." Gus repeated, waiting for Prue to acknowledge anything.

Gus stopped and looked at Prue who was still looking away. "Prue, I need you to focus. You can take us right where the time warp is but we need you." He took Prue's hand and placed his hand on top of hers. "We need you." They were standing in the hallway with the lights flickering around them. "I need you to remember the airplane accident, where we were. Not inside the plane, but outside on the dirt lot." Prue winced; she shook her head refusing to imagine anything but Kaleb alive. "Please. This is the only way to take us there so we can give him another chance and save those other people."

Prue was hesitant but she wanted more than anything for Kaleb to be alive. She would give anything and everything she had to make him okay. She closed her eyes, trying to imagine the lot again. Gus whispered quietly, holding Devon's hand. "Remember the mountains and the hot sun and the dirt blowing in the breeze, and the dry grassy areas."

Shortly after he didn't need to finish. They were already there. They were on top of the lot, this time overlooking the airplane wreckage and the cars that were still damaged. It was taped off. Police and investigators were everywhere. "Don't stop. Keep thinking back. Think back before these people were here. Imagine what it would look like if these cars weren't here, if these aircraft pieces weren't here, if no one was here but the three of us."

Prue concentrated, she couldn't wipe the tears from her face, they continued to fall but her focus was on bringing Kaleb back, by whatever means necessary. She did it. They were in the same place but the vehicles were gone, the aircraft wreckage was gone, the caution tape was gone, the orange cones were gone, it was just the three of them.

"Great job, Prue. Now, let's look around. It's gotta be here somewhere."

Moments later, Devon approached a cracked boulder that had surely been impacted by the crash landing. Devon tried to move the boulder when he almost fell into the time warp. "Guys, I think I found it."

Gus and Prue ran over to him, Prue stretching her hand into what appeared to be the boulder but would lead them to another dimension or plane as her arm disappeared, opening a magical time portal. "This is it."

"Okay, so we found it. Now what?" Devon asked.

"Now you go back to find your friend Dwayne, and Prue and I will try this day again."

"But how will you go back to the start?" Devon seemed concerned.

"I'm not sure. But we will figure it out. Go find your friend. Prue and I can take it from here." Devon sighed, looking at Prue, immensely concerned, her head down, still feeling the pain of losing Kaleb not once, but twice.

"Good luck." He looked at Prue. "Believe in something greater." Devon turned and walked away.

"Good luck Devon." Gus turned to Prue, "Are you ready?" Prue took one last look at the quiet hiking trail, looking around at the sun and the clear skies, feeling the heat on her skin, the slight breeze in the air, and then she walked into the time warp, Gus walking right behind her.

Once inside, it felt like they were in a tunnel or an elongated cave. They could see interactive videos of themselves leading up to the moment they entered the time warp, as if they were replaying them on video. The videos floated and changed so quickly. Some scenes were going by much faster, appearing like hieroglyphics and taking the entire wall.

Everything moved so quickly with bright orbs floating and dancing around the inside of the magical tunnel. They could see their lives before their very eyes. Some sections of the tunnel had earlier experiences before they appeared to have even been born, others with scenes and stories with people they had met in their lives.

One scene in particular Gus remembered from when he saw his brother as his father in another dimension. All were in color, and they were moving so fast. Prue and Gus tried to move through the tunnel, but they felt a voracious wind trying to suck them through. Prue and Gus carefully turned around the tunnel, watching their step, holding on to each other. The wind sounds were so loud.

There was only one sense that Prue could truly listen to, the feeling inside her heart. Gus was incredibly scared, but he knew he had to put on a brave face for Prue, so he did. Prue would have known better but she was too busy looking for the moving images that would take her back to the day they started.

With great difficulty, she had finally found it. The more she watched it, the larger it became, but it moved so quickly. Before she knew it, it gravitated from their heads to a wall directly in front of them and materialized into a door. She could see herself crying in the hospital, then arguing in reverse with her friends, then waking up from her coma then holding Kaleb. Seeing these forced her to compartmentalize her feelings. She couldn't save him if she continued to let herself feel all of them. Something made her turn back to her watch.

Everything else in the time warp was moving in rapid motion but her watch seemed to rewind time at a steady pace. She knew the time she needed to return to. She had one hand holding a very frightened Gus and her eye on her right arm that was keeping track of the time on her watch. It would tell her when to open the door.

Just then, she felt a large gust of wind trying to suck her and Gus in again. It had to be now. Gripping Gus's hand, she opened the illuminating magical door and rushed out of the portal. To their disappointment, they found themselves not exactly back in time but running out of time, as they were now themselves falling through the sky.

30

Turning Point- A Defining Moment

Devon had finally arrived outside Dwayne's dorm. He had caught a lift from one of the hikers to the College Grove area and luckily for him, he knew Dwayne's RA who let him into Dwayne's dorm. Waiting inside Dwayne's dorm for Dwayne, technically a ghost, to walk through that door felt like both an absurdity and an eternity.

Looking down at his watch, he knew Dwayne was probably studying at his last class and heading there any minute. He didn't know what it would be like to finally see his friend, standing up, alive, walking, talking, being. All this time they had played with magic, cast spells, rewound time, forwarded through time, protection spells, exchanging powers, and not once did he even fathom that there would be a moment where he would actually see his friend, his brother, alive again.

Sitting on his living room couch, he anxiously walked around, pacing, reality starting to set in what was about to happen. He was going to see Dwayne alive again. Dwayne was alive again. Mrs. Harris would be so happy. He started to feel the excitement bursting at the seams along with the anger setting in of the reminder that this would be his last day, Dwayne would be killed tomorrow.

Devon heard the familiar jiggling of the keys and he prepared himself, staring at the door, trying to not stare at the door but staring, nonetheless. He could hear his voice before the door was even cracked. And then he opened the door, wearing his favorite denim shirt, blue jeans and books in his hand.

"Hey Dev. Who are you hiding from now?" Devon felt like he was looking at a ghost, all he could do was stare. "Dev, you been smoking something again?" Dwayne laughed it off, placing his mail from on top of his books to the kitchen table and then moving through the hallway to his bedroom to take off his bookbag.

Devon had to shake himself out of this. He knew exactly what was going to happen, his friend was going to walk through that door this evening and he would never see him alive again. *Pull yourself together.* He couldn't. He ran to the backroom and hugged his brother, tight. Dwayne felt this as the sincerest hug he had from one of his closest friends.

The two had been through Devon's struggles in the service, transitioning to civilian life and dealing with PTSD that Devon dealt with ongoing. They had been through Dwayne's continued struggles achieving higher education despite racial injustice in his program, semester after semester finding ways to turn pennies into dollar bills to afford all his expenses.

Plus helping Dwayne overcome patterns that didn't serve him as an adult anymore. Dwayne and Devon embraced, enjoying the moment they were in. The two pulled apart. "Dev, you good? What's up?"

Devon felt the tears swelling up in his eyes. "Man, I'm just glad to see you."

Dwayne chuckled. "Is that so? Well, I'll be here all week," he joked. Devon was unable to laugh. He knew the truth. "Are you hiding out from Stephanie, Veronica, or Cynthia?"

"Huh?"

"You know, whichever new girl it is. You've got so many. It's a wonder you can keep your head straight about who they are."

Devon needed to think of something. He hadn't gone to his dorm that day so he didn't have a script, he didn't have anything particular he needed to say. Or maybe he did. "I really can't keep up, but I was thinking how about we take a road trip, you know, drive off to Arizona, see the Grand Canyon."

Dwayne angled a look at him and laughed. "What I look like driving to the Grand Canyon?"

"What? It's a place to go, a lot of people say it's a spiritual experience."

"Who?"

"Uh, who?" Devon searched for an answer.

"Yeah, who?" Dwayne eyed him to put the pressure on.

"I'm sure they are out there."

"They?"

"What is this, a Judge Judy episode?" Dwayne burst out laughing.

"As funny as that is, you know I've got my midterm to study for. It's the day after tomorrow."

Devon looked disappointed. "Oh, right."

"But I'll see you for the Aztec game at my place tomorrow night, right?"

"Oh yeah. Sure." Devon did a double take. "Actually no, I think I'm meeting with Melissa for uh..."

"Don't even finish that sentence man."

"But let's do something later this week, right?" Devon dapped him.

"Of course, man. I'll see you later. I'm just going to be up wasting my life all these hours in these business books."

The two chuckled, Devon started to walk out then immediately stopped. *What am I doing?* He wasn't seeing Melissa or anyone else tomorrow night. If he didn't prevent

Dwayne from going to that store tomorrow night, he would be dead and this would all be a waste. He had to think of something.

He turned around. "Dwayne, why don't you let me pick up some groceries for you for the game tomorrow?"

"Huh? Oh, it's all good. I can take care of it tomorrow." Dwayne moved to the living room, starting to open his Financial Accounting book.

"No, I really don't mind, D. Just tell me what you need and I'll get it right now."

"Dev, the corner store is just two blocks down."

"Oh, that old gross place. They have rats and shit, cuz. You don't want to go there. I actually heard that someone was attacked by a rat while they were looking for a candy bar there. You definitely don't want that."

Dwayne had to hold back his laughter. "That's the worst piece of bullshit I've seen you try to pass off as the truth, Dev. What's going on?"

Devon was running out of options. He was never good at the planning part. Gus and Prue excelled in that area. Devon was going to have to lay it out straight. "If you go to the corner store tomorrow, you're going to be murdered."

"What?"

"Yeah, you are going to be shot dead by Lt. Hunter, so I need you to not go there tomorrow night."

Dwayne scanned his friend up and down. "Whatever you have been smoking or drinking, you've got to stop, Dev. This isn't good for you."

"I haven't been smoking or drinking anything, D. I'm honestly telling you that if you go to that corner store tomorrow night, you are going to be killed by Lt. Hunter."

"Lt. Hunter? Campus police? And how do you know this? Why would he want to kill me?

Devon tried to sound as calm and confident as possible, it was the only way to help his friend believe something so fantastic. "He kills you because he's a racist fucking pig. And just trust me." That came out nowhere near how Devon would have liked.

"Dev, you sound psychotic right now. How do you know this?"

"Because Prue, Gus and I went back in time to save you from dying again. We used a protection spell to keep us safe and went back through time, first to save Gus's brother David, which we did, and then to try to save Prue's Kaleb, which is a work in progress. So now I'm here to save you but I don't have my magic power, Gus has my magic power. I'm getting used to Prue's magic power and I don't have time to explain all of this to you. I just need you to believe me." Dwayne gazed at Devon in a way he had never before. "I know you don't believe me."

"You sense that? I can't understand why after telling me about two friends I have never heard of before helping you go back through time to save people from dying with your magical powers that I never knew you had."

"D, it's true."

"Show me."

"Show you?"

"Show me," demanded Dwayne.

"Okay." Devon opened his hands. Nothing happened. He closed his eyes and tried again, trying to remember how Prue did it. Nothing moved, nothing broke, nothing froze. "Hmm, okay, so it's not working right now."

"Really?"

"You have to believe me, D."

"Dev, I think you need to go now." Devon was beside himself. He didn't know another way to tell Dwayne the truth and there wasn't any other alternative to make it sound more believable. He would have to figure out a new plan to save his friend, he wasn't going to give up without a fight.

Devon turned to walk out of his dorm when abruptly he stopped and turned around. "Wait, you know Lt. Hunter?"

"Dev, leave now!"

Devon walked out of his dorm, feeling sudden defeat. If only he had Prue and Gus with him, they certainly could have helped prove that this was real. As he walked down the stairs of Dwayne's dorm and began walking through the college campus, unsure where he would go next, he found his attention focused on a patrol car a few cars down.

As he got closer, Devon saw the officer exit the car. Similar stature, although his back was to him. Devon followed after him, feeling something strong in his soul, feeling the heat rising. He saw the officer enter the store. Devon went quickly after him, feeling the rage shooting through him banging on the front door. They were both inside the corner store now, the same one Dwayne would be killed in front of the next day.

Never No More.

31

Forward to Time Past

"I didn't say we were actually falling, but that I saw something falling in the sky," said Gus who was thanking his lucky stars that they were even alive after his latest premonition.

They had exited the portal and miraculously returned back to the tarmac, standing where they had stood once before, surrounded by various aircraft, stretching out for miles. Planes that were black, planes that were white, planes that looked as though they only flew the most elite passengers, planes that looked like they could occupy an entire city, and just one private jet with a seagull painted on it.

Prue and Gus were amazed. They had done the impossible. They had successfully used the time warp at the crash site to rewind time to the very moment they needed to start the day over again. This meant that the charred bodies they had seen, the violent ferocious fire that killed over a dozen people and caused an unsuspecting town to evacuate had never came to exist. This meant the hikers who had no suspicion their lives would end there were once again alive.

This also meant that Kaleb was somewhere, alive again, sharing the same breath, the same air. Prue and Kaleb were breathing the same air, breathing at the same time on this earth, both alive again. The terrible tragic images she had of Kaleb, the image of seeing the emergency nurse staff over his amputated body, trying to shock him back to life never happened, the crash landing, the celebration of life, none of it ever happened, it was all but a dream. Holding his hand, seeing those nicks into his scalp, knowing he would never be able to walk or be the same person again, all of that was nothing but a nightmare.

Prue was determined to make sure this wouldn't happen again, this time he was going to live. She looked at her watch, it read 6:30am. She looked around and knew it was time to devise a new plan to save him.

"So, what's the new plan?" Gus impatiently asked.

"It's 6:30am. That gives us some more time than we had yesterday or last time or whatever."

"Well since we know when the accident happened, we've got a little over an hour to come up with a new plan."

"Wow, this is a lot of planes," said Prue, walking around, taking a closer look at the aircraft on the black tarmac that morning.

"What can we do? Why is he flying anyways? Where is he supposed to be going?"

Prue stopped. She had never considered why Kaleb and Marco had flown before, and she remembered thinking soon after if he had only gotten there some other way, any other way, how he could have been fine. She peered at Gus, "I know what to do now."

Gus looked startled. "Okay, what's that?"

"I'll show you." She took a long look around, inventorying all the aviation aircraft around them, the sun rising on what was initially a cloudless day. She tried her hardest to remember the horrific airplane wreckage she saw yesterday, the wreckage that had been burned into her brain for the past several months as the media had showed it over and over again, across every possible platform, experiencing it as undoubtedly trauma porn.

She tried to think hard, remembering what it all could have looked like intact. Finally, she was able to remember

212

the airplane was originally white with a pelican engraved in blue and gold. She had never paid attention to what it looked like when the pieces were still intact before the crash, she had only seen it once when she was floating out of her body and she'd have to trust her instincts and believe in herself that she wouldn't let him or herself down. She had to give herself a chance. Crossing her heart, she said a prayer, and then uttered the words:

"Light as a feather, clear as the sea, if it's white, blue and gold, make it disappear, so no one can see."

Just then, several of the planes and helicopters disappeared from the tarmac. All the aircrafts that had a color combination of white, blue and gold vanished in thin air, leaving only the planes and helicopters that were of a different color or color combination. Gus examined the tarmac in utter amazement. "Wow. You think this will do the trick?"

"Yes. They were supposed to taken an airplane that was white with a blue and gold pelican across it. If we get rid of the plane, they won't be able to use it, which means they may just drive instead."

Gus interrupted. "What if they end up just taking another plane?"

Prue paused to reflect. "I don't think they can do that. These other airlines are probably already booked, especially with all of the other passengers of the aircrafts that we've made disappear needing new flights. And I don't think you can just decide you're going to take aircrafts that weren't scheduled to fly today. Don't they have to do tests and make sure it's safe and filled up and everything?"

"You're looking at me? I have no idea, but it may be a good idea if you can just make them all go away, that would mean he won't have any other option."

Prue thought about this for a second, seriously considered it, and finally agreed with Gus. "Okay. So how would we do that?"

"Probably the same way you did that spell but instead, try something like this." Inspired by Prue, Gus created his own impromptu incantation to incite,

*"**Light as a feather, clear as the sea. If it can fly, put it in hiding.***"*

Nothing happened. "Gus, what the hell was that?"

"What? It was a spell."

"If it can fly, put it in hiding? You call that a spell?" Prue retorted.

"Well, your spell was just a rendition of your other spell. I mean how many times can you use 'light as a feather, clear as the sea'? I mean why does it need to be light as a feather anyways?"

Prue rolled her eyes. "You have a better idea? You try."

Their conversation was interrupted by a deep male voice that appeared to originate from loudspeakers through the tarmac airport control system. "What the fuck are you guys, aliens? Stay right there."

Prue and Gus panicked, fear holding them under duress. While they had been standing there arguing, the airport crew and security had been watching them, most likely on watch after Prue made about six aircrafts completely disappear. They could see the airport crew looking at them through the distant glass windows that were far in front of them. Their secret was out.

Now Prue and Gus had to get out of there. In a panic, Prue opened her hands but nothing happened. She tried again. Then she remembered, she didn't have her power, she had Gus's. Devon had left to save his friend with her power. Now what were they going to do?

They didn't have time to think about it. They did the only thing they could think of, run. Prue and Gus ran as fast as they could, seeking a way to get off the tarmac.

"Stop!" the man's voice demanded. "You've just committed three federal offenses. The FBI is on the way to investigate you. There's nowhere for you to run."

Prue and Gus had no time to care. They had come too far to be stopped by something as minor and miniscule as the law. Quickly, they became tired, the tarmac stretched for miles, but they kept pace. Dogs barking in the far distance coming closer and closer, Prue and Gus always stayed together.

What a time to not have an active power, Prue thought to herself. They were just about dead when they finally reached a tall metal fence. Gus was confident he could climb it, it was about ten feet tall, and he was already six feet tall. He was, however, unsure about Prue. Looking behind them, they had no choice.

They could hear the roaring of an engine chasing after them not far away, and they knew the dogs would be onto them shortly. What did these people think they were? What were they after? Did their magic scare them? They were just trying to save Kaleb. Kaleb?

Then it occurred to her. Now that all the planes had disappeared, there was no way for him to fly that day, least not that morning. He would have no choice but to drive or reschedule.

Moments later, a new feeling was taking over her body. It grew and quickly gravitated to every area of her body. She hadn't felt this feeling in a long, long time, relief. They had done it. He wouldn't be getting on that plane this morning. He would live today. He would live to see the night, he would live to see a new day. Her heart was overjoyed, tears starting to swell on to her face.

Barking ensued closer. "Prue, we don't have time." Gus was higher up on the metal fence, holding his hand out to help lift Prue up. "Prue, grab my hand." Prue only came back to life once she heard the barking only feet away. She returned back to her body and quickly went to try to reach Gus's hand. It was getting far out of reach. She wanted to reach it so badly. She could feel something grabbing her. She tried to look back and it all faded away.

Prue found herself awakening in a gasp with a device over her nose and mouth. She was lying flat on her back. She could feel the concrete or tile beneath her was cold. Several people wearing masks and uniforms had surrounded her. Oh no, had she been captured by airport security, or worse, the FBI to dissect them because of their magic? She tried to move her head but was told not to move. Had she fallen trying to reach Gus' hand?

She gasped again and tried to move but it was too late. The people with masks were now holding her down. So many voices, she could barely make out what anyone was saying. She tried to look around but it wasn't until the people helped prop her up that she saw what was going on.

Dozens of people were gathered around her, and not just her, Gus who appeared to be waking up and Devon who appeared to be more conscious. They had resuscitating equipment on her and her friend's faces. Sitting up, she was finally able to place herself, they were back at the Plaza Del Balboa. But why? The huge crowd of people were park goers watching as if they were witnessing a show.

"What-What's going on?" Prue asked the EMT.

"You're going to be okay. We're going to take you to the hospital."

"Wait, why? What's happening?"

"Ma'am, can you tell me your name?" Another EMT asked her.

Prue was happy to be addressed properly, a freedom few trans women get to experience, but still wanted to know what was going on and if her friends would be okay. "My name is Prue. Tell me what's wrong with me."

"We aren't sure. Several people called because you all were just laying here and you were unresponsive," the EMT answered.

Prue was confused. Prue and Gus were just at the tarmac trying to get away. Why were they here and why was Devon here when he had gone off to find his fraternity brother, Dwayne? Why were they right back at where they had started from? Prue opened her hands but still nothing. She yelled to Devon, "Devon, open your hands!" The EMTs looked puzzled at her.

Devon could barely hear her but when she said it again, he understood what she meant, and he tried. But nothing happened. The three were trapped, once again powerless and now forced to a one-way trip to the E.R.

An hour after being admitted and with the guards at their doors, the group had regretfully and with much resentment, accepted their fate. They would be in the hospital until they found a way to escape. All their tests came back negative, it appeared there was nothing wrong with them. And that wasn't a shock.

Prue snuck out to find Gus and Devon who had been placed in the same room with a curtain in between them. "So, there's nothing wrong with us?"

"Sure, there's lots wrong with us," Gus answered. "We have or had each other's magical powers that decided to just disappear, again."

"But they disappeared because we altered time. As soon as Kaleb was unable to fly, we changed..."

"Destiny," Devon answered.

"Well, I don't really think we should think about folks dying as destiny," Prue said.

"But we are all destined to go at some time."

"The immediate question is how did we end up leaving the tarmac and end up back at the park?" Gus interjected.

"Because that is where we came out of the time portal we created to get here after we left your time ten years ago," Prue said. "We then astral-projected to the tarmac so when we lost our powers again, technically, because in this time we haven't met yet, and we changed what was going to happen we came back here."

"Did that make sense to anyone else?" Devon scratched his head.

"All of us? Devon wasn't with us," Gus pointed out.

"I don't think that matters. Because we changed what was going to happen, we lost our powers, so we all came back to the beginning," Prue rationalized.

"This is weird. If we lost our powers, why didn't we just go back to when we first cast the time travel spell?" Gus asked.

"More importantly, how are we going to catch up with the month we are actually in if we don't have any powers to get back there?" Devon piped in.

"Hold on. When we saved my brother, we didn't lose our powers. If changing this one event caused us to lose our powers, since we technically haven't met yet, does that mean that we won't actually meet now? Is that why our powers disappear?" Gus inquired.

"We've already met, dummy," Devon said. "I'm looking at your weird little face now."

"Hey, you shut it, okay. I'm serious. Have we like, changed our own destiny then?"

Prue opened her mouth to answer when suddenly all three were shocked with electricity, rapid, flowing energy charging through every crevice of their bodies sending waves of vibration through their spines. Penetrating every fiber of their being, the numbness was instant, sudden and unsuspecting. The light in the ceiling above them began to glow, increasing in brightness, shining for a long moment before becoming so bright that it blinded them. And when they didn't think they could take the brightness any longer, the lights faded away. For a long pause, the room was dark, devoid of sounds and movement.

After a few seconds, the electricity seemed to return. Prue could hear a distant television in another room. "Breaking news: An airline carrying passengers from the James Dean airport unexpectedly crashed this morning. The airlines stated aircraft at the James Dean airport magically disappeared. Several folks were able to transfer over to Brown Hawk Jet Lines for an emergency flight. On board, included local baseball star Marco Jackson and his father

Kaleb Jackson, former director of a local afterschool teens program. Tragically, there appear to be no survivors. Our news anchor, Katie, is at the scene reporting."

Prue couldn't believe her ears. This had to be a mistake. She must have been hearing things. Judging by the looks on Devon and Gus's face, they all heard the same thing. Suddenly, the phone next to Gus's bedside started sharing a live news feed. "Two mysterious people have escaped the tarmac. They are people of interest and may be involved with Brown Hawk Jet Lines crashing today. Investigators say these two individuals made quite a few aircraft 'disappear,' causing a reshuffle of the airports entire flight schedule. The company reports that the Brown Hawk Jet was not cleared and approved to take off this morning which may have led to it not having enough fuel for the flight. Currently, if you have seen these two suspects, call the police immediately." Just then, Gus let out a sudden gasp.

"What is it?" Prue asked.

He handed her the phone. "It's us." The live feed showed images and video footage of Prue and Gus saying their spells to make the airplanes disappear, then images of them running away before vanishing in thin air.

"We're fugitives now? What? Now I'll never make the Olympic Swim Team."

Devon started laughing.

"This is not funny. They think we are responsible for tampering with that jet. Wait, what? They crashed again?" Gus said aloud before realizing the impact of his words. "I'm so sorry Prue."

It didn't matter to Prue. She had already left her body. She was no longer there. Not only had she lived through him dying once but now she had lived through the same day where he died two different ways, twice. Was she cursed? Why wasn't she able to save him?

"Prue, I think we're going to have to go back in time again," Gus said to her.

"Are you crazy?" Devon asserted. "They have you two using magic now all over social media. You two look like you're murderers."

"But we aren't!" Gus shouted.

"What difference does that make? You think those people care what the truth is? They'll come after you just like they go after anything else that scares them. They won't rest until they destroy all of us."

"Devon, we have no choice. If we go back in time, we can reverse all this like we did before."

"But how many times can we do that?"

"As many times as it takes," Prue said. "I'm not giving up until he survives."

Devon paused and tried to use a softer tone. "Prue, he may not be meant to survive."

Gus looked down; he had pondered the same thing but felt so guilty speaking the truth into existence.

"Devon, did you save Dwayne?" Prue glared at Devon with fumes of anger rising from her ears.

"Honestly, I don't know. With all this magic stuff, I'm back here with you all instead of stopping the officer that is trying to kill him."

"Well excuse me, Devon. I am so sorry you both are able to save the people that you love, while for some reason, Kaleb is 'destined' to die. Thanks for having my back."

"Prue, we do have your back. We care about you. I just...I don't want you to get hurt," Devon said.

"I'm already hurt. I'm dead on the inside now. Nothing else matters but saving him." Prue left the boys in their hospital room. Gus and Devon stared at each other.

"I guess my power isn't helping you any," Devon said.

"It is. I saw something falling from the sky. It had to have been them. I just don't understand why it seems we can save our two friends but not him."

"I don't get it either. It seems like he's destined to die. Every time we try to change destiny, it seems to get worse," Devon stated.

"She's going to keep fighting to save him, you know."

"I know and I need you to protect her."

Gus and Devon silently agreed and made a pact, they would keep their thoughts to themselves not to upset Prue any further, and Gus would do whatever he could to keep her safe. Gus went after Prue, knowing exactly where she would be, trying to find the time warp to try that day again.

Devon looked to find a way to escape the hospital. As soon as it was clear, he would make his exit. As Gus left the hospital to find Prue, he found himself with another vision. His fears were confirmed, Prue's life was in jeopardy.

32

Grieving Enraged

When Devon returned to the corner store, he didn't know what time it was. He didn't know if he was too early or too late, but he remembered Lt. Hunter would be there. He wondered if all this time changing meant that Dwayne wouldn't remember Devon telling him the truth. One way or the other he was going to make sure Dwayne survived the next day.

He couldn't fault Prue for not giving up on saving Kaleb. It was all too much, having to deal with loss, unexpectedly losing someone who just hours ago was a living, breathing person who had caramel macchiatos on Tuesdays and snored like a hog when you stayed over, and would smell his hands after he wiped, and would answer the phone each and every time you called. A person who was living his life, his goals to become someone, his desire to prove that his life mattered, his grand goal to prove that Black Lives Matter. A person who was just going to a corner store to get snacks ends up dead in seconds.

It was all too much to fathom and understand, and then how the world just carries on as if nothing happened, as if your world wasn't just shaken to its core and after three days of bereavement, you're expected to resume your daily living and responsibilities, ignoring this hole in your life and this pain in your heart that is so deep, you yourself can't even see the end of it. .

Devon looked around the store, aisle after aisle, trying to see if the Lt. was there. He hadn't made it yet. Aimlessly checking out the magazines, sudoku, and crossword puzzles, he could only ask himself if it would make a difference if he tried to make Dwayne understand. He came to the conclusion however that it wouldn't matter. They had gone back in time, but all of this still sounded crazy, irrespective to what time it was. It was easier if he just didn't see him again until after this was all over, until after he had saved him. This was for the best.

Holding the crossword puzzle in his hand, he was too consumed with his inner thoughts that he just decided it best to leave right now and return later this evening. As he exited the corner store, to his surprise, the man he was looking for was already there. In case he had forgotten, he was reminded he was Black when he saw the Lt., along with several other officers, pointing their millimeters at his head and chest.

It startled him to the point that he dropped the crossword puzzle to the ground. Though it was made of paper, he could hear the thud as it hit the floor. He realized his mistake; he had forgotten to pay for it. But another mistake became more apparent to him, his real mistake was existing as a Black man in America.

He had just left the store. How could the police already be outside pointing guns at him mistaking him as a shoplifter if he only opened the door seconds ago? The clerk must have called the police when he saw Devon hanging around, looking through the aisles. If a fight was what they wanted, that's what they would get. Devon shouted, "It's not a crime to be Black in America."

"No, it isn't, but it is a crime to shoplift," the Lt. said.

"Cut the bullshit. You were here waiting for me. I just stepped outside. You're not here because I shoplifted. You're here because that clerk in there thought I looked suspicious!" Devon shouted.

"Just calm down, son," another officer said, still pointing his gun.

"Right. I should calm down. That's real easy to do when officers are pointing a gun at your head. And I'm not your fucking son!"

Lt. Hunter didn't appreciate his sarcasm nor his outspokenness. "Put your hands up, son."

"I'm not your fucking son!" Devon shouted. "I have done nothing wrong. You pigs are gonna shoot me for $4.95? That's how much my life means to you, less than a $5 bill?"

"Put your hands up NOW!"

Devon refused. Standing in the same spot where his friend Dwayne would lose his life the next day, the same spot where they spent hours protesting, feeling the energy of that crowd yelling for equal rights, Black Lives Matter, rising above the fear, Devon wouldn't turn back now.

Looking Lt. Hunter dead in the face, "Why are you a racist pig? Why are you out here killing innocent Black men?" Lt Hunter's face appeared to have gotten rosier, the red quickly spreading like a contagion from his forehead to his cheeks. "Take off your shades so I can look you straight in your eyes, motherfucker. You murderer!!"

Devon knew everyone was watching and he didn't mind making it a showdown now. He had been waiting for this moment since he received the text that Dwayne was murdered. Somebody had to finally do something. The nerve of police to tell people to relax and calm down while they have a gun pointed at them.

Devon was so full of rage. The pain, the sadness that he felt for each and every person who lost their life to a police officer for walking, talking, living while Black. The sorrow and empathy he had for each and every family member, friend, community member affected by that loss; mourning them, being afraid to drive a car, being afraid to move to a new neighborhood that could improve their life, every Black person attending a school to gain a higher education and being faced with security being called on them because someone thinks they don't belong there.

If it's not any of that, it's the white people liking you only for what you can do for them. To help make them feel less guilty about what they have done and what their parents have done. For the macro and microaggressions that are still happening in this world, donating to causes so they feel less bad about how they benefit from white privilege, using the Black male body so they can receive pleasure, so they can feel better about themselves, cooler, happier with themselves. Devon was ready to take a stand.

He didn't make it here because his ancestors just gave up and rolled over. He had the courage of Harriet, the intelligence of Martin, the resilience of Marsha, the motivation of Malcolm, the perseverance of Bayard, the creativity of Josephine, the power of all the Black Leaders that carried him forward. He was walking in the steps of Eric Gardner and George Floyd, and he wasn't going to stop. He took a step forward. "You're going to shoot me over $4.95? No. You're shooting me because you're racist and you're trying to kill as many Black men as you can."

"One more step and it's over," Lt. Hunter yelled at the top of his lungs

"Put your hands up now!" one officer shouted.

"Prepare to fire," he heard another officer call out

Devon was going to be the example. "Black Lives Matter! Black Lives Matter!" He took one last step. Sooner than he could imagine, the bullets shot out of the guns faster than the speed of light. Devon closed his eyes, knowing what would happen, but feeling a resolve, knowing that he would die for what he believed in.

He knew this was being recorded somewhere and would go viral, showing the world the truth, the whole truth, and nothing but. There would be few lies they could say to justify killing him, a graduate student seeking higher education in business. No one could argue that he was murdered because he was Black and the police were racist, instead of continuing to be protected by the badge.

Devon waited before opening his eyes. He wasn't even sure if he still existed to have eyes to open, but he did. When he opened his eyes, the scene amazed him. The bullets were frozen in midair, sixteen of them directed at him. Sixteen damn bullets? They must have really wanted him dead. But he wasn't, at least not yet.

He didn't understand how this was possible, but he concluded they must have gotten their powers back in the hospital when Kaleb passed away again, and Prue's power must have returned to him. Instinctively, he must have opened his hands as a reflex, causing him to freeze everything and everyone.

This felt surreal, standing in this spot where he was supposed to die, where who knows how many Black men have died and were going to die here, at the hands of this man and this man's descendants. Devon glanced to his left to see the clerk holding his phone recording him. Devon looked around and saw more customers in the store watching from a distance at the door and over the counter, pedestrians walking past, cars going by, a few holding phones out. Devon hadn't noticed any of this before. All he could see was Lt. Hunter's red face in front of him trying to kill him. Not today.

Devon went to touch the nearest bullet that was less than a second from grazing his neck leading to internal hemorrhaging, fatal. The bullet was hot like fire. He immediately dropped it; it nearly scolded his fingers. Not today. Today was not going to be the day the police officers killed an innocent Black man. Oh no.

Devon stepped away from the direction of the bullets, motioned his hands, and without a second passing by, time had unfrozen, the bullets aimed at Devon now returning to the officer who had shot them, landing in each officer's chest who had fired them, killing most of them instantly. Devon was calm and he looked for Lt. Hunter who at this point was injured on the ground. Devon took three steps forward, closer to him. He kneeled to the concrete edge, in front of the Lt. as his head was on the ground, blood gushing in several streams around him. Devon picked his head up to see if he was still in there. To Devon's disappointment, he had already departed.

Devon knew this wasn't how he was raised, that this was morally wrong, but he felt such a feeling of satisfaction not just for him, but for all the innocent Black people who had been murdered by the hands of a racist cop and the families left to mourn them. Dwayne wasn't going to die by the hands of a racist cop today, nor would anyone else who might have encountered these racist assholes again. As time had caught up with itself and Devon heard the final gasp from the last remaining officer bleeding to death, he opened his hands and fled the scene.

33

Try, Try Again

The inside of the church looked exquisite. Beautiful cherry wood with an open vaulted ceiling. A wooden flank ceiling with Venetian plaster and Eurospan fabric walls. The church had a 48' high interior ridge, revealing forms of gothic arches throughout the sanctuary and the nave. Natural light beaming in from the skylight above, highlighting the polished floors of concrete and majestic stone. The altar was made of 40' of wood, metal and brass fabric. Large and wide wooden polished cherry pews centered around the pulpit made of concrete and majestic stone. The outside had a gathering plaza with a fountain flowing with water of purity and forgiveness. The church also had an 85' bell tower that served to ring the Lord's truth to the ears of those who felt forsaken. Prue and Gus sat in one of the church pews alone, the exalted glass doors not open for service yet.

"What are we doing here?" Gus asked.

"Because this is a place he often came to try to find his hope again, especially after his injury set him back, particularly after his injury. I read it in the comments." Prue looked up into the skylight, almost motioning for God to step in and take the wheel.

"I don't understand. Why don't you just call him and tell him not to get on the flight?"

Prue placed her hand in her pocket and pulled out a piece of paper that was folded. "I can't."

"Well why not? This is literally a matter of life and death," Gus affirmed. Prue held great hesitation. "What aren't you telling me? How do you even know him anyways?"

"I don't."

"You don't what?" Once again, Prue hesitated. "Spit it out, Prue."

"We've never met. I've never met him." Prue looked down.

"What? What do you mean? We've been busting our asses to save him and you've never met him?"

"Yes, we've been busting our asses to save him and I've never met him. I don't need to meet him to know this is wrong and this is a great tragedy and God shouldn't have allowed this to happen."

Gus held back the next few words, knowing they would only make matters worse. He said the closest thing he could, knowing he needed more information. "If you haven't met him, why do you care so much about what happened to him?"

"I can't explain it, Gus. I didn't know him but what I did know was that after struggling to find himself again, trying to get out of the despair of depression, he found a way to start putting the pieces of his life back together again. After his divorce, he tried to rebuild his relationship with his son, and that was starting to happen, he started to find a new destiny to help others and then out of nowhere it all ended. All of a sudden, I felt this tremendous grief. I felt this grief like no other, like I had lost someone I had loved for decades, like I had lost my best friend, like I had lost someone who was somehow a part of me, connected to me."

Gus sat there, processing, trying to understand the words he was hearing. Prue tried to hold back her tears; tears Gus knew were very real. He had seen her crying all three versions of the same day. "I can't explain it, but the moment he died, it was like my life just stopped. My heart felt this intense, immense, irreversible sorrow. It didn't make sense." She stood up to turn away from Gus. "He was in his prime. He had so much left to do and he was doing so many amazing things with his life. He was helping other people. He was saving kids that otherwise would have been on the streets or became involved with drugs or crime. He parented fatherless kids who look like us who had no father to love them, who had a mother at home but provided guidance to them at school to keep them on the right path. He was trying to be better each and every day. This was his time to live." The emotion was too much; she felt the pangs in her heart. "Why would God choose that moment to take him away? He didn't deserve that. And God took him away in the most horrific way possible."

Prue tried to walk around but the pain was all too much. She didn't know what to do. She had never been able to fully let it out. "He didn't deserve that. Why, God? Why would you do this to him, to all of them?" She hit her fists on the seating. "There were kids on that plane. They were supposed to grow to be adults. Their parents were on that plane. They shouldn't have been forced to sit there and die with them. All of this is wrong. Kaleb didn't deserve this. He was in the prime of his life, he was doing so much good, his son was about to take off in the MLB. He surely would have made history." Prue fell to the floor, swallowed up in ails of defeat and despair. "Kaleb died, he felt all this pain, he lost his life when all he was trying to do was be the best man he could be."

Gus ran over to hold Prue. He wouldn't act like he understood this, but he could tell the emotions were real and that her pain was real, and maybe it wasn't his place to understand it, maybe he didn't need to. Maybe all he needed to do was acknowledge that this was how she felt and be there for her, "Prue, I'm sorry. I'm so sorry." She cried even more. "I don't know why this happened. I don't know why we lost any of the people we lost but I have to believe that

God wouldn't have let them feel pain. He was a good man and I have to believe God would have protected them from feeling any pain. God does things that we don't understand for reasons we only learn about later."

Prue continued to sob but Gus told her it was okay. "You think I'm a freak."

"No, I don't think you're a freak. I think you're an incredible woman who loves so much that you can do so unconditionally, who cares so much that you can care for someone you've never met and push to the ends of this earth to save them. No, you're not a freak. You're exactly the kind of woman we need more of. If there were more people like you, there would be less hate and less pain in the world." She continued to sob, finally feeling safe and strong enough to break down.

"I feel like I don't know what to do now. I just..."

Gus stopped her. "It's okay. You'll figure it out, or we'll figure it out together." He rocked her.

"I feel like a mess that I need you to tell me this."

"You're not a mess. You're showing all of your strength right now by trusting me to help, reaching out for help. You're so much stronger than you think you are when you do this than keeping it all inside where it can bury you alive. And I'm going to be here to remind you that you're going to pull through this, we will together, no matter what happens."

Prue heard these words and something about this comforted her. She was able to show how she really felt, what she was really feeling to another living soul, and he didn't turn it against her. He didn't use her; he didn't use it for his own advantage. All the years she had been alive in this world, this felt so rare. But she wasn't sure if it was as rare as she thought, to see it in others, she would have to let herself go and trust in her own power of vulnerability, knowing she would be okay and get through it no matter what.

"I think about Kaleb, the wonderful lessons he has taught us and continues to teach us. Many years after he has gone, we will still see new articles and stories and lessons that he has taught us coming out on the daily. This was his legacy, this was what he wanted, to motivate and inspire others. Even though his body isn't here anymore, his soul still is, the parts of him that made him who he is, is still here with all of us. It's in that kid that wants to give up on school but doesn't. It's that college student that wants to take his own life because he's depressed but doesn't because he thinks of him and it encourages him to seek out help that he is finally open to receiving.

"It's all the people that want to give up on something, that want to dream but are too afraid, or are so close to the dream that they almost lose it out of fear but they press on, looking fear into the face and continuing no matter what. That's Kaleb. That's Kaleb speaking through all of them. He's speaking through you now, every time you've wanted to give up but haven't, you refuse to. It's you trying to save him. It's you trying to save us. It's you trying to help make the world a better place. He's living in you right now and he always will. He will never be forgotten." These words brought so much relief to Prue. It didn't take her pain away but she felt some level of peace nonetheless.

"You two never met but maybe you two are connected somehow. Maybe you weren't destined to meet in this life for a reason, for something that has to do with the big picture, but you two are connected, like soulmates." Prue continued to listen. "I saw my brother in another life, but in that life instead of being brothers, he was my dad and I was his son. We were still connected, even though it was another life. Of all the gazillions of people out there, it can't be coincidental that the same two people connected in one life are connected in another. People that are connected, they have to be like soulmates, connected to each other's soul through love, in whatever shape or form, in each and every life. But that doesn't always mean we walk together in the same life, or even meet, but we can influence each other in different ways even if we aren't on the same plane at the same time. A part of us is always connected to that other person until we see them again, and we will always find each other, whether we know it or not."

Prue looked at him in awe. She had never heard him talk like this. She could hardly recognize him. The words he said still staying with her. "You two didn't share a life together but maybe in the afterlife, he is connecting to you. Maybe you felt this pain because you are so connected. All I know is each and every day you continue forward, you're honoring him and giving him another chance at life through you." Gus heard his own words, words he wished someone had said to him. Hearing them out of his own mouth, he knew he had said them, although the words felt like they came from someone or something else, something that knew more, emerging from a calm all-knowing place that he knew was speaking truth.

The doors opened for services, Gus still sitting on the floor made of concrete and majestic stone, holding Prue in his arms. The image of Jesus Christ nailed to the cross made more obvious and apparent by the natural light of the open glass doors as others walked in.

"Come on in."

34

No Turning Back Now, Nowhere to Run

His photo was all over social media. They didn't have proof that he had killed Lt. Hunter and those other police officers, but they knew he had and, in this country, they didn't need evidence to convict. Others had been killed for much less. Luckily, the video footage from the camera phones also froze and didn't show any delay.

He might as well be a criminal because he knew what he was doing, and he had no intention of talking to the police. After what they had just done to him, the only talks they were about to have were from the other side, because Devon was going to make sure that no Black person in this city was going to lose their life innocently by a police officer again.

He ignored the phone calls and the text messages, was never happier that phones had the "do not disturb" feature. Sitting in his car, there wasn't much for him to do but to wait. He wanted to make sure that all of them had arrived at their shift to do their police briefing before he came in.

With a bulge in his right coat pocket, he would affirm all the Black lives that had been lost in America at the hands of an ill-equipped, racist pig. They seemed to think it was okay to shoot at Black bodies first and ask questions later. Never No more.

Start with one city at a time, then move to the next until all of them learn to ask questions first, then shoot with non-lethal rounds, before moving to killing. No more innocent killing. No more killing unarmed Black men. No more killing unarmed Black women. NO MORE!

His phone said 8 pm. He had to check twice when he saw a text from Dwayne who had been trying to call him for a few hours. Devon wanted to celebrate that his friend was basically back from the dead, he didn't want to ignore him, but he knew what he had to do.

He had saved his friend but he remembered the young Black men he had saved using his power of premonition, which sadly could have helped him right now. At least he could see what the outcome would be. He doubted he would survive much longer but if he saved anyone, it would be worth it.

He stepped out of his car, camouflaged in black shoes, black pants, black sweater, black coat. Swiftly, he moved to the front entrance of headquarters, passing by the window that he would crack months later with the rock he would throw, starting the revolution. He moved quickly and quietly and opened the door.

From his right, he was stopped in his tracks by the one person he didn't think he'd see. "Dev, where have you been? I've been trying to call you since I saw you on the news."

Devon was awestruck. "Dwayne, you really should get out of here man and go home."

"Dev, what are you talking about? What's all this about man?"

"You don't belong here, D. Just go home okay."

"I'm not going anywhere Dev. You don't belong here either. They're saying they think you killed police officers. Is that true? Why would you do that, to get out of our business exam tomorrow?" Devon looked away. "Dev, look at me. What's going on, man? Talk to me." The two stood there.

"D, there are some racist ass cops out here."

"Yes, Dev there are. Some. But not all of them. Most of them are not like that."

"D, you don't even know what you're..." Devon stopped himself. It was possible that Dwayne didn't know but it felt completely wrong to tell him so considering Devon had to go back in time to save him from being killed by a police officer.

"What I'm talking about, Dev. I'm a few years older than you. I don't need to be older to know that some police officers use their badge to exert power and control over people and act out their bias. But we can't turn into those monsters, killing all the ones we think are bad and evil. We will become bad and evil just like that, except worse. We will lose any support we have to stand up against the bad ones and say they are wrong."

Devon was dumbfounded to hear this, of all people, from Dwayne. "Dwayne, you really don't get it."

Dwayne moved closer to him. "I don't need to get it. You need to turn yourself in if you did anything. I'll support you, but don't do anything else. We have no right to take the life of someone unless we have no other choice. But that is in very, very few situations and going on a rampage to kill all the bad police officers will not work, it will only end with you getting killed." Dwayne held a stern expression on his face, one of concern and worry.

"Rather me being killed than you." Devon flailed his hands and time froze. He went through the call center where the police dispatchers were, up the stairs to where the police officers of the night shift were having their nightly briefing.

With his Glock in his pocket, he said to himself, *NO MORE.*

35

The Last Goodbye

He had walked in with his son, Marco. Prue couldn't believe her eyes, he had came here before his fatal flight? He couldn't have looked more normal, seeing him now, she felt she had to be two thirds insane. She had to have dreamt up this whole thing with magic and time warps and the Book of Spirits Past, if it wasn't for Gus sitting beside her, she could have just floated away in an abyss.

Kaleb and Marco sat in the back pew, closest to the exit. Prue felt like she was in a trance, sitting in the pew that was far enough from him where she blended in with the others, but finally close enough where if she wanted to walk over there and touch him, she could. He was alive, he was living and breathing and, in this church, praying.

Prue couldn't understand why God would listen to him pray for whatever he prayed for that Sunday morning but not protect him an hour later and completely abandon him. She heard what Gus said, but she was still angry. What's the point in being a good person if God is just going to abandon you and won't stop you from unexpectedly crashing and burning into a mountain? What more could he have done?

Prue needed to stay calm. Her eyes and cheeks were puffy as she had been crying only moments ago before the early morning service that filled the church with its patrons.

Everyone looked so devout and devoted. She couldn't find it in herself. She wanted to, but so many times hearing the bad guys win and the good guys lose, this morning, losing Kaleb was the tipping point. If God was who they claim he was, he should be here for everybody. The good guys should be the winners, the champions, not the bad. Instead, Kaleb was left forsaken that morning, along with Marco, and all the other passengers and staff of that aircraft.

She rubbed the folded paper in her pocket. Prue had to affix her eyes. She caught herself nearly staring at him and she didn't want him to notice and feel uncomfortable. The fight within herself was real, whether to go over there and talk to him, say something to him, warn him, but she felt this would be futile. She would look like a crazy person. She wanted more than anything for him to be safe.

The preacher was talking about God's sovereignty. Prue heard bits and pieces, but she couldn't pay attention to it. Listening would lead her to the familiar friends she had become accustomed to since her grief: helplessness, hopelessness, anger, and despair. She couldn't have these friends here now. She needed to feel the most powerful she had ever felt if she was going to save this man from dying this morning.

Starting to feel her friends popping out again, she thought it was best to walk outside and get some air. And then her eyes connected with Kaleb who had been looking at her, an experience she never had. She had seen him thousands of times but this was the first time he had seen her. She decided to stay until the end of the sermon. If Kaleb was going to hear it and come all this way for it, she would at least keep herself open to hearing it and try to understand it too. It was important to him, so it became important to her.

She watched him stand up only once to go to the pulpit to be blessed with holy water. She saw the wetness of the holy water on his shiny forehead. Then Kaleb and Marco left. Prue sat there with Gus, battling with herself about what she should do. Should she let this go and give it to God, or should she try to save him a third time from dying this morning, since God clearly wasn't going to do it? She knew what Gus wanted her to do, she could tell. But she didn't want to be stopped.

"Hey Gus, I'll be right back. I'm going to get some air."

Gus turned to her. "Okay. Do you want me to come with you?"

"Oh no, I'll be okay." She stood up and left the church, closing the double glass doors behind her.

Curious, Gus noticed the Bible in the pew in front of them and opened it. While flipping through the pages, suddenly, the pages became his next premonition, Gus completely immersed in the scene unfolding before his very eyes. His friend needed him now or it would be too late. Numbers 35:16-21

36

What Goes Around...

He was seconds from blowing their brains out, their guts would be dripping with blood, oozing all over the tables and chairs before they had a chance to see what was coming. There was nothing stopping him now. They were already frozen, defenseless, just like all the other innocent Black people they had mercilessly killed who didn't have a chance to survive after encountering them.

But he wanted to wait until time caught up with itself. He wasn't going to be a coward like they were. He pointed the barrel of the gun straight at the group of officers sitting at their desk where once they unfroze, anyone could have gotten shot. Death was the great equalizer. His hand was on the trigger. Within seconds, time caught up with itself and the nearly three dozen officers jumped to their feet. It was too late.

"No more killing unarmed Black men."

He said nothing else. He heard footsteps behind him but it was too late. He fired several rounds with his left hand, swinging it aimlessly left and right to kill as many people as possible. He opened his right hand to freeze time. It worked. He saw over a dozen officers wounded, bleeding, bent over holding their abdomen, their chest.

Several were slumped over the table already dead, dripping from the blood gushing from their arteries. The blood made its way onto the carpet, creating a real mess that would never truly be cleaned up. The officers had fired back, stray shots flying through the air were frozen still.

Devon knew he would use telekinesis to guide them right back to the officers, they were racist pigs anyways. He gestured his hand, return to sender, the bullets flew back at the officers. He turned to his left. A limp and unconscious Dwayne was now on the ground, holding his chest, suffocating in his own blood. Devon was horrified. How could this have happened? Dwayne must have come from behind him, no doubt trying to stop him from killing the officers, trying to protect them. Now he was laying lifeless on the ground, bleeding to death.

Devon couldn't process what was happening. He couldn't fathom that after all this work to save his dear friend Dwayne from being killed by the police, he, himself, would end up killing him at the police station. How could he end up killing his own best friend, his brother like this? How could this have happened?

37

A Twist of Fate

She followed close behind him, dodging between the other cars to not be noticed. She had devised a new plan. If she could follow him home, she could do something with his car so that he wouldn't be able to even make it to the James Dean airport in time. Maybe if she just hit it once he got out of the car so he couldn't drive there. Perhaps pouring sugar into his gas tank or slashing his tires, something that wouldn't be too noticeable until it was too late for him to make other arrangements. This would stop him from being able to make it to the airport and force him to stay home. Done deal.

Following close behind him would also give her access to his technology. She could cast a spell to interfere with his WIFI. He wouldn't be able to contact anyone that day, he'd have to just stay home. He would be safe after 8am. He would live. All she had to do was make sure he lived passed that time and a new destiny would have to be created where he would stay alive. Gus and Devon would have to understand. The time warp couldn't help them any further.

After multiple attempts Prue determined that it would never allow her to go any earlier than today. Anything else would require a power of three spell which she couldn't do without Gus and Devon anyways who would only just be huffing and puffing the entire time. She had to do this on her own.

Racing in the car, sliding behind the steering wheel so as not to be seen, she thought she had almost lost track of him when miraculously she was able to catch sight of his car once again. *Thank God.* She had hot-wired this Nissan, justifying to herself that this wouldn't matter because she would return the car after the day was over when she was sure Kaleb was safe. Hopefully him never getting on the flight would save them all.

She drove, trying to stay hidden so as to not make it apparent she was following him. A steady bright light captured her eye and stole her vision for several moments. At once, she could feel something rising out of her. When she regained sight, she saw Kaleb's black SUV four cars ahead, just passing through the intersection. Her luck, the light was turning yellow. She knew she could catch up to him, she had to. She couldn't lose him again. Swerving ahead, she cut off two cars and was right behind him.

The yellow light was turning red. She had to pass through it to stay on track. It turned red, her foot still heavy on the gas petal, knowing she would pass through it in a second or two. Suddenly, a 32-ton, 12-wheel, large fuel tanker carrying 20,000 liters of fuel entered the intersection, right as Prue tried to drive through the red light. The semi t-boned her vehicle, followed by a violently loud fiery explosion, killing her instantly. The fuel from the truck poured all over the streets, setting the intersection and adjacent cars ablaze.

A driver swerved into two pedestrians at a nearby bus-stop. Another driver crashed into the tanker, his life ending abruptly. Glass windows of adjacent buildings were blown out, people running through the streets screaming for their lives. Thick, black smoke filled the air, burning embers floating throughout the morning sky, soot falling about them.

Prue's car was engulfed in unrelenting flames, her lifeless body imprisoned from escape. The flames continued to burn, nothing but the violently orange flames to remain in sight. Prue was no more.

38

When Preparing for Revenge...

Devon was pleading with Dwayne to hold on, carrying his deceased body to anyone that could help save his brother, beseech in a loss so great and significant that he wasn't sure he could ever truly recover. He was in utter disbelief. How could this have happened? How could in this altered reality be the one who killed his brother? He didn't deserve to live anymore.

A light seemed to emerge out of Devon's body, hovering before disappearing. He was too preoccupied with trying to carry his friend to safety that he hadn't noticed. Then suddenly, he couldn't seem to move his legs and his thoughts didn't make sense to him anymore. For some reason, he was now laying on top of Dwayne, continuing to try to get up and awake his friend to take him to the hospital. Then it seemed like nothing mattered anymore. His soul was gone.

The remaining officers walked over to his lifeless body spread out on the asphalt, face down. Seconds ago, time had caught up with itself. Devon had been shot multiple times in the back and skull and now only his body was laying on the ground bleeding out. He was dead.

39

Flying Over the Sun

She sat, swinging her feet back and forth over what appeared to be a bridge so tall and high up that she couldn't see the ground, even the birds and the clouds were below her. The clouds moved irrespective to time, moving fast, or going slow, time didn't seem to have any value here. Watching below, she could see the birds soaring, the eagle in the distance, the black crows, and it was odd her lack of surprise when she saw a cluster of bright butterflies expanding their wings and flying over the sun.

Prue felt light, with a calmness within her soul, her long, black curls blowing briskly in the wind. She watched and observed things but she had no personal experience, no memory, nothing tying her to them. Not entirely. She could feel some sort of connection within her trying to come out, but the calmness was hypnotic.

Insidious fog was surrounding her. Sitting there in the haze long enough, her eyes had adjusted, and she could see through the fog. For once, she was unafraid to look down and that fear of falling was far removed. For once, she felt no fear inside of herself, no fear of pain, no fear of sadness, no fear of sorrow.

All the pains that she had been accustomed to while living, the decades on earth that had tired her, all those pains had evaporated into the light. Everything sounded so peaceful, everything smelled incredibly fresh. The thoughts in her own head were plenty and none at the same time. Even her memories felt they were both escaping her while grasping on harder than ever before.

She had no idea how much time had passed since she was here but she felt no need to know, she didn't much care. A sound of a motor seemed to take her attention away from her own thoughts. It sounded near and far and throughout her experience, she had this feeling of being split in two places at once, connected to the earth, looking up, while floating higher than ever before in the sky, looking down.

She allowed her attention to wander as she looked around at the gold and blue pelican symbol on the white airplane flying at an angle below. Her brain didn't see the significance, but something inside of her drew her near, she had to be there. Watching the aircraft, it was both below her and in front of her, and then suddenly she was inside of it.

She could see the pilots with their shades and headset on, the cockpit and all the controls. In the main seating area, she spotted Kaleb wearing his sweatpants and sweatshirt, looking down at his phone texting. Seeing Kaleb, she could feel her heart beating louder and faster than ever before. Her mind didn't know but her heart had to follow. She could see his son, Marco, looking out the window, trying to see through the thick fog that had completely surrounded them.

Prue knew where it was heading, that it was going down. It was clear to her that no one on board knew this was happening. She could hear the sound of a voice that was far, far away, and one of the pilots speaking through the headset. It was too noisy in the airplane to hear much of anything.

Prue knew what was going to happen next but everything in her felt different. She was sad, she was filled with trepidation, but she also had a calmness and acceptance about her that told her somehow everything was going to be okay. It felt like there were two parts of herself, a loud part that was writhing in shockwaves of throbbing pain that she was beseeched with through her time on land, and a quiet part that felt in peace, something new that was emerging that felt like a different, all-encompassing energy trying to save her.

From inside the plane, she knew she was now powerless, she couldn't do anything to change what was destined to happen no matter how much her insides wanted a different future. There was no more that she could do. She looked at Kaleb, who was still texting, her heart breaking while the new part of herself was gluing the pieces back together so as not to break and shatter completely. It was imperfectly healed.

Well, if they were going to die, Prue decided she would have to die right there with them. And then the quiet part of her took control, when she accepted that this was going to happen, she didn't have to like it, it was totally valid for her to hate and despise it, but she had to accept she couldn't fight this. She could only deal with it as best as she could and she at last felt the permission to be angry at God. Parts of herself wanted to curse, scream, yell, throw things at God, but the quiet part reminded her how useless this was.

Just then, she noticed a glimmer from her eye and looked to the head of the aircraft, outside of the window. She expected it any second, a painful fiery crash that would take them all away. What she saw, instead was unexpected. Above the clouds, she began to see a warm light striving to break through the clouds.

The insidious fog began to dissipate. The airplane was rising above the clouds and out of the thick hazy fog that had been smothering it. Prue was overjoyed. They were actually flying above the clouds. Maybe something she had done had changed God's mind, had altered the course of destiny to allow them all to live without taking anyone else.

She peered into the warm light that appeared to be so comforting and soothing. The airplane was lifting up and up, over each and every light puffy cloud along its destination. And then it went steady, Kaleb, Marco, and all of them onboard looking out the window at the most beautiful sunrise that anyone had ever seen.

She saw Kaleb smiling with his son, witnessing the sunrise that their plane was illuminating across the skies. She had done it. She had done something to change God's mind. The plane and all on board disappeared into the sky, flying over and above the sun continuing forward. Prue felt the wetness on her face, her last glance seeing them all smile as they carried over. They were flying free.

But she also found herself confused. While she saw them fly off, she couldn't explain why she also saw a blue and gold pelican on a white airplane crash below her and was spread across miles of the mountain below. She could see the ball of fire, she could smell the jet fuel, she could see the thick smoke that was emanating.

This didn't make sense. They were flying free, higher than the sun. She saw it, she felt it. She saw the crash site, she heard the sounds of sirens, she smelled the fuel, but the quietness would not leave her. She knew what she saw and the calmness allowed her to override what was bursting at the seams.

She had seen Kaleb smiling, and she knew he was going to be okay. Knowing this helped her now harvest a new ability to tune out the images, the sounds, the smells now. She had seen the image of them flying into that warm comforting light, watching the sky open up for them to pass through, and she continued to remember. The quietness that had been living inside of her now began to emerge as her own warm light, where she could finally see it in all its beauty. And then it set her free. She could feel it's warmness in every crevice of her body, knowing she had lived. She had lived and now they were all free.

40

Back to Life

Gus came to with a sudden gasp. Finding himself trapped, encapsulated in a dark, hollow place, he had no idea where he was but feared he would lose all oxygen and suffocate to death. He tried to move his hands but there was hardly any room. He could tell wherever he was, he was laying down flat but he didn't know where. He couldn't really hear anything. But he could feel something tied to his toe. He began to feel cold.

Wherever he was, he needed to get out of there quick so he could save Prue and Devon. He was certain that Prue would be killed in some sort of crash if he didn't get to her in time, though he hadn't thought of a plan to stop her yet. He was also certain that Devon would be shot to death, but he was torn. How could he save them both? The premonitions never had a time stamp and they happened with very little time to stop them.

As he started moving around more, he found that something started to open, particularly where his feet were.

He continued trying to move more, forcing the weight to give. Little by little, it worked. The shelf was open, and he frantically leapt up. There Gus stood, in all his glory, his hands, his light brown, cream colored skin, his chest with its tiny hairs on top, his thighs, his semi-hard penis, all exposed and all looking a bit lighter than they usually did.

He was biracial, but this was the palest he had seen himself. He investigated his body, having no idea why he was standing in this place nude, and he noticed a tag on his toe. He bent down to take it off but he couldn't, so he read it from his position: *Gus Brooks, 26, Date of Death: 7-2.*

What?! Gus became frantic, anxiously looking around for any sign that this wasn't true. In the chaos, he started to notice the all-white walls, the various white drawers in the room, what looked like medical equipment on a tray in the center of the office and large silver metallic doors with levers on them.

The room felt cold, he couldn't tell if this was because he didn't have any clothes on or because the A/C was on, but it was colder than he ever felt before. He looked around for his clothes, he'd have to figure this all out later. He couldn't be dead. That didn't make any sense.

Just then he heard the voice of a staff member coming in. Gus looked for somewhere he could hide, anywhere, but it was too late. He was face to face with this staff member, standing all 6 feet, 2 inches, with his bare chest, lean build and semi-erect penis. He would have been horrified if the staff member hadn't fainted.

Thankfully, it gave him more time to look for his clothes to get the hell out of there so he could figure out how to save his two friends. As he exited, he pulled open a door where an embalmed body laid in rest, the shelf moving towards him. Gus screamed and ran as fast as he could.

*   *   *

Gus was never able to find all his belongings, but he had found a few things that he had been wearing, along with his phone, which was the most essential thing he needed right now. He wandered the city, unaware of where he was most of the time as all of it looked unfamiliar. It didn't look like anything he had seen before, during any of their travels back or forward in time.

Because he didn't have his own power back, his attempts to imagine a place didn't transport him there. He tried multiple times to remember the place he thought they would return to if their powers were taken away, Plaza Del Balboa, but he had no luck. His feet never moved. His soul never transported.

He tried imagining Stone Mountain, the parking lot where the airplane had its crash emergency landing, but nothing. He tried imagining the church they were last in before everything seemed to go dark. All were without luck.

As he walked aimlessly around town, no money on him, no cash or credit cards, he wondered if he could touch something to give him a premonition. He didn't usually but he had been walking for what felt like hours, he could see the evening sun, and he knew he had to figure out where he was and find a way home.

He had tried to call Prue and Devon several times, but all calls went directly to voicemail. The only person he could think to call now would be his brother, David. This was the only bright spot, and Gus was ecstatic that he was alive finally in this time where they could be brothers again, he didn't have to love someone that couldn't receive his love back. He had to call him now. He needed his big brother now; he'd know what to do. He'd help him.

Naturally, he didn't have his number, so Gus went to social media to find him. Researching his brother's name, it took him no time to find an answer. Gus, who was aimlessly walking through the city had to stop immediately. Before his eyes, he read the words, "David Brooks died in a drug overdose, fentanyl poisoning ten years ago. He was survived by his parents Mr. & Mrs. Brooks and his younger brother, Gus." Gus's name also had a hyperlink.

Gus was dumbfounded. This clearly had to be a mistake. He had gone back in time. He had talked to his brother. He had told his brother he was there for him. He had stopped his brother from hanging himself. How could he have then died from a drug overdose?

Yes, Gus remembered that it looked like he had been using some kind of drug the day he went into his room, but he told him not to use that stuff. He even offered him help. How could this have happened? Fentanyl? What in the holy fuck? No, this couldn't be right. Gus refused to accept it, he refused to believe it. He left his brother as he was preparing for his Olympic trials. He wouldn't do this, not after everything Gus did to help save him.

It was time to go home. Going home, he would be able to get to the bottom of this and understand why social media was spreading these lies, and then David could help him save his two friends.

"Hey Gus, what are you doing all the way over here?" Gus heard a familiar voice behind him, coming from a Black dodge charger. He turned to get a good luck at the driver but didn't immediately recognize the man. Yet the more he spoke, the more familiar he became. "Wow, you must really be tripping, Gus."

Gus thought it best to play it cool. "Sorry, I just need to get home."

"No worries. I'll take you. You're a long way from home. Hop in."

Gus let out a sigh of relief. He could figure this out when he got home. "I'm just glad you're okay. This is why I don't watch the news, man. All lies."

Gus looked at him. "What do you mean?" as he buckled up.

"They said you died, man. Just lying in some park, you just fell down and never got up. Crazy man, I'm looking right at ya."

The familiar man lent him a newspaper. Gus looked at it as he passed it to him. It showed a picture of Gus, one he had taken for the swim team, all smiling and shit, with the headline: *Found Dead Last Night in Plaza De Balboa, Under Investigation.*

"Wait, what? What about Prue and Devon?" Gus found himself instinctively shouting.

"Who?" The man started up the engine.

"My friends. Weren't they with me too?"

"I don't know who they are, but you were alone. They thought you were attacked or something and we were just waiting for the autopsy cause that's weird, a cat your age just dropping dead like that."

Gus was beside himself. If he was alone, where were Prue and Devon? The man passed him a brown bag that had something in it. Gus opened it. It was then, he remembered who this man was, and how he had hoped during all this time travel, that he could forget. But you can't run away from your past, it's always right there in front of you.

The car took off. Of all the days.

41

Deja Vue

The water was cool and calm and forgiving. Stroke after stroke, climb after climb, he became one with the water, losing his thoughts, losing his memories, losing his emotions. He became one with the ocean as he swam to the deep parts of the pool, dive after dive, no one in sight.

It was dark now. Gus was where he belonged, where he always went whenever he felt these strong emotions and urges to give up. Instead of using what his drug dealer had so politely given him in the coveted brown bag, he had decided he would go to the place he knew would calm him, the Sapphire Elite Athletic and Swim Club. He loved to go there and practice when it was dark, when he was alone, where it was quiet, and he could silence internal conversations.

Right now, what he needed most was to forget about learning that his brother, who he thought he had saved, had decided to kill himself anyways. Instead of the sadness that he was accustomed to feeling, he felt sudden rage and unfathomable anger. He did all of this, going back in time and saving him, told his brother about resources, told him he was there for him, just for his brother to turn around and still choose to end his life anyways because he didn't want to be an Olympic swimmer.

What the fuck!!!

Just the thought required Gus to run to the highest
dive platform there, the 50-meter, and jump. He climbed to
the very top, darkness seeping through the large, gigantic,
curved windows above. Once he reached the top, he jumped
in as deep as he could dive. This wasn't his specialty dive,
and as he flopped into the water, it was taking him longer
than usual to reach the surface.

He could see bubbles in the water. In the deepest
blue, he looked to his left and right, trying to swim to the
surface. Something seemed to be weighing him down in the
pool. He didn't feel anything attached to him though, and he
was starting to feel much lighter than he ever had, similar to
when he gained his power to astral project.

Although he started his dive very much alive, at this
point, he wasn't far from dying. The longer it took to reach
the surface, the harder it was for him to breathe, losing the
energy he even had to swim. He started to fall further down.
The colors of the water changed from clear to a royal purple,
lilac, blue and indigo.

He could see something coming into his line of
vision, becoming closer and closer. It appeared to be
reaching out to him. The colors appeared to get fuzzier
followed by a light that seemed to come from above. Gus
could barely recognize this as a hand trying to reach out to
him.

Gus seemed to fade off into sleep, until he heard a
familiar voice, "Gussy, wake up. Wake up, Gussy. Grab my
hand." Gus didn't have any energy left. "Gus, wake up. Take
my hand."

Gus finally recognized this was his brother David's
childhood voice turned adult. Gus opened his eyes. Before
him was his brother David as he last remembered him,
floating in front of him, trying to reach out to his baby
brother. Despite being moments from death, Gus was too full
of seething fury that he refused to reach out.

"It's not your fault," David communicated to his
brother, never moving his lips.

"I know it's not my fault. I did everything I could," replied Gus, telepathically.

"I'm sorry."

"You are sorry. Only an idiot would do what you did. I was right there. I would have done anything for you. You didn't even talk to me. You didn't seek help. You just decided to end it all."

"It was a mistake. But you ending your life here will be more of one if you don't take my hand." Gus moved further away from him. "Who's being the idiot now?" David asked.

Suddenly, they were back at Emerald beach, back at the memory where Gus had pushed his brother David down and then ran off. They started out the ages they were in that memory but then Gus returned to the age he was now, leaving David the same age he died. Gus was now older than his big brother.

"I'm not an idiot like you. You straight up just left us, you left all of us." David sat arms folded in the sand. "Was it worth it? Was the pain you were feeling worth the pain you inflicted on all of us by leaving us like this?"

Smoke might as well be coming from his ears. He was like a hawk, and he was going to let his brother have it. "The problem with you people is that you think of only yourself. You may think of us a little, but you mainly think about yourself, and then you make these stupid decisions that cause us to grow up without you, forever missing you. Not a single day has gone by where I have forgotten about you. Every goddamn day, I am missing you.

"Our family is completely torn apart without you. Mom's depressed. Dad drinks. They're divorced. And then you people just leave, you overdose, you kill yourselves to spare yourselves the pain that you've passed on to us. Your life ended, but every damn day I'm left with the pain of what you did, the pain in my heart, the sorrow that never ends. That's not fair."

Gus knew he was being hard on his brother, but he didn't care. He knew his brother had to have been in significant pain to take his own life, but he was feeling pain too. He had been feeling it all these years. "Aren't you gonna say something?" Gus stared down his brother.

David shook his head. "I don't have any explanation for what I did except I'm sorry. I didn't know that I would actually die from it and I didn't know it would hurt you and our family this much. If I could have done this again differently, believe me I would. I never meant to hurt you, Gus. You're my little brother, I love you."

This was unsatisfactory for Gus. No. He wanted to fight now. He walked over to his brother and without a second thought, punched him square in the face. "There. Fight back!" Gus pushed David, then took another jab, hitting him this time directly in the nose. David refused to fight. "Why aren't you fighting?"

David's face was gushing blood, his nose appearing contorted. He spoke while holding his nose. "Because you have every right to be upset with me. I know you're hurting and I'm sorry that I did this. I never, ever meant to do this to you."

This admission only made Gus angrier. He took three more jabs at David who didn't try not once to block any of them and allowed Gus to attack him. This didn't satisfy Gus. Hearing I'm sorry didn't make him feel any bit better. He knew he was sorry. He knew his brother was hurting. He didn't understand that kind of hurt because he was too busy feeling the pain of his own but he knew David's pain was real.

Then he thought of Prue and remembered what he said to her:

You're not a mess. You're showing all of your strength right now by trusting me to help, reaching out to help. You're so much stronger than you think you are when you do this than keeping it all inside where it can bury you alive. And I'm going to be here to remind you that you're going to pull through this, we will together, no matter what happens.

He remembered what he told her next, *I saw my brother in another life, but in that life instead of being brothers, he was my dad and I was his son. We were still connected, even though it was another life. Of all the gazillions of people out there, it can't be coincidental that the same two people connected in one life are connected in another. People that are connected, they have to be like soulmates, connected to each other's soul through love in whatever shape or form, in each and every life. But that doesn't always mean we walk together in the same life, or even meet, but we can influence each other in different ways even if we aren't on the same plane at the same time. A part of us is always connected to that other person until we see them again, and we will always find each other, whether we know it or not.*

It was easier for Gus to show anger than sadness because the anger made him feel stronger. But he knew the strength was actually in showing your true emotion. He knew what he was doing was wrong. He was punishing his brother, but his brother didn't need to be punished. He had already made his decision and he recognized that he made a mistake, but maybe he was in so much pain that this seemed like the best decision to him at the time.

Unfortunately, when you kill yourself, you end your own story. There isn't a tomorrow or a few days or weeks later to see the things that can change that may cause you to see or feel things differently. Gus loved his brother very much; he was just so incredibly sad and disappointed that for a moment he thought he had him again only to find that he had lost him in the end. . He ran to his brother, sobbing and wanting to make amends.

"David, I'm sorry. I, I..."

"You don't need to apologize. I should apologize to you." David grabbed his younger brother and embraced him. "Gus, you have grown to be such an amazing man." He looked at him deep into his brown eyes, rubbing his hair, "I am so proud of you. I promise you, next time, I will get it right." The two chuckled.

But Gus didn't know what he meant by "next time."

"Gus, I need you to take my hand."

"What do you mean?" Gus looked confused.

"No seriously, Gus, take my hand. You have so much more that you are destined for. My story ended here, but yours in so many ways is just starting. And I'm going to be here on this side to help push you to achieve your dreams and help you live your life as happy as you can, to make sure you make it everything you want it to be. You need to be brave, never ever give up, and take my hand."

Gus didn't understand what his brother was telling him. Then suddenly, he was underwater again, a hand reaching out to him. He didn't feel like he had any energy left to reach out, but he remembered what his brother told him, "Never, ever give up."

That was all he needed. Somewhere deep within, he found the energy inside himself to move upward and reach his brother's hand. It became easier this time, whatever was holding him back he was now set free from. He grabbed the hand and allowed it to pull him up.

Finally free, he laid on the cold tile floor, coughing up water that had filled his lungs, trying to regain control of his breathe. He wasn't sure if he had just hallucinated or if the experience was real.

Out of nowhere, a white pelican appeared above the waters, in the center of the swimming pool. Gus eyed it, its beautiful, gorgeous wings. It sat still. Gus tried to get close to it but each time it looked like the pelican would flap its wings to fly away so he stayed where he was.

At once, a brown duck appeared next to the pelican. Gus understood now. As the pelican flew away, the duck stayed. He knew his experience had been real. He knew what was happening now.

Drifting away from this moment, Gus couldn't help but notice the early morning sky appearing through the Athletic club sky windows above. In the next moment, he heard splashing from the adjacent pool, the same one he, Prue and Devon had used to teleport through time.

These kids that practice at all hours just to do whatever it takes to win. He walked over towards the direction of the adjacent pool. From a distance, Gus could see someone on the 30-meter diving platform. He was doing incredibly well with his posture, position, dives and strokes. He had great timing and stamina, diving into the water with grace and then back on the diving board in what seemed like seconds.

Gus definitely would need to refocus his efforts onto the Olympic Swim Tryouts if he wanted to earn a place on the team and by the looks of it, he had serious competition. Gus watched him though a few seconds longer before the feeling of fear began to set in. And once he realized it, he had just about lost his mind. Gus was watching himself. He had to get out of here.

Frantically, he ran towards the locker rooms to get his clothes and his keys so he could drive off. He noticed the locker next to his own with the same lock. No time, he grabbed his clothes and his keys and ran out as quickly as he could to his car. Miraculously, not a soul was outside and his other self hadn't noticed or heard him. With relief, he pressed the key fob to find that nothing was happening. He tried again, this time noticing the sound of another car unlocking. "Damn it!"

Things were beginning to make sense. He now knew exactly where in this time he was. He was reliving the same day again. He had gone back to the early morning at the pool before his crash. Today, he had grabbed the wrong car keys and had opened his own lock but that original day, someone else had used his locker, so he had used a back-up lock in his car and used the locker next to his.

Now he was holding the keys to his own car instead of the keys to the car his dealer had hooked him up with. Why was he seeing himself now? If the magic hadn't worked, weren't he, Prue and Devon supposed to return back to the moment when they first cast the Time Travelling Spell?

Gus didn't know how, but he had to fix this. If he saw into the eyes of his past self, he would become him again, changing everything they have done and altering time. If he changed time now, after all they had already done, all would be lost and what they had done would have never happened.

He snuck back into the locker room, opened the other locker which had the same code, and initially only switched the keys until he realized, he'd also have to change his clothes or the other him would be suspicious. This must have meant that on the original day, the other locker had to have been from his future current self.

Wouldn't that mean that he had already gone back in time twice and relieved the same day three times now? His head was starting to ache. Gus tried to change clothes as quickly as he could but before he knew it, he heard himself walking inside the locker room. He had to hide.

Quickly, he went into one of the stalls, closed the door, and stood over the toilet, being as quiet as he could be, hoping the other him wouldn't notice. It worked. He heard himself passing by, changing his clothes and closing the locker-room door behind him. Gus held his breathe until he finally felt he was in the clear. This was way too much excitement; Gus's heart was racing like a freight train.

After a few minutes, Gus sneakily made his way outside and crept into the right car this time. It was parked on the street which may have been why the original Gus hadn't noticed this when he left. Oh no. More of that day was coming back to Gus. His sigh of relief was now a fleeting memory.

This was the morning he crashed his car. Gus needed to leave.

       *   *   *

Trying to get ahead of himself, he tried to remember the path he took, the signs he saw, most of which was a blurred memory because he had been driving under the influence. But he heard the words of his brother in his mind's eye, "Never, ever, give up" so he allowed whatever in him to continue to guide his path.

He tried to understand the little bit he remembered now with a sober mind. He remembered something about hexagon or yellow shapes. What looked like hexagon or yellow shapes? Signs? Could they be school signs? The closest one was Thurgood Marshall Elementary. That was along his typical driving path as he left the Sapphire Elite Athletic and Swim Club.

He also remembered something about colors yellow, red…red, maybe these were the traffic lights. Gus changed directions heading to the school, knowing his past self was already minutes ahead of him. He would have to drive faster.

Surprisingly, Gus made it to the school before his former self had. Thankfully, it was not busy but there were a few people walking around, mostly working parents who were dropping their kids off early for school. Gus waited. He knew he would be coming through there shortly and he wanted to make sure that he didn't hurt anyone, that everyone was safe.

David had made his decision, but Gus was still alive to try to make better decisions. It didn't take long before he saw a pair of quick moving headlights and heard the familiar bass blasting from his stereo. He knew it was time to make sure everyone got out of the way. He couldn't stop what needed to happen but he could make sure that no one else was hurt in the process of his own mistakes.

He yelled as loud as he could at the parents to get in their cars and drive off. He pulled a few homeless individuals and redirected pedestrians out of the way of where he thought his car would crash through. Less than twenty feet, he used all of his human power and strength to make sure no one would be hurt in this crash.

As his car drove through the red light on Grandview and Park Boulevard, he watched himself crash into a truck that was halfway in the intersection, then another car colliding with his car into a nearby fence and tree. Just then, he saw the light pole next to the tree falling on top of his car, followed by 1,000 volts of shockwaves, electrocuting him. Everything in the car was shocked. He couldn't see himself because he knew the risk, but he watched as his car was hit by those 1,000 volts of electricity, and everything lit up.

How did I survive that with only a few bruises and bandages?

A few of the people that Gus had cautioned to get out of the way ran over to the car. Their mouths were frozen in place when they saw him again inside the car, unconscious. Gus had to hide. He headed back to where he had parked his car when he stumbled over a newspaper blowing under his feet. The headline captured his attention, he had to pick it up. On the cover, it showed Kaleb's airplane that had crashed yesterday morning. Gus's heart broke, knowing how lost in grief Prue must have been when she read this.

As Gus flipped the pages, he saw more tragic news. *An unidentified transgender woman was killed near Stone Mountain in a fatal car crash.* On the next page, he saw two Black men had been fatally shot at the local police station. The newspaper read: *It is believed the two Black men entered the police station to kill the officers. Devon Blackstone was involved in a police shooting earlier today that killed eight officers including Lt. Hunter and tonight about fourteen more were killed, including Dwayne Harris who is of interest in this case.*

Frozen in shock, Gus knew that his premonitions must have come true. Prue must have been killed in the car crash that he saw and Devon must have been killed by the police officers in his other premonition before everything went dark. It was too much for him to bear. Prue and Devon were dead, this couldn't be true. They had magic powers.

They had saved people from being killed. *They* had travelled back and forth through time, casting and concocting spells and incantations to help save the people they had lost and now Prue and Devon, the only two friends he had that knew were dead? He needed to get high now. He couldn't deal with this much sadness. Enough was enough.

When he made it to his car, he started to text his dealer, but as if his brother were right there with him, he heard the words, "Never, ever, give up" and the comment his brother had made about helping him from the other side seemed to echo in his mind. What difference did this make? It was over. His brother was dead. His friends were dead. Even if this wasn't their original destiny, he didn't know how to bring them back from the dead.

He didn't have any powers now. Their powers had to have vanished because they weren't all alive anymore, they had crossed the great divide. They crossed the great divide? And then he had an idea. What if he didn't need to bring them back to life? What if Prue and Devon were still walking around, just like he was, living their lives and they just hadn't met yet? A smile crossed his face. *Where did we all meet again?*

42

Back to the Beginning

It was a few weeks later when Gus knew that it was safe to return back. He wanted to make sure he had his timing just right and he remembered that it took a while before he was well enough to move around after the crash. Timing was essential and everything had to be perfect. There was no room for mistakes.

Retracing his footsteps, he remembered the address of the building, parked a different car that he was using and walked inside early before the others arrived. It was now nighttime. There were details that he had forgotten, when the group actually started, what time he had arrived, the exact timing of the others but he would have to play it by ear.

He entered the counseling room, noticing right away the plastic plants, the impressionism artwork on the walls, and the dreaded fish tank. To his surprise, the fish was actually alive. He could see the rainbow-colored fish swimming around the tank. He went over to look at the fish closer but when he touched the tank, mysteriously this wave of electricity came out of his hands and shocked the entire tank, the body of the fish now floating in the water.

Gus was astonished. He was the reason why the fish had died and was left in the tank just floating around. Where was this electricity coming from? He had to get this energy under control.

Just then, he heard voices stirring about and knew it was time for him to hide. There was a nearby suite adjacent to the counseling room where the grief and loss support group took place. He believed this would be his best chance. He kept himself hidden, watching from a nearby window as Marci, Shawn, Mx. Thomas, and the other group members entered the room for the support group that night.

Gus prepared for the emotional rollercoaster that would ensue by compartmentalizing his feelings. He had to. He knew it was the only way he'd be able to focus to get his task done to save his friends. Of course, he could have left them as they were but wouldn't they just repeat the same cycle over again?

Except it was by some unknown coincidence that Gus recognized what was going on. Despite Gus's armor, the compartments all opened at once when he saw Prue walk in. Seeing her alive again made him remember exactly what he was doing. He wanted to walk in there, pull her aside and tell her everything, but he knew he had to wait.

Then he saw Devon walk in and he felt overjoyed to see him alive too, reunited again. His heart nearly stopped when he saw a figure of himself walking in with his crutches and eye patch. They were all here now. It was time to set his plan in motion.

He waited, listening through the wall and air vent, overhearing the start of the group and then the bickering that ensued between the three friends as they were just starting to get to know each other, an ongoing theme that nearly threatened their ability to work together in the future.

Anticipating what would happen next, when Devon stormed out of the room, Gus held his hands to the light switch that connected both rooms. This caused the lights to flicker in the rooms. He now had to do something to get Devon in the elevator. He left the room to go after him.

"Devon, you always were a little chump."

Devon was on the third step down on the staircase when he quickly turned around, undoubtedly pissed at Gus.

"You're talking to me, asswipe?" Devon looked up and down at Gus. "Why do you look different?"

Gus tried to play it cool. "Different? I don't know what you're talking about."

"Where's your pirate eye and your crutches, fucker?"

"I think you're hallucinating. It must be all that anger you're hiding deep within. You really should talk to somebody about that."

Suddenly, both Devon and Gus could hear Gus's voice from inside the counseling room. Devon had a peculiar expression on his face. Gus had to do something to get the others out, but he needed Devon to hang around. "You know Devon, I think we should fight downstairs because you really are such a little fucking bitch."

"Have you lost what's left of your fucking mind kid?" Devon headed towards the stairs.

"Wait!"

Gus needed a new plan. He ran to the adjacent counseling room and touched the light panel, causing them to flicker again. Hearing the uproar, he quickly pushed Devon into the elevator and then hid out. Seconds later, he saw both Prue and himself enter the elevator before the elevator door closed.

At last, they were finally alone in the same space. He pressed his hand on the elevator up button, then waited a few seconds until he touched the control panels once again; this shocked and disconnected the electricity from the elevator, causing the elevator to shut down midstream.

He remembered something about he and Devon trying to loosen one of the top tiles in the elevator. He couldn't figure out how to reach the elevator tiles since the elevator was now stuck between floors, but he had to think fast. His brother told him, "Never, ever, give up." He took the stairs to get the closest to the elevator. Then he crossed his fingers, said a little prayer and touched the elevator control panel one final time, sending the elevator crashing down.

He took the stairs to follow it all the way down to the base floor. Then he could see this glowing, fluorescent light coming from the elevator. He looked around and then pressed the button to open the door. There all three laid on the floor unconscious. It had worked. Together again, their powers were reconstituted, the power of three.

Gus lifted himself up off the floor. His past-self appeared to come to, starting to awaken from the trauma of the accident. And then he opened his eyes. Gus was startled, he had helped himself up but now was looking directly at himself, as was his former original self. The two stood silently for a moment before a smile crossed his original self and like magic, Gus caught up with himself, slamming into the previous version and then jumping back into his body. The two Gus's were now one.

Gus began moaning and aching, now feeling the pain from the car accident that he had relived. It was now clear to him that the elevator crash had really happened, and it was their magic that had protected them. But Gus didn't want to think too much, or it would only hurt his head again, opening infinite places of nonsense and magical dimensions that need not be entered. Gus was himself again, his friends were alive, and now they were back, back to the beginning.

43

Together Again: Reunited

Everything was dark. The light that had surrounded her was gone. There was nothing for her to see, it was as if there wasn't a Prue to interpret anything to see in the first place. And as swiftly as there was darkness, she felt this overwhelming presence, this need, this desire, something in her telling her it was time for her to finally open her eyes and see again.

So, she opened her eyes and to her surprise, the rays of light that were beaming in, that warmth, that presence she felt, was the sun peeking out of her window, trying to shine through her black-out curtains and covered blinds.

She was surprised to find herself in her bedroom, drooling on her pillow, pressed against her life-sized corduroy teddy-bear that made her feel she was finally not having to sleep every night alone. This was the closest she had ever come to having a man in her bed the morning after.

All of what she had felt the moments before opening her eyes, the terror, the fear, the confusion, felt like a daze, felt as though she was in a fog and must have dreamed the whole thing up. She rationalized to herself that this had to have been a dream. Last she remembered, she was headed face-first to the metal floor of a man-made inescapable deathtrap, plunging to her end. The irony of surviving her difficult, life-altering surgery, only to then meet her maker trapped in a death box with strangers.

She made several attempts to lift herself up out of bed, still getting used to the heaviness on her chest. She turned on her television to hear the relaxing voice of Alex Wallace forecasting the next east coast storm in Philadelphia. She walked over to her bathroom mirror and took a long look at herself, finally seeing herself now. Standing, unclothed, she saw her body, the shape of her breasts, her medium waistline, her long, curly black hair that she bought from Malaysia, the scars on her chest. The shape of her virgin vagina. Her vulva, her clitoris. The smoothness, the softness of her vagina. She could even sense wetness…

And then she heard a strange sound of a male voice from outside the door.

She felt panic and fear. Swiftly, she grabbed her nightgown and her stun gun, prepared as she opened the door. The sounds seemed to be coming from downstairs. She grabbed her phone just in case of an emergency. Walking down the stairs, she could hear their voices becoming louder, but more importantly could also hear the sounds of bacon frying, the smells of bacon frying and coffee being brewed.

"What the fuck are you doing in my house?" She pointed the stun gun.

"Oh, relax Prue. It's me, Gus. And Devon is just over there deciding if he's going to get off your couch or not. He's a big time drooler," Gus enthusiastically shared while cooking breakfast in her kitchen.

Prue recognized them from last night. "What are you guys doing in my house?"

"That's really a good question," Devon interjected. "I just woke up here."

"What? How the hell you just wake up in my house?"

"I don't know, princess. I just woke up here after our little elevator incident." Prue stopped. "Can you put that down?" Devon pointed to her stun gun. She really felt silly holding it now. She thought the elevator experience was just a nightmare but how could he have known it too?

"I can explain everything guys, I mean Prue and Devon. Just give me a second to finish these pancakes. Do you have strawberry syrup?" Gus asked, delighted to be himself again and to see his friends alive once more. His two friends, on the other hand, were completely caught off guard by his chippy demeanor and what was happening.

Prue lowered the stun gun. "I'm surprised you'd want to be in MY house, Dedrick."

Devon rolled his eyes, "Sure. Act like you don't know my name."

Gus prepared their plates with bacon, hash browns, sausage, sunny side-up eggs, chocolate scones and blueberry pancakes with strawberry syrup, his own tribute to his brother in that final breakfast they shared together. Prue and Devon looked amazed.

"Where did you learn how to cook breakfast like this?" Prue asked.

"I'll tell you all in a second. First, I need you all to sit at the table and say prayer before we eat breakfast, so grab each other's hand." Prue and Devon sat down but hesitated to hold each other's hand. Gus sat in between them. "Come on, we hold hands and pray."

No Book of Spirits Past in their time yet, but Gus had a rhyme of his own. While holding hands at Prue's dining room table, Gus uttered the words:

"After all this time, let them remember so they can understand why."

44

Grieving Still

It was sometime later. He was taking his typical 30-meter dive, zoning out the way only he could to focus on his competitive spirit and doing the best he could. He maintained his skill to be able to tune out the rest of the world at a moment's notice when he needed to most. Dive after dive, he felt free with the water.

The gymnasium was full with onlookers, competitors, fans, their family and friends all in the stands, after all he was trying out for the Olympic National Swim Team. He needed to tap into his greatest power of all, the one that he held inside all along when he silenced his thoughts. It's a power he wished his brother had tapped into as well, but it was okay. He would win this for the both of them.

As Gus took his final dive deep into the deepest blue, he thought for a moment that he had made a mistake. He felt this fear in his body, he recognized it was because he was worrying. *What if I don't score, what if I didn't do enough, what if I'm not good enough?* All the what ifs were sinking him.

He had to tap into his power again, as if no one else was there, as if the what ifs didn't matter because they don't. He had to silence his thoughts; it was okay to be scared, but the fear alone didn't make it true. As he accepted this as truth, that he'd have to simply do his dives scared, and that was okay, he saw an amazing cool light from inside the water.

Before he could recognize it, he heard the words, "Never, ever, give up." He felt this heaviness drop as if something was lifting him up. The voices in his head were quiet. He knew his brother David was lifting him up, the only way he could from the other side.

As Gus touched the surface, he saw an image of a duck sitting on the water. He was okay being who he was. Although he wasn't born with wings, nevertheless he found a way to fly. He returned back to reality and when he arose from the water, he was reminded how real it was.

Gus could hear the echoes of applause and the cheering in the stands. He even noticed the maintenance man that had saved him that day when he began astral projecting underwater. He would have to buy that man a cup of coffee or something. He smiled and waved.

"Gus!"

"Whoo! Olympic boy."

Gus turned to his left where he immediately recognized the voices of his two best friends, Prue and Devon. They were so excited watching him do what he loved, cheering him on every way possible. Gus finally had someone to cheer him on at his swimming trials, and it felt like they had become family. He walked over to them sitting in the stands. "How do you think I did?" he asked.

"I think you did terrific. That's very impressive Gus, especially after all we've been through," said Prue who seemed overjoyed and seemed to feel more like herself.

"Yeah, very impressive, Olympic Boy. Even more impressive would be if you stopped doing that little head thing you do with your hair," Devon joked.

"You mean, like this?" Gus shook his hair, spreading water all over the place. Prue lifted her hands up and time froze. "Oh, Prue. You really have got to control that. Why didn't you do that when I was actually swimming in the race?" Gus joked.

Devon laughed.

"Very funny guys." Prue looked around in the stands and the swimmers. "You know, there really should be more people that look like us here, watching and competing." Gus nodded his head. Prue flailed her hands, unfreezing time. The sounds and myriad of conversations and movement returned to the gymnasium.

"What are you both doing after?" Gus hinted.

"You mean after your celebration?" Prue smirked. Gus grinned.

Devon explained, "We're going to City Hall to talk to the mayor about the research we've been doing on police that have killed unarmed Black people. I get it, all police aren't bad, but some of them still are for sure and there's still something wrong with the system.

"If the bad police are able to stay protected, then nothing stops them from continuing to endanger the lives of the Black community, and it may not just be limited to us. There has to be accountability, there has to be a separate entity that investigates these killings, body cameras must be on at all times and transparency is needed.

"We continue to lose unarmed Black people because officers think they see a gun. You can't shoot just because you think you see a gun, and if you shoot, it shouldn't be lethal. Ask questions, don't shoot first." Prue placed her hand on Devon's shoulder.

"I'm in. What happens after talking to the mayor?" Gus asked.

"We're going to Washington, D.C. We can't be silent about this, but we can't become the enemy either. We have to do what we can to protect our community. No one understands more than us. Allies are good too, but we have to lead this and they really need to use their privilege and resources to support. But we, as the Black community, all shades of us, have to stay together, united."

Gus understood the message that Devon was saying. Even though Gus was biracial and was still working to accept both of his identities, Gus knew Devon was affirming that he too was Black and was part of this community.

"Dwayne would still be alive today if the police hadn't mistaken him as a criminal and asked questions first before shooting. He'd be alive along with countless others that were just living their lives until they encountered the police. What about those that have mental health challenges and can't calm down when they do encounter the police?

"I get it, they aren't all bad, maybe most of them are good. But the system was based on slavery to protect only some of us, and if they have to continue to follow and protect the bad apples, how long before all are contaminated? Lt. Hunter is still out there and there are more of them."

Prue and Gus were in full support. An attack on one of us is an attack on all of us and Prue being transgender knew this significantly. Every year there is an attack on the rights of the transgender and non-binary community. They are granted rights, rights they should naturally have as any human would, because trans rights are human rights.

Then the people that don't want the world to move forward, always try to bring it back, repealing rights, attacking rights, releasing anti-trans legislature where the trans community must always be aware of what's politically going on. Even harder for Black Trans women, that in many states are at risk of losing their lives just for existing, those same women who may have harder challenges finding work because the government doesn't protect them, causing them to work in areas that put their lives more at risk than anyone else.

Prue would vow to do what she could to protect those rights. To always uplift those lives and with every breath she took, using the philosophies that Kaleb had instilled in her to do the very best she could. To grow and become better each and every day for the greater good.

"Well, it sounds like we have a lot of work to do. How odd that once you earned your bachelor's degree, you became even more interested in social justice," Gus said, throwing a towel at Devon, chuckling.

Prue smiled. Everyone could tell the difference. Since she had won her insurance case and had Facial Feminization Surgery, she was walking on air, able to show herself and see herself more than ever before. She encountered misgendering less and less often, which made her feel that she was finally being seen authentically as herself.

Suddenly, Devon was taken back. The walls of the gymnasium disappeared, and he could hear and see someone asking for help. Moments later, he returned from his premonition.

"Looks like the magical trio has another person to save," Gus laughed. He stood up headed to the locker room then turned around, "What are you guys still sitting there for? Let's go."

45

The Other Side: A New Beginning

She stood on the upstairs balcony looking up at the night sky. It was quiet and she could smell the fresh night air. Right away, she noticed the two stars that were far away in the night sky but seemed they were always in the same position when she went to look out at them. One star was closer and bigger than the other, the smaller one reminded her of a child.

When she opened her eyes more and really looked, she also noticed other smaller stars in the distance, but these two stars stood out the most, in particular the biggest star that seemed to make her feel this warmth and calmness in her spirit.

Above the house, she could see the full moon glowing as brightly as the sun. She just allowed herself to look up, she knew who she was thinking about, she knew she was still hurting and missing him. She had given her all and had lost, but she didn't feel the loss in the same way she had before.

Time passing by didn't mean that she stopped loving him or stopped missing him. She never would stop missing him, she never would stop loving him, the only parts of the man she could know. If there was a way, she'd still try to bring him back. Prue looked up into the night sky, looking into the stars, looking for him, trying to find him.

As she went to sleep that night, she closed the book that she would read to feel closest to him. He cared so much about his work and influencing the next generation so she would let him do that through her. She had hoped that Gus was right, that maybe he was alive in some other reality, some other plane of existence and that if they were connected, they would have another chance to meet in the next lifetime.

Before she went to bed, she went downstairs to turn off the lights but passed the Book of Spirits Past on the dining room table. Something always did bother her about their time travel. She flipped open the book to find the spell. She could see the time travel spell and there it was, the other page she knew was attached but hadn't read.

In elegant font, the second page that had been attached to the time travel spell read: *Caution. Changing the past is futile. You cannot change the past. Many have tried but have only found changing one thing changes everything else, often making it worse. We can't change destiny. We can accept the past, grieve what we have lost, but we can only live for today, today is all we have.*

Prue walked upstairs to her bedroom, pulled out a dresser drawer to reveal the folded paper she held in her hands to give to Kaleb that day in the church. She opened it. It read: *Please don't get on that flight this morning. Drive instead.* She held it in her hands, remembering why she didn't give it to him in the church that morning.

Before she laid her head down, she knew it was time for her to write her own story next, to continue his legacy, to help comfort the many people that have lost someone, to help bring hope into their lives and into their hearts again. All things start with a seed of hope. And most importantly, "Never, ever, give up."

*   *   *

Out of that warm, comforting, soothing light, the sun continued to surround itself around the aircraft that was in the sky. It flew with a smoothness and with a quietness.

Before there wasn't a cloud in the sky, but as the sun began to set, the warm bright light became an amber dim glow as the plane began to shift downward however remained steady, appearing to prepare itself for landing.

Inside the airplane were five people. In particular, a young girl that had her hair back in a ponytail wearing headphones, drinking an orange soda. She had very light skin, appeared to be in her early twenties, wearing a denim top and white blouse. She was sitting really close to a darker skin man who appeared to be looking after her, both peering out the window at the setting sun. The man had pink and blonde hair and was wearing gear that looked like he was a skater. There was a skateboard between his legs that was overwhelmed with stickers and logos.

On the plane were several TV mounts. It was all happening very quickly, but the anchor mentioned the hard work and creative genius of a particular man, judging by the tall man's expressions they were referring to him. It was impossible to hear the name of the man but he believed in never ever giving up and doing your best, no matter what.

Looking closer at him, it was hard to tell if that was his actual hair or some kind of disguise. He had something bronze on his face as well. Something about this man looked very familiar.

As the plane landed, it passed over a sign between the mountains. The man shed a tear only when he saw a bronze statue of a young man wearing a baseball cap and holding a bat. And then he did the oddest thing, he smiled as he looked up. It was time to get off.

Suddenly he and the young lady were on the railway, grabbing their seat before the railway doors closed. He and this young lady appeared very happy. All the people around them appeared happy as well as they headed to their next destination. He finally got off.

9 798218 782443